# Filthy Rich Lawyers

*It's More Than a Novel. It's a Lifestyle.*

Book One

## The Education of Ryan Coleman

Books by Brian Felgoise and David Tabatsky


**FILTHY RICH LAWYERS**
Book One: The Education of Ryan Coleman


Coming 2023!
**FILTHY RICH LAWYERS**
Book Two: In Due Time

# Filthy Rich Lawyers

*It's More Than a Novel. It's a Lifestyle.*

Book One

## The Education of Ryan Coleman

Brian Felgoise
and
David Tabatsky

SPEAKING VOLUMES, LLC
NAPLES, FLORIDA
2022

The Education of Ryan Coleman

ISBN 978-1-64540-782-9

To anyone who has ever needed a lawyer . . .

# Acknowledgments

*Brian*

A loving and heartfelt thank you to Lori Felgoise, my soulmate and loving wife for 26 years. Without you, my life would be empty. With your support, I have been able to thrive, both personally and professionally. Thank you to Bethany and Brianna, the ultimate muses who drive me to become a better and more caring person.

Thank you to Marla A. Joseph, Esquire for proofing the manuscript utilizing skills you learned from your loving father, one of the greatest lawyers I have ever known. Thanks, too, to Steve Shoff, Lawrence Bergman, and Rabbi Ari Goldstein who offered valuable criticism and suggestions. A special thank you to Michael Broudo, who challenged me to come-up with a better storyline.

Thank you to David Tabatsky, who agreed to take on this project because he believed in me and the story I wanted to tell. I feel lucky that we wrote this book together.

I apologize to anyone who may be offended by any aspect of *Filthy Rich Lawyers*. I merely wanted to pull back the curtains on the legal arena I was involved with for many years and make the story more compelling and comical. Please remember, this book is a satire. I hope it provides a much-needed escape from the crazy world we live in.

*David*

Thanks to Brian Felgoise for trusting me to do what I do. Thank you to Hank Rosenfeld, Wendy Garfinkle, and Meghan McEnery for their supportive feedback. And thanks to Google for saving me numerous trips to the library, not that I have anything against libraries. Please support them, along with independent bookstores and book fairs.

We would like to thank Nancy Rosenfeld for agenting this book series and our publishers, Kurt and Erica Mueller at Speaking Volumes.

# One

## Into the Fire:
## Do Not Speak Unless Spoken To

My first mistake was wearing a pair of handmade Alden shoes into the courthouse. They are ridiculously comfortable and look like a million bucks, but unfortunately, they have a metal shank in the sole. While these black beauties provide essential stability, which my father always stressed, this feature also made passing through a metal detector inside the Earl Cabell Federal Courthouse in Dallas a major problem.

On the afternoon of August 23, 2018, I was heading inside what I knew might become a contentious courtroom to claim my share of a class action lawsuit. You could say I was a typical lawyer, trying to dupe the system, like, it's a dirty job and someone's got to do it, but it's more complicated than that. I mean, I'm a good guy. I've been taking care of my sick mother for years.

In any case, I figured I should be stepping pretty for the occasion. Not by choice, however, I became the only attorney on the premises who had to remove his perfect, jet-black shoes, forcing me to step aside and watch a parade of slick, well-dressed lawyers and an assortment of clerks enter the tenth floor, unencumbered by any issues with their feet.

As I was pulled aside for further scrutiny by two rather large security guards, I felt thankful to be wearing such handsome, designer socks. They featured a green and white rendering of an eagle in flight, set against a backdrop of Independence Hall in Philadelphia, the City of Brotherly Love. I was a huge fan of my local team, dreaming of owning my own AFL franchise someday, but for now, showing off a pair of limited-edition, cotton blend socks to honor my hometown team as the ultimate champions, would have to suffice.

I hoped someone would notice, especially a miserable Cowboys fan. One of the guards glared at me as if my feet were offending him. I smiled and made some comment about hoping the Cowboys might one day rival the Eagles again, just for the sake of good competition.

I hoped even more that there would still be a seat at the Plaintiffs' attorneys' table when I finally made it upstairs into the courtroom. From my calculation, there had to be a place for me because I would be presenting to the judge at this Fairness Hearing.

As a young, brash but somewhat naïve lawyer, fresh from grinding my way through Temple Law School in Philadelphia and setting up my own firm with my friend and partner, I was about to be thrown directly into the fire of plaintiffs fighting for their fair share as they encountered the larger-than-life world of a corporate war zone.

Fairness, my ass. Where was the fairness when it came to my choice of shoes?

It had already been a hectic afternoon since arriving 30 minutes late at the courthouse, due to the nasty Dallas traffic. This was a legal proceeding I had been anxious about for quite some time because a judge was about to decide whether to approve my settlement. This case was my first big securities class action, and I was itching to have my share secured by the judge.

Just to set the record straight: I was supposed to receive $275,000 as a fee because I had gotten the Defendants to agree to pay back $2.5 million to the company in question as a result of their actions, which caused the company to spend $5 million for attorneys to represent them.

If you're thinking that's a shitload of money, you're right. But considering how the system works, it was an appropriate amount and I had earned it fair and square.

As soon as I entered the courtroom, Bill Waterman, who I had met a few years earlier when he filed one of my first cases for me, stood up and waved me to my seat. Bill was the local counsel for the law firm Schwartz, Bennett, Golden & Kiester, LLP, better known as Schwartz & Bennett. He had wanted to meet me early at the courthouse to have a coffee and discuss the hearing. As a local counsel, he was a designated attorney who would be admitted in court to serve as a representative for an attorney (me) who was not officially licensed to practice in a specific court in an out-of-state proceeding.

Schwartz & Bennett, who must have had at least 75 lawyers on payroll at that time, was a law firm located just outside Philadelphia, and I referred a lot of cases to them because they were rock stars in this field of law. In exchange for bringing them clients, the firm paid me a referral fee anytime they received a fee for litigating a case I had referred to them.

It was a sweet arrangement, especially since I was still paying off loans from putting myself through law school. This work I was doing would allow me to settle my debts within another year or two, which was a huge relief for me, personally and professionally. I needed to accrue capital if I was going to expand my law firm and become a serious player, and that also meant keeping my wife feeling secure and happy because most of the hot shot lawyers I looked up to were married, and what woman wants a husband who still has a ton of loans to pay?

I had to get my shit together in a major way. That afternoon, I was already off my game from the whole security scene I had to endure by the elevators. I was a little uncomfortable, too, because my hotel was just a block away from where President Kennedy had been shot, even though it happened a lifetime ago. I knew the tragic incident well because when I was an undergraduate at Drexel University, majoring in political science and minoring in economics, I saw video footage of the motorcade and the shooting hundreds of times because one of my professors was obsessed, so I must admit, I was spooked just being in Dallas, in the shadow of all that rotten history. I mean, who goes and shoots a president, even if you don't like him or agree with him? That was insane and it still freaked me out a little.

When I finally arrived in the grand courtroom, I was relieved to see that there was a place for me at the Plaintiffs' table next to the jury box. The Defendants were seated at a table further away from the jurors. The judge would be seated about 20 feet away from our table, raised above us all, on what is commonly referred to as the bench, which was close enough that one would be able to clearly see and interpret the judge's facial expressions. All the spectators, who were just lawyers on this occasion, sat behind the railings in rows of five benches. It looked like we were at a convention of bankers or some meeting of accountants, showing off their suits. I was happy to be wearing my Aldens again because they always made me feel like a million bucks.

Just as the proceedings were about to begin, Waterman, not missing his chance to remind me that he was more experienced, leaned in and whispered intensely into my ear what would soon become sage advice.

"Whatever happens today before Judge Glynn, please remember one thing."

I stared at him as he furrowed his forehead and moved in even closer. I could smell the caffeine on his breath and wished I had the time to go get a quick cup myself.

"Do not speak unless spoken to."

That sounded like one of the sisters in my cousin's Catholic school.

"You mean . . ."

"Don't say one freaking word unless Judge Glynn asks you a question."

I felt like I was back in first grade, about to be tried by my teacher in front of my entire class for questionable behavior, like talking out of turn. I had a habit of doing that, sometimes at the worst moments, so maybe Waterman was right. I should cool it on the verbal impulses.

As I adjusted my imported silk tie, which featured a multi-colored, Andy Warhol style print of Benjamin Franklin, I surveyed the courtroom and saw a row of legal all-stars, the big guns in this arena, looking polished and ready to roll. I had watched a few of them breeze through the security checkpoint while I was delayed because of my shoes.

I was a young, up-and-coming lawyer, looking fresh and spiffy, and ready to score my first big payday in the world of class-action lawsuits. I would soon discover that the Honorable Brenda Glynn, our presiding federal judge, suffers no fools.

# Two

## The Fire Burns:
## Judge Brenda Glynn, The Honorable, Presiding

As I mulled this over and settled into my seat, I wished I had gotten to the courthouse early enough to slug down a coffee, but I was pretty jacked up on adrenaline. This was a big deal for me. If everything went according to plan, I would be receiving official confirmation of the biggest payday in my life to date—by far! I could return home with a new bounce in my step, with even a little swagger, as I relaxed into my new role as a bona fide player in this game.

I was about to ask Judge Glynn to approve the shareholder derivative lawsuit I had filed against the officers and directors of the company in question for allegedly misrepresenting their potential liability, which happened after their merger with another defense contractor. I know that's a mouthful, but the truth is I created a benefit to the company by getting the Defendants to pay that $2.5 million back to the company.

You might be asking, what exactly did the company do, and why was it so rotten? Those were reasonable questions I had done my due diligence to answer. Basically, the officers and directors of the accused company had learned all about the asbestos liability during its acquisition of the other behemoth corporation, but it had failed to adequately disclose the potential problems to its own shareholders.

Whoops!

The plaintiffs alleged that they learned of the exposure to asbestos one month before the shareholder meeting to vote on the merger. Instead of disclosing the information to its investors, which they obviously should have done, the company issued positive press releases to them and the public. They also filed documents with the SEC one year after the merger was completed and failed to disclose any information about the asbestos liability.

Whoops!

Not disclosing the information to its shareholders cost the company more than $6 billion. During a 15-year period, Selwyn Drummer, the CEO, was paid $277,189,018, which was obviously unjust, and depending on who you asked, even perverse. His annual income averaged $14,588,896. Pure greed! I had to wonder how many members of the board of directors approved of this absurd compensation, or if Drummer had managed to leverage those payments in exchange for hiding the company's malfeasance. Either way, he was one lucky bastard.

Judge Glynn took the bench, and after exchanging a few pleasantries with both parties, she addressed the legendary lawyer I had never met and was anxious to watch in action. Robert Smalley was a man I had admired from afar ever since he became the de facto king of winning class action cases, with judges awarding his clients monetary packages never seen before, most of which apparently went to him and the high-powered law firm that brought him in to work his freelance magic. Some attorneys I knew, who were pretty wealthy themselves, always referred to Smalley as that "filthy rich lawyer." They said it with reverence and fear, as if his awesome prowess in the courtroom was not only impressive; it was intimidating. I was fascinated and couldn't wait to see how he would work the judge.

Robert Smalley looked so dapper and cool he must've come straight from filming a TV show about some badass lawyers. Without a doubt, he appeared as if he owned the courtroom. This was a relatively small case for him, certainly when it came to monetary value, but it posed potential ramifications for a related action that could yield him hundreds of millions of dollars later.

As for me, I was there to get my money, and Smalley was the lynchpin *and* the sideshow.

Judge Glynn got right to the point.

"Mr. Smalley, how much money from the $9.5 million settlement will the clients specifically receive?"

It was as if she had been waiting anxiously for the hearing to begin, itching to bait Smalley with her question.

"I do not know, Judge," he said.

I heard a distinct murmur among some people in the courtroom when Smalley said that. At the time, I had been practicing law for nearly 10 years and had never heard any attorney address a judge that way, as "Judge." I had only heard them use "Your Honor." Smalley's response struck me as odd and shocking. Was he messing with the judge to show her that he was in control of her courtroom? I wondered if she would let it slide or chop his head off, right then and there.

BREAKING NEWS: "Smalley Goes Down in Round One!"

Little did I know, in the midst of my own panic, that she was saving that for me. I had stepped directly into the fire of a contentious courtroom, as I quickly realized that the Plaintiffs in this class-action lawsuit weren't the only ones encountering the larger-than-life world of corporate greed.

I watched Judge Glynn consider Smalley for a moment from the raised perch of her bench, as if she was debating in her head whether to chew him out or save it for a future moment. I had no idea if she knew who he was, but I figured his reputation must have preceded him all the way to Texas.

Smalley jumped in before she had a chance to continue.

"Well, the cost to administer the settlement will be approximately $2.7 million," he said, "plus the attorney fees will be $3.5 million and we also have the $275,000 attorney fee to Mr. Coleman on top of that."

I almost stood up, ready to make my claim. I was scared, because when I heard Smalley incorrectly answer the judge, I panicked. I thought she would never approve my fee because his client lost a ton of money and was going to walk away with pennies. I figured if I could sell the judge on the fact that my fee was not going to be an additional cost to the settlement fund then she would approve it.

Smalley turned slowly and stared at me. Then, he nodded as if he knew who I was and was telling me to cool it.

Judge Glynn raised an eyebrow.

That's when a chorus of boos broke out behind me.

"Fucking greedy lawyers!"

"You all suck!"

"Kill all the lawyers!"

The screaming continued until Judge Glynn rocked the room with her gavel.

"Enough," she said. "Order in the courtroom, please."

The chorus of boos stopped for a second. I hadn't noticed this handful of protesters when I came in and wondered how they had gotten past security and who had organized them.

"What about us? What about us? What about us?"

The chanting became quite loud until Judge Glynn slammed down her gavel again.

"Enough! And I mean it!"

She had quite a set of pipes when she chose to use them.

"Bailiff, escort these troublemakers out of here immediately. I will not tolerate this kind of dissent in my courtroom. Ever!"

As the uniformed officer of the court moved to the back of the room, the shouting started again until two policemen showed up out of nowhere and gathered up the screamers who had managed to get inside and raise holy hell. I was still wondering who had organized them and what they were trying to accomplish. After all, there was nothing illegal, or even controversial about what was happening. Lawsuits are for lawyers. Everyone knows that they make a ton of money doing this stuff, so what's the big deal?

"Order!"

Judge Glynn banged her gavel one last time, just to remind all of us who was in charge.

"Thank you, officers. Now, let's get back to business. We've got some math to do with this case, concerning these administrative costs and the lawyer fees, despite what a few people in the peanut gallery had to say."

Shit! I felt like she was never going to approve the settlement. At that point, I was sweating in my best clothes, as I really thought my $275,000 fee would be gone. Based on what Robert Smalley just told Judge Glynn, coupled with the fact that there were 860,000 shareholders listed as class members, I knew I had to do something. I figured Smalley was in it for himself, and definitely not caring one way or the other for me. It felt like my fee was slipping away fast and I just couldn't let that happen. Guys from Philly can't let shit like that slide, not in a courtroom or on the street.

Now, this might sound like I'm some kinda tough guy, but I'm not. I grew up in a rough neighborhood, but I'm really a cupcake. Being the youngest kid, my mother pampered me and wouldn't let me get into any fights at school or on our block. If I had, she would have cracked me harder than anyone else. That didn't automatically make me a mama's boy, but I was close.

After Judge Glynn determined that from the $9.5 million settlement there would only be approximately $3 million to distribute to the 860,000 class members, I figured there was no way she would ever approve the settlement. To me, that meant I was not going to receive the $275,000 legal fee, which I had earned and had been promised I would collect.

I tried not to panic, but I was not feeling too good as the judge continued the proceedings.

"So, it's $9.5 million, less $2.7 million to administer the settlement," she said, "less $3.5 million in attorney fees to the Plaintiffs' counsel, less $275,000 for attorney fees sought by Mr. Coleman. Is that correct?"

That's when my nerves got the better of me, and I did what any relatively inexperienced lawyer would do while attempting to save a hefty $275,000 fee. I stood up, totally unsolicited, completely ignoring everything Bill Waterman had told me just minutes before. I wasted no time getting my head chewed off by a smooth, acidic judge with no patience for rookie attorneys who talk out of turn.

"Your Honor, respectfully," I said.

I was using the correct terminology, but I still felt blood rushing to my face. This was no game for me. I didn't come all the way to Texas to go home empty handed.

"Excuse me. I am Mr. Coleman. Ryan Coleman. Allow me to point out that the attorney fees in the derivative case are paid out of the attorney fees that you award to counsel for the class case. So, it would *not* be an additional $275,000 of fees and expenses. That clarification is important here."

The judge stared at me.

"I'm just saying, Your Honor."

I guess I was hoping that if Judge Glynn knew that the attorneys' fees awarded in my derivative case were not an additional charge to the $9.5 million settlement fund, that it would help her approve the entire settlement, which would mean that I would receive the $275,000 and I could leave Dallas a happy and much wealthier man. My wife would be thrilled.

Judge Glynn glared at me, as my panic, and maybe greed, were probably obvious. From my perspective, she looked dumbfounded, which reminded me of a famous scene from the 1995 film *Apollo 13*, when, after an explosion on the ship, the character played by Tom Hanks says, "Houston, we have a problem."

11

Shit! In that moment I wished I was inside mission control a few hours away at NASA and not appearing before Judge Glynn in Dallas, where she was about to teach me a lesson, deservedly so, for attempting to deceive the Court. Her questions to me, recorded in the official transcript, do not adequately reflect her attitude, as the court reporter was not able to capture in words the judge's acidic facial expressions, which she directed straight at me.

"Well, now, Mr. Coleman . . ." she said, trying her best to control herself, ". . . if I am supposed to understand that from your papers, I certainly do not."

She was referring to the brief, a legal document I had filed before the hearing, which specifically detailed the terms of the settlement, which was my not-so-subtle effort to convince Judge Glynn to accept the terms of my full settlement.

Basically, she had just said to me that when she reviewed my brief, it didn't state that the attorneys' fees are paid from the amount awarded to Schwartz & Bennett. She was correct. My brief did not say that because I made up that fact before her in court that day, hoping to convince her to accept the settlement, specifically my $275,000. I did not anticipate that Judge Glynn would be fully aware of the settlement terms.

"I stand corrected, Your Honor."

I probably sounded as sheepish as a kid who gets caught with his hand in a cookie jar. I wanted to shrug innocently at her, as I might have done with my mother when I screwed up, but it wasn't a good look, for me or my expensive suit.

"Well, Mr. Coleman, how is it that you don't know that?"

At least she was being civilized and hadn't thrown me out of the courtroom for some contempt charge, which she could have just made up if she had wanted to. I mean, who was going to argue? The Plaintiffs and my fellow lawyers would have been happy to have my share added to theirs. Still, I was impressed that she hadn't yet shut me down completely.

"Your Honor, that was my understanding."

I watched her eyebrows move. I had spoken way too fast, but as I said, I had an agenda and I wasn't about to let anyone mess it up, not even a judge.

"Well, I must say that I'm mystified by how I could have a different understanding about how you will get paid than you do. How is it that you do not know that?"

I waited for the protesters to give me shit on that one, but thankfully, they hadn't returned, which left me stuck with the judge.

She seemed to surprise everyone by raising her voice to ask me that question. I was sweating by this point from her line of questioning about my mistake. My bad. I had thrust myself into the frontline way too quickly, without thinking any of it through, and had wasted no time getting my head chewed off by this smooth, acerbic judge who had no patience for young attorneys who talk out of turn.

I had no idea that she could see that I was trying to bullshit her. I also had no clue that she would consider my bogus attempt so offensive.

I wanted to say," Judge, it's not a big deal, okay, in light of the value of the settlement, right? So, can we move on now?"

No, I wasn't getting off that easy.

Judge Glynn seemed to take pleasure in belittling this rookie lawyer, maybe because she was an unhappy person and made herself feel better by ripping into others.

That wasn't my only concern. What kind of crappy impression had I made on Robert Smalley, too? That upset me even more because I had fantasies about working with him someday, side-by-side, raking in obscene buckets of cash from corrupt corporations who were hurting innocent consumers. I would be a hero, too, like him, a Robin Hood for the people, robbing from the rich and giving it to the poor, I mean their attorneys, or something like that, even though I have personally never met a poor attorney.

I had been involved in the preparation of the Notice that was mailed to every one of the 860,000 shareholders, all of whom were official class members, so I knew about where my fee was coming from. But in the heat of the moment, inside that literally steamy courtroom, I just panicked, completely obsessed with the money, which meant all rational thought, which lawyers are supposedly trained to maintain, had been thrown out the window.

"Your Honor, my understanding was that the fee you will award me will come from the settlement fund. The company is not paying it in addition to the $9.5 million, but it does come out of Counsel's fee, so I stand corrected, Your Honor."

I knew I had botched it good and could only hope that she would do me a favor and make things right—for me, at least. After all, that's why I was there—for me and my money.

Now, normally I would provide a footnote here in my word-for-word transcript of what transpired in court that day, but then you would miss out on how the official court reporter had such a hard time keeping a straight face as she noted every single word of Judge Glynn dressing me down. The stenographer nearly spit up her coffee trying to keep up with barrage of bullshit I had to endure in front of all those people, including Robert Smalley.

Her rebuke came so fast and to the point that I had to check for a second to make sure I was still wearing any clothes. Thankfully, her legal magic stopped short of rendering me naked, so I was merely left embarrassed and humiliated in front of the entire courtroom.

I was still fully clothed, of course, in my impeccable Canali tonal pinstripe classic suit and those excellent and impressive handcrafted Alden dress shoes, what any nattily dressed lawyer would prefer to be seen in but knew well enough was a stupid idea to wear through a government building metal detector. Obviously, I still had much to learn when it came to practicality and fashion, as well as legal skills.

# Three

## Barbecue in Texas:
## A Lawyer's Rep Is All He's Got (Besides the Cash)

Judge Glynn would not overlook my desperation. She was not content with my answers and probably did *not* enjoy watching me get so sweaty in her courtroom. Then again, from my vantage point, she was being a bully and probably enjoyed watching me squirm.

"Well, Mr. Coleman, I understand you are correcting yourself, but I'm going to ask you one more time. Can you explain to me, please, how it is that you would not know how your fees are going to be paid, and that I would know because I read your papers? Excuse me, but how is it that you don't know?"

Looking back on that day, I think Judge Glynn made such a big deal about the issue of my legal fees because when I stood up and said my fees would be paid by Schwartz & Bennett, a fact which was not included in the papers I filed, she knew I was trying to BS her in her own courtroom. Bad move! Due to my inexperience, and lack of a seasoned, wily mentor, I never anticipated that she would respond in this manner.

I wasn't used to being berated like that. The Philly Street in me was ready to punch back, but I knew that would be an extremely bad idea. Instead, I chose to keep it civil.

"Obviously, the paperwork does detail where my fees are coming from, so it must have been a mistake on my part, Your Honor."

She looked at me as if I'd memorized my excuse for cheating on a term paper.

"And for that, Your Honor, I humbly apologize."

I figured I had gone that far, so I might as well pour on the bullshit and see if it worked. While she played me like a puppy, I was doing a great job of demonstrating how a relatively inexperienced lawyer can mess up big-time in an intimidating arena that provides little to no room for anxious stupidity and lame excuses.

I bowed to her, hoping our little back and forth was finished, but Judge Glynn threw me for a loop when out of nowhere she asked me about my flights from Philadelphia to Dallas.

"Once again, Mr. Coleman, I recognize that in the big picture this is not a substantial amount, but you listed airfare of $2,600."

She was referring to the itemization of my expenses, which I had included in my brief.

"That's correct, Your Honor. I can present the receipts to the Court."

"Is that $2,600 for you? Just *you* Mr. Coleman?"

She took her sweet time repeating the number, as if it were a curse word.

"Two thousand, six hundred dollars?"

"Yes, Your Honor. What happened is, each time I came to Texas for a hearing, when you don't stay the weekend, the airline charges $1,293. That's correct."

I bit my tongue because an associate I knew who worked at Schwartz & Bennett told me that Robert Smalley flew only with charter airplanes after 9/11. So, while Judge Glynn was taking issue with my airfare budget, she likely would have fainted when she heard what it cost him and what he billed. Then again, if Smalley was paying for the flights out of his own pocket, Judge Glynn would not have cared. I believed then, and still do, that Smalley, and others like him, would not do anything that was not in the best interest of the class he was representing, so if he did fly on a charter plane, it was paid for by him personally or he had to fly like that so he could go back and forth the most efficient way possible, which is something that lawyers working cases like this have to do from time to time, at least according to the man himself. As Smalley used to say, it's just another human cost of doing this kind of business.

He may have appeared to Judge Glynn to be a slick lawyer from the elite Northeast, but according to some associates of mine who had seen him operate behind the scenes, once you got to know him, you would only say that the man is a mensch, even if he does wear incredibly expensive suits. I mean, when a colleague's wife was battling breast cancer and was on her deathbed, Smalley apparently drove an hour-and-a-half each way to have dinner with the guy one night a week, just to be there to comfort a friend. That's the kind of guy he was, and I wish someone could've told that to Judge Glynn, but I was already in a jam of my own.

The whole time I was speaking back and forth with Judge Glynn, I was standing at the Plaintiffs' table. Right next to me, sitting in a chair, was Bill Waterman, who couldn't seem to stop shaking his head and rolling his eyes. In fact, he handed me a note.

I WARNED YOU!

Yeah, he was right. I should not have spoken out of turn.

Later during the hearing, Judge Glynn asked me another loaded question about the lawsuit, which I had filed six months earlier in Federal Court.

"Mr. Coleman, does that take into account the facts that were just stated, which I believe to be correct, and my statement to be incorrect, so does that help you in your derivative case?"

This was a compound question, which kind of stumped me for a minute. Once again, I wished I had run out for a coffee before this all began because I was struggling to keep up.

"Your Honor, I think that's a three-part question."

"Excuse me, Mr. Coleman, but you can't object to a judge's compound question. Objection to my question is overruled."

I heard plenty of laughter when she said that so quickly. I wasn't sure if it was with me or against me, but at that point I was sweating like a pig, and my anxiety was out of control. It was way too hot in Dallas in August, but for me it wasn't the heat. It was pure nerves, embarrassment, and full-fledged panic about getting the money.

Judge Glynn never forgot the issue of my mistake about where the $275,000 in fees was coming from, because at precisely two hours and 48 minutes into the hearing, she reminded everyone in her courtroom, including more than 30 lawyers, about my blunder.

"The concern that I had," she said, her voice dripping with sarcasm, "was that Mr. Coleman did not know where his fees were coming from."

I wanted to roll my eyes, but I stuffed it. Let's just say, I was lucky not to be thrown out of the courtroom. And thank God I ended up receiving my agreed-upon fee.

Two-hundred-seventy-five-thousand-dollars.

Looking back, I am pretty sure that Judge Glynn took great pleasure in exposing me as a greedy attorney, trying gamely but lamely to dupe the Court.

Ironically, I ended up receiving a much more positive result compared to Richard Schwartz, the chief partner in his firm, which Robert Smalley had elevated to near mythical status. I found this out two weeks later, when Judge Glynn issued her official Order, which not only affected Schwartz's professional reputation because the effects rippled throughout his entire firm.

She stated that Smalley, by merely arguing that none of the Plaintiffs' claims are likely to succeed, had offered no concrete evidence at the Fairness Hearing in Dallas to justify his position. Judge Glynn also pointed out that Smalley had relied on a declaration from one of his associates, who only had been practicing law for seven years, stating that the settlement was fair and reasonable. How that happened is anybody's guess.

Judge Glynn made a subtle point in her Order, which also served to embarrass Schwartz and Smalley. She stated that Don Stovall, the attorney for the company being sued, was a bigger advocate for the settlement than

Schwartz and his firm. To me, it is embarrassing if an attorney representing a defendant is considered more passionate about a settlement than the
plaintiffs' counsel. Then again, perhaps the biggest passion these lawyers
share is using the system to make as much money as possible, and to be
honest, that includes me.

The Judge's Order also mentioned that she had attempted to determine how much the client, Secure Asset Management Group (SAM),
would receive from the $9.5 million settlement for their calculated loss of
approximately $870,000. She determined that SAM would receive no
more than $1,000, which was shocking. Why? Because SAM loses
$870,000, agrees to serve as lead Plaintiff, and at the end of the case is fine
with receiving $1,000, whereas Smalley, on behalf of Schwartz & Bennett,
received $2.5 million.

Nice work if you can get it.

This was a classic example of why I felt so excited by the entire field
of class-action law, where even though clients receive next to nothing, the
lawyers reap millions. I mean, I can't help it if we're lucky.

In the conclusion of her Order, and I'm telling you this just so you
won't think things go the lawyer's way *all* the time, Judge Glynn ordered
the parties to engage in mediation so they could try to resolve the lawsuit.
She believed a fair, reasonable, and adequate settlement could be achieved.
She appointed a Guardian Ad Litem to represent the class at the mediation, and to advise the Court as to the fairness, reasonableness, and ade-
quacy of any settlement proposal they reached through the mediation.

Let me explain some shit here. It's not like I'm showing off, but I did
learn a few things in law school. A guardian is a person designated to
protect or help someone. Ad litem means "for the lawsuit." A Guardian
ad Litem refers to an attorney appointed by a judge to act in the best
interest of a party when they are not able to do so on their own, which is
usually in settings involving children. Fees for the mediator and guardian
ad litem were to be shared equally among the defendants and plaintiffs.

What Judge Glynn did to Smalley and Schwartz was tantamount to a public castration. I mean, she screwed them by appointing a Guardian ad Litem, whose job was to oversee the settlement negotiations of a class-action case, something I had rarely seen done. Judge Glynn did reference a few cases in her Order where this had been done before, but it was a surprising move she made after that loaded day in Dallas.

She simply did not trust Schwartz & Bennett to do the right thing by the class. Why else would she have appointed a babysitter? Her decision rendered Schwartz & Bennett relatively impotent in court for a few years, as they could not file for lead plaintiffs because any opposition they faced would cite the 2018 Dallas result as a means of disqualifying them.

But amazingly, Smalley, as a ringer that day, avoided the worst fallout and continued doing his thing and racking up enormous payolas. Good to be independent, right?

In every securities class action, a number of law firms jockey to serve as lead plaintiffs' attorneys because they receive almost all of the attorneys' fees. Nice, huh? This probably cost the firm many millions of dollars because they could not be appointed lead counsel. If they had attempted to pull it off, their efforts would have not only been negated; their reputations would have been harmed.

As I've learned the hard way, a lawyer's reputation is all he's got, aside from an excellent wardrobe, so it's a fine line to tread, no matter how fancy your shoes may be.

As Mortimer Zuckerman, the real estate magnate and media billionaire, once said, "Practicing law is the exact opposite of sex. Even when it's good, it's bad."

# Four

## Biggest Payday Ever:
## Not Too Bad for a Kid from Philadelphia

Luckily, Judge Brenda Glynn did not throw me out of the courtroom. I guess I demonstrated how a rookie lawyer can mess up big-time in an intimidating arena that provides little room for anxious stupidity and a speck of avarice. Okay, more than a speck, let's be honest, but that's the name of the game. After all, I didn't come all the way down to Texas to buy a Dallas Cowboys hat. I came to claim my share of the pie, good old-fashioned American pie, the kind you bite into to swallow the cash. Of course, the plaintiffs deserved their crumbs, which they invariably received, months or years later, after all of us lawyers had received our hard-earned compensation. So, when it came to following in the footsteps of Robert Smalley, I wanted the rich part with just a small side of filthy.

Since the Defendants representing our adversary wanted to settle my derivative case, things took a turn for the better that day after being raked over the coals by Judge Glynn. I had become an unwitting minor celebrity and easy to pick out among the coterie of slick lawyers and their well-appointed lackeys. I was flattered for a second, but then I wasn't sure if they wanted to meet me or avoid me.

During a brief recess, I went outside to get some fresh air, if you can call what Dallas offers in August a form of oxygen. As I exited the courthouse, I noticed a line-up of limousines, all getting pelted by a barrage of water bottles and fake money. One of the drivers jumped out of his car to yell at a group of protesters gathered on the other side of a police barricade. They were jumping from one chant to another, trying to rile themselves up as much as anyone else.

"Power to the People!"

"Steal from the rich and give it to the poor, tell those lawyers we're not their whore!"

"Corrupt! Corrupt! The system is Corrupt!

This one driver, who told me he was waiting for Robert Smalley, was having none of it. He whipped out a fire extinguisher from the trunk of his limo and hit the lot of them with a blast of chemical smoke. By the time I wiped away the residue from my eyes, the protesters were gone and the only sounds they were making were coughing, wheezing and cussing out whoever just gassed them. The driver looked satisfied, and as he put away the extinguisher he told me that the other limos were waiting for Schwartz, a few corporate bosses and the judge.

I went back inside, wondering if Smalley had any idea of what his driver was capable of doing. That was some real Masters of the Universe type stuff, so if the driver acted like that, who knows what his boss might do when he's in a position to "remove" someone? Smalley was becoming more and more intriguing to me.

At the next break in the action, an attorney by the name of Rick Boyles approached me. He said that it did not matter whether Judge Glynn approved the class-action settlement or not because the Defendants were interested in settling my case. At that time, Rick worked for Baker Botts, a firm with more than 700 attorneys that was a major political player. It's crazy to imagine 700 lawyers, mostly men, mostly white, all with something to prove or flaunt or manipulate, all working inside one building.

The testosterone levels alone could have probably blown the roof off and the competition within the firm must have been dizzying. On that day in Dallas, they wanted to end the case, according to Boyles, which meant that it was essentially a done deal, as long as Judge Glynn signed off on the particulars, with the biggest one, according to me, being my fee! Like I said, why else would I be in Texas unless I was chasing the biggest payday of my life?

I had put significant time into the case, having flown down there on two separate occasions to prepare the briefs. Then again, when I think again about my actual time spent on the particulars, I didn't exactly spend a commensurate number of hours to match the amount of money I received. Not even close. To be fair, which is an obscure concept in most of these situations, maybe even an oxymoron, I only spent enough time working on the case to merit earning a $50,000 fee, but I ultimately received more. Much more.

Call me oxy, but I'm no moron.

Before Judge Glynn would approve the final settlement of my lawsuit, she required a telephone conversation, arranged by her law clerk, which took place less than two weeks after the hearing. I was on the call with Judge Glynn and Rick Boyles. She made herself crystal clear that she wanted to be certain that the Release, a legal document that serves to terminate any liability between the parties, was properly handled. The call lasted less than ten minutes and Judge Glynn was not exactly friendly, pleasant, or nice. It's hard to say if that was her usual style on the phone, but when I hung up, I was not feeling too good about the chances of her approving my settlement.

"Honey, you're gonna have to drive your stupid Honda a little while longer."

I figured I might have some explaining to do to my wife, who seemed to still be under the impression that money grows on trees or simply falls out of the sky if you have a law degree and a good suit. She probably learned that growing up in a rich family. Daddy bought her whatever she wanted, and so she expected her husband to do the same thing.

I had been promising her a new car for quite a while, so this windfall of cash was coming at a perfect time. Of course, I had my own Benz, which was necessary for appearances and all, not to mention how comfy it was, but I needed more dough to get a new ride for the wife. If there's one thing you don't want to do to a woman who grew up with a silver spoon up her ass it's breaking a promise, whether it's for a brand-new car, a fancy dinner, or some exotic vacation in fucking paradise.

Much to my surprise, it didn't take long for Judge Glynn to sign the Order approving my case and all the "costs" requested from the court. That meant I received my $275,000 in attorney fees, all in one big fat transaction. Holy shit! Not too bad for a city kid from Philadelphia. I was lucky to get caught up in that legal storm, which turned corporate corruption into a fountain of cash, for me and a handful of other lawyers. I was relieved to receive the entire fee because one never knows how things can turn out in the practice of securities class actions. While the hotshot attorneys look like they rule the courtroom, it's really the judges who run the show.

That day in Dallas was just the beginning of my education, an unexpected introduction into a world of legal mumbo jumbo, courthouse theatre and huge settlements, with unheard of rewards for the filthy rich lawyers and other players in a system that enables it all to thrive. I not only won approval of the full terms of my settlement. I had the unique good fortune to meet the one-and-only Robert Smalley.

He entered the courtroom that day believing that the Judge would have approved a settlement and dismissed the case, which explains why he had recommended to Schwartz & Bennet that they enter into settlement negotiations with Drummer and his company. Smalley turned out to be right, because the case eventually went all the way up to the United States Supreme Court on two different occasions, which could have resulted in an adverse ruling, affecting the Plaintiffs' ability to recover money. But it didn't, and Smalley and everyone else ended up "earning" even more money than Judge Glynn initially awarded them.

The second highlight of my trip to Dallas came the following day when Bill Waterman arranged for me to play golf at the exclusive Northwood Country Club. I was an avid golfer and welcomed the chance to play such a magnificent gem of a course, home of the 1952 U.S. Open, won by Julius Boros, who walked away with $4,000 for his efforts. Sixty-five years later, I'm not sure I could even buy the shoes I want for that kind of scratch.

Considering all the money I expected to receive, I felt as if I belonged in that club. I was also relieved to be far away from that steamy Dallas courtroom. For all I knew, I was on my way to bigger and better paydays, which meant pricier and better clothes, too.

Oh yeah, there was one catch. I suppose I should 'fess up here and explain how this really went down. I couldn't use my name to solicit clients—just in case any lawyers in the Plaintiffs' Bar alienated me. The whole thing was sticky, at best. I had originally managed to move the suit forward with an alternate email, along with a friend and front man who didn't mind me using his name for a 10 percent share of my fee. I mean, you gotta do what you gotta do, right? I was lucky, though, that my buddy, Stan, did what he did because he could have said no, which would have risked the whole enchilada.

A move like that would piss off lots of lawyers, but Stan was too cool for school and didn't care. Then, I called Bill Waterman, and asked him for a client. He referred a shareholder to me and didn't even ask for a percentage of my fee, but I ended up sending him a payment which amounted to approximately 20 percent of what I ended up making. That's a cool 50 grand for Waterman, just for a reference, which took him five minutes to do. As I mentioned, since I was not admitted to practice in the Northern District of Texas Court, I needed a local counsel, because that's where the class-action suit was situated. Waterman became responsible for filing all the case documents. Okay, that took him more than five minutes, but I think I made my point. He and I developed a close personal relationship, and now I feel fortunate to call him a friend.

By the way, Rick Boyles was appointed general counsel for the defendant company and eventually received $8.85 million in 2019 for his services. Schwartz & Bennett suffered a few flesh wounds as a result of that day in court and felt the aftershock of Judge Glynn's wrath, but no one is shedding a tear for one of America's most legendary class-action law firms. They made a ton of money on other cases and left Texas and Judge Glynn in their rearview mirror. In fact, Schwartz sold one of his houses for $20 million, so I guess he did relatively okay. And before the leaves started falling on the streets of Philadelphia, Judge Glynn was appointed Chief Judge of the Northern District of Texas, a prestigious position, which probably came with a few perks.

Shortly after receiving the $275,000 fee, I attended my 10-year reunion at Temple University Law School. I ran into a friend I hadn't seen since we graduated who said he did legal work for a non-profit, facilitating their mission of feeding the poor and disadvantaged. I was a bit embarrassed for a minute. What did I do? I helped myself to a large legal fee. Did I change anything? No. Did I make the world a better place, even a little? No. Not at all.

Well, come to think of it, maybe I did. Think about the people who will benefit when I spend that $275,000. You got your golf clubs, car dealerships, shoemakers, tailors, and salespeople, not to mention the illicit, under-the-table relationships that naturally evolve out of these circumstances. I'm talking cash tips and all kind of "thank you" gifts for uh . . . use your imagination, okay?

As I drove home from my reunion, I had to reflect on what I had been doing that led me to the best payday of my life. Luckily, I only had ten years to consider, one marriage, two cars, a house, a law partner and a few part-time secretaries. As far as I knew, I didn't owe anybody any money and I took decent care of my peeps. But as I said, I was no moron. Naïve, okay, but not an idiot. I knew I was working in a world bathed in greed, and at the end of the day, I was no different than those other lawyers. I willfully participated. Granted, I was fighting against the worst behavior of the greediest companies and the individuals who made them that way. While it's true that I was not on the bad side, I can't honestly say I was on the good side either . . .

I don't know. That revelation, and a good pair of shoes, might get me a cup of coffee.

Meanwhile, the best thing that came out of my time in Dallas, aside from the big bucks, was meeting the hotshot of hotshot attorneys, Robert Smalley, a legend in the making, who knew precisely what I had attempted to do in bullshitting the court.

He flashed a hint of a smile and winked at me on his way out of the courtroom that day and said four words I'll never forget.

"You got balls, kid."

It wouldn't be long before he introduced me to a world I never imagined being privy to, one that would eventually test my moral code of ethics and change my life—not necessarily for the better.

# Five

## Hear That Whistle?
## Bunny Greenhouse Spills the Beans

My wife says I'm a quick learner, and who am I to argue? With that in mind, let me provide some historical context for how class action lawsuits come about in the first place. Imagine a defense contractor, like Halliburton, for example, who have a history of going to great lengths to circumvent the legal system in order to maximize their shareholders' profit, that is, until they end up in court on the wrong end of a class action lawsuit.

As I previously pointed out, the stars of these complicated proceedings are the manipulative, high-powered lawyers who routinely work the levers of power like no one else, and not only for their clients. In fact, they do it for their own egotistical satisfaction and to create unimaginable wealth, mostly for themselves and their exclusive firms.

But these lawyers cannot operate in a bubble. They need at least one individual to raise a stink, someone those of us in the biz affectionately call a whistleblower. Regular folks get dazzled by the idea of a single person raising a ruckus, as if they are some kinda one-man-band taking on the system all by their lonesome. Granted, it does take courage to step forward and deal with the consequences of blowing that whistle, especially when it's a company like Halliburton, that notoriously does not play fair.

Let's go back a few years to examine what happened with them and a single adversary who decided that enough was enough. In June 2005, a genuine patriot and courageous employee, Bunny Greenhouse, spilled the beans on a Halliburton corporate subsidiary, which had just received a $7 billion, no-bid contract from the U.S. Army.

She eventually testified before a Congressional panel about chronic fraud, waste and irregularities inside Halliburton, and surprise, surprise, their boys club, facilitated by a cutthroat team of lawyers, retaliated against Bunny the whistleblower.

The former CEO of Halliburton issued a statement that he had broken all ties with the company when he threw his hat into the ring with George W. Bush. But that didn't stop the puppet master of the Iraq war from whining about how Halliburton was being treated unfairly by the American public. Poor guy. First, he has a lousy heart condition and then the people who voted for him have the nerve to break his failing Halliburton heart.

Let's do a quick contextual review of history. In 2003, we supposedly went to war in Iraq for two reasons: weapons of mass destruction and Saddam Hussein's support of terrorists. It doesn't take a rocket scientist to figure out that there was a third reason, perhaps the biggest one of all: money! Contractors like Halliburton always want war somewhere because of the profits they make. Who cares about the lives lost, limbs blown off, and countries all but destroyed? Despite the opposition to the Iraq War, the neocons pulled the right strings in the White House, Congress and the Pentagon to make the war a cash cow for them and their pals.

Fact: KBR, a subsidiary of Halliburton, earned $38 billion during the Iraq War.

Fact: The U.S. Army was heavily criticized over contracts they made with Halliburton.

Fact: Bunny Greenhouse blew the whistle on a no-bid, $7 billion government contract.

Fact: Jamie Leigh Jones, an administrative assistant serving in Iraq with KBR, claimed to have been drugged and gang-raped while working for the defense contractor. She testified before the House Judiciary Committee about the incident in 2007, and after a painful trial, especially for her, the jury found in favor of the defendants.

The judge awarded the defendants $145,000 in court costs, much less than the $2 million the attorneys requested. I think Jones would have fared better in front of an arbitration panel instead of a jury. It's likely that a panel of three lawyers would have found in her favor.

Either way, the controversy for Halliburton seems to know no bounds. But they're not the only gigantic corporation playing devastating games. A few years earlier, newspapers exploded with reports of Enron executives hiding a billion in debt, which caused them to file bankruptcy and fire 5,000 people virtually overnight.

In that case, the judge awarded lawyers' fees of $688 million, more than five times the billable hours they submitted. Hey, I don't fault the lawyers for getting as much money as possible, but why did the judge agree to give them *that* much? I mean, isn't it ironic that a private company suddenly collapses from hiding all that debt while another one has the United States government give them a $7 billion no-bid contract?

Stranger than fiction? You bet. Does it happen every day in the dark shadows of corporate boardrooms and government think tanks? You betcha. How do I know? I've seen email chains that would blow your mind, with top execs and government officials agreeing to shit that should never fly in the light of day.

For example, imagine if the CEO of a company invites a cabinet secretary to go hunting and offers to pay for the whole thing. Sounds innocent, right? It might be, until the next email says, "Can't wait to shoot some profitable holes in your department's budget. LOL." Then, the government official responds, saying, "Sounds like we're aiming for the same damn target!"

Hey, it takes two to tango, especially when the dance card is full of worms like these two guys. They put the shit in shithead if you know what I mean. They make lawyers like Smalley look like saints, coming to the rescue to save the day for those whistleblowers!

But let's go back to those judges awarding class action lawyers astronomical fees. How can that happen? If a painter comes to your house and charges $400 to paint a room, do you choose to pay him $2,000 just to be nice? What the hell were these judges thinking?

In every one of these perverse decisions, a team of razor-sharp lawyers worked in secret with company execs to pull that shit off, and they devised the language to make everything appear just right for anyone nosing around to find any fault in their behavior.

This raises a big question about self-respect. Then again, if we're being honest, self-respect is not a priority for *all* lawyers, including me, at least not all the time.

For example, Joe Jamail, Jr., maybe the most successful lawyer in the country, had his own set of standards. Once listed by *Forbes* as one of the 400 richest Americans with a net worth of more than $1 billion, he left the Texas D.A. office to make a fortune as a personal injury lawyer. His first big corporate payday came with the Texaco-Pennzoil case in 1987, when he received an estimated $345 million in fees.

"There's no limit to how big a whore I can be," he said, when he was 73 years old. "And it's hard to quit. There's still some loose money out there."

Indeed, there is, and I'm still wondering if Bunny Greenhouse saw any of it.

# Six

## Medium Rare:
## Smalley Takes Me Out to Tear Up the Town

I must have done something right inside that Dallas courtroom because Robert Smalley, the brilliant attorney, told me I had balls. I guess he was impressed because a few weeks later he invited me to meet him for a night-on-the-town in New York City. I was thrilled with the invitation and anxious to experience "life with the big boys" if you know what I mean. Robert Smalley! Are you kidding? Asking me to hang out with him in The Big Apple?

I had looked forward to a night like this for a long time—stepping out in public into rarified society air with a man of Robert Smalley's stature. Every colleague I knew would be jealous of my unique opportunity. His reputation as a wild partier was fairly well-known among lawyers, and I was excited to find out first-hand what made a guy like him tick. I hadn't really met him yet, aside from our brief exchange in that courtroom, but from everything I'd heard through the grapevine, when it comes to the world of class action abuse, Robert Smalley is the poster child for unprecedented shenanigans and unexpected victories.

Somehow, those two characteristics went together when it came to Smalley's outrageous legal techniques and the gigantic set of testicles he possessed, which must have made him believe he could get away with just about anything, which apparently he did.

He and I were half a generation apart. He was born ten years before me, in 1972. I knew he had made millions in the class-action field before he even turned 35. A real wunderkind. He claimed in some media outlet featuring him as the new celebrity face of the legal world, that his take home pay was only $10 million. Anybody who knew anything knew that was pure bullshit, but I bet he said it as a joke. I considered asking him about it when we met in New York.

Smalley was the quintessential example of a lawyer who became filthy rich by exploiting corporate greed and the judicial system for his own best interests, without really affecting any significant change or improving the problem at the center of the action. His attitude about his clients in several on-air interviews demonstrated the problems people were talking about when it came to securities class-action lawsuits.

I didn't give a shit about what a bunch of critics and nerdy academics thought. It wasn't the money I was interested in hearing about, either, although I have to admit I was a little curious about what expensive toys he might enjoy. What I really wanted to hear about on our night out was his methodology, how he was able to do what he did, and what he really thought about the class-action practice of law.

Okay, okay. I also wanted to know how I could make money like him.

As an up-and-coming attorney, I wanted to impress a man like Smalley from the jump, so I arrived at the famous Sparks Steak House in midtown Manhattan 15 minutes early. As soon as I mentioned his name to the hostess, I heard a distinct and loud voice.

"Coleman, here you are. Welcome. You finally made it."

I was so excited I could hardly talk. I reached out to shake hands, but Smalley was already holding a drink in each one of his large mitts, as if they grew naturally right out of his fingers. He offered me a glass with a warm, extremely confident smile, stretching from ear to ear. His teeth looked perfect, much like his hair, which was exquisitely combed to fit the exact contours of his head. I figured he was happy to see me, and I was still quite curious about why he had invited me to meet him.

He explained that were starting off our night with a bottle of Dom Perignon P3 Plenitude Brut 1984 champagne, which I later found out goes for more than four grand.

"1984 was a very good year for me, Ryan. I fingered my first girl, and the rest is history."

"She was a lucky girl, I'm sure."

"Yeah, I was in sixth grade, and she was in eighth. Needless to say, I became a legend right then and there."

"Wow, most guys don't even kiss a girl until they're in high school."

"You better believe it. Lottie Shackelford. We're still friends, too."

"Here's to Lottie, then. May she enjoy more historical fingers."

Smalley laughed. Yes! I made him laugh. Good start.

"A toast to Lottie. Drink up, Coleman."

I rarely drink champagne. I'm more of a domestic beer guy, with a can of Bud in one hand and a Philly cheese steak in the other. But in this case, considering Smalley's reputation, I wanted to get off on the right foot, on the perfect right foot, no less, dressed in an impeccable designer shoe, so I accepted the flute and toasted to his good health. I figured the champagne must be top shelf if he was drinking it because Robert Smalley was known to be a man of excessively good taste.

"Coleman! Boy, do I have a night planned for you."

"Sounds terrific. I can't wait."

"That's what Lottie said."

I laughed. I remember thinking, "Great, what the fuck have I gotten myself into?"

I had told my wife that I was heading up to New York City for a few hours to attend an important business dinner and would be home by midnight. I had a feeling I might have to update my ETA.

Then, Smalley asked me about myself. I told him about my humble childhood, growing up in a mixed neighborhood in West Philadelphia, taking care of my sick mother and staying home to get my law degree from Temple University. Smalley didn't really respond, except for toasting me and my mother and making some snide comments about Temple, which I let pass.

After ordering a 2016 Cakebread Cellars Dancing Bear Ranch Cabernet Sauvignon from Howell Mountain in Napa Valley, California, he regaled me with the history of the mob boss of the Gambino crime family, who was executed outside Sparks in late 1985 by John Gotti, known to many as "The Teflon Don" because no prosecutor could make any charges against him stick. That move elevated him to become the boss of the most powerful mafia family in New York, which of course was the Gambinos.

Smalley sounded so infatuated with the mob, like he wanted to be a member—or maybe he already was, I don't know. I didn't ask. He regaled me with so many stories of these kooky, psychotic characters, like Salvatore "Sammy the Bull" Gravano and Robert "The Fist" DiBernardo, guys who did shit that would curl your toes or make you wonder why you were alive. I don't know why Smalley was so enraptured by these criminals, as if they had contributed something good to society or something, but I guess it worked for him, like it made him feel fierce or invincible, or whatever it was that enabled him to be such a wicked good lawyer.

I have to admit that while we were sitting there in that exclusive restaurant, rubbing elbows with some big-time, A-list individuals, like Rudy Giuliani, Megyn Kelly, Sean Hannity, Eli Manning, and the newest New York Yankee star, Aaron Judge, I was feeling my oats and wishing that some of Smalley's "mafioso legal magic" would rub off on me.

"This is quite a place here, Mr. Smalley."

"Call me Bob," he said. "But never in front of strangers. Got it?"

I shrugged, as if a request like that was completely obvious. He smiled and nodded to a waiter to pour us another round. As soon as the gentleman came to our table, Bob asked if they could rush the meal service because we had big plans for later that evening. I asked him how he knew so much about organized crime, with all the history he was telling me and the stories about all these crazy criminals, with names like "Legs" and "Bones" and "Dead Meat Dave."

Smalley said he had read every book written on the subject. That made me wonder even more if he was into that shit more than anyone should be, which was a scary prospect.

When I asked him how he had achieved so much success in the class action field at such an early age, making many millions before he even turned 35, he told me that because he originally worked out of Little Rock, Arkansas, other attorneys thought he was a hick and did not take him seriously. Apparently, most of them doubted his potential as a high-powered, whip-smart attorney, that is, until he blew right by them and took over the field.

"Sounds like they underestimated you."

Smalley smiled and slugged down another glass of wine.

"Country bumpkin, my ass!"

I shrugged.

His face got red.

"Fucking idiots."

Those were his words, not mine. Then, almost out of nowhere, he looked at me intensely. His face became quite animated, and as he raised a glass of the most expensive wine I had ever tasted, he lowered his voice to an unusually low register, as if he were showing off some new vocal technique. He didn't speak. He bellowed.

"Do not go gentle into that good night. Rage, rage against the dying of the light."

I vaguely remembered that poem from seeing *Back to School*, a movie with Rodney Dangerfield, but I had no clue who wrote it, which was embarrassing, as Robert Smalley seemed so worldly and smart.

He waited a second for me to respond, but I had nothing.

"Dylan Thomas," he said.

I shrugged and nodded, as if I had surprised myself by not knowing the name of the author right away.

"You see, Coleman, when I establish my position, no matter what it is, I will go to the end of the earth with it. I will fight to death. I mean, shit, I am not ever going to give up. You hear what I'm saying?"

That sounded both funny and a little scary because I had heard that Smalley was extremely difficult, so much so that other lawyers did not want to deal with him at all. One lawyer had told me that if he saw that Smalley was on a case, he would find a way to get out of it because he refused to work with him. Basically, the lawyer felt that it was more productive for him to *not* be on a case with Smalley.

Over the years, people said a lot of horrible shit about him, but I bet most of them never even met the man. He was the real deal. Smalley was extremely gracious and generous. He refused to let me pay for anything the whole night, and our tab from Sparks must've run into several thousand dollars.

His response to my offer to pay was classic.

"Coleman, your money is no good here."

He even sounded like a Gambino. That was kind of cool, but also a little disconcerting. A combination of champagne and wine took the edge off pretty quick, so I was good to go.

"Drink up, my boy. We're just getting started."

Normally, I would not tolerate someone within ten years of my age calling me by my last name or referring to me as "my boy." I would tell that person that my correct name is Ryan, so please address me that way, like a normal, respectful person. And I would remind them that I haven't been called a boy since elementary school, and that if I'm anybody's boy, it's my mother's, God bless her living soul. I mean, she had a habit of tormenting me to make sure I was perfect, but I know she had my best interest at heart and all that nagging paid off, I guess.

I did not say any of that to Bob Smalley that night, but each time he said Coleman, it sounded like he was scratching a blackboard with his fingernails right in front of my face.

After wolfing down a couple of perfectly cooked, gorgeous looking steaks and drinking another bottle of absurdly expensive wine, we headed out for what Smalley called "a night to remember before it's forgotten." He explained that in these times, if and when things get a little out of hand, it's best to let the memory banks go loose so "the party stays tight."

I wasn't sure what that meant, but who was I to argue with Robert Smalley? When a dude like that invites you out for a night on the town and foots the preposterous bill, you say thank you, try to stay reasonably sober, and do nothing to embarrass yourself. The last thing I needed was getting into any kind of trouble that my wife could use against me, in a court of law, no less.

Our party tour began as soon as we stepped outside Sparks, when Bob asked if I had ever been to Rick's Cabaret or Scores, which according to him, a self-described expert in the field, were the two best strip bars he'd ever been to in New York City or anywhere else.

"Uh, no, never been, Bob, but there's always a first time, right?"

Smalley laughed and beckoned his limousine, which glided over the curb to where we were waiting. As we tucked ourselves inside, he told his chauffeur where to go.

"Listen, my boy, I can tell from your reaction that you may have no burning desire to go to Rick's or Scores but let me tell you something. You've got to keep an open mind if you want to be successful in life. That means welcoming new adventures, like this one, and reconsidering the contributions to society that these well-trained dancers actually make."

"Yeah?"

"Fuck, yeah. Without them, we wouldn't be the masters of the universe we've been so fortunate to become."

I found out later from another attorney that Smalley hired strippers to work as secretaries in his law firm. One can only imagine the craziness that took place there behind closed doors.

"Are you ready to get lucky, Coleman?"

# Seven

## The Bowery Ballroom:
## Do Not Go Gentle Into That Good Night

My pulse shot up as we entered the Bowery Ballroom. *Rolling Stone* magazine ranked this kick-ass joint number one on its 2018 Best Club in America list. It had a history of presenting some of the greatest bands in my opinion to ever put on shows, like Metallica, Red Hot Chili Peppers, Talking Heads, and Lou Reed.

On that autumn night in downtown Manhattan, Aldous Harding, Aerial East and Ancient Ocean were playing, but Smalley wasn't too interested so we headed upstairs for a round of drinks and what he like to call "selective socializing."

As soon as we were seated in a VIP area, I excused myself to go to the bathroom. That was an adventure all by itself. I wasn't used to hearing people fornicating inside a toilet stall or watching men use make-up to become something other than what I had grown up perceiving a man to be. But I was pretty looped by then, and well into a spirit of anything goes.

Luckily, I still had enough of my wits about me to remember to contact my wife and tell her I'd be staying over that night because Smalley insisted on drinking more and discussing the law. She didn't question me, at least not then. When I came back to the table two minutes later, I was surprised to see a guy and a girl sitting there with Smalley, looking quite comfortable.

"Coleman, say hi to my new friends, whoever you are. Say hi to my boy, Coleman. He's a hotshot lawyer from Philadelphia."

I blushed. I wasn't used to being blown up like that, especially with total strangers.

Although New York City is less than two hours from my hometown, it's a different universe when it comes to the high-powered intersection of Wall Street, Broadway, and the literal law of the land. Among the celebrities who swing effortlessly between the worlds of finance, entertainment, and policy making, lawyers like Smalley are always welcome, even required, at this elite level of deal-making.

The man and woman looked exceptional, dressed to the nines for a night out. I had no idea who they were, but I suspected they were well-connected. Otherwise, they never would have been admitted inside the upstairs VIP room.

The four of us shared a few drinks together. Smalley dominated the conversation, trying to get everyone to laugh at his off-color jokes. He didn't have to work too hard because the three of us were in hysterics responding to his outrageous stories.

When it came to holding court and "selective socializing," he was a natural. It seemed like he could charm the pants off anyone, including opposing lawyers and even a judge, if he had to or if he just enjoyed the challenge.

"I hear you're quite a practical joker," I said.

"Oh yeah? What did you hear?"

The man and woman sat up quickly and demanded I spill the beans.

"You heard 'em, Coleman. Tell us a story. And it better be good."

I took a deep breath and swigged my drink. I was feeling loose and ready to have some fun. Had I been sober, I'm sure I wouldn't have risked embarrassing Smalley with a story I'd heard about him, which I couldn't exactly verify.

"Well, according to a lawyer I know, you were traveling one time by plane on business with one of your associates. Supposedly, and I can't verify this shit, but I heard you took a 13-inch dildo along and wrapped it in aluminum foil. Then, you somehow managed to hide the thing, this love toy, at the bottom of your associate's carry-on."

"Yeah, you got it right so far. Keep going, Coleman. Looks like our friends are quite interested, aren't they?"

Both nodded, took another drink and encouraged me to continue.

"Okay, so can you imagine the guy's reaction when a TSA worker took out the dildo after it showed up in the metal detector? I heard you laughed so hard you cried, and soon enough the entire security area knew about it and they were laughing their asses off at your associate."

"True, true, I couldn't stop reliving the incident to the poor sucker during the rest of the flight. I kept bringing it up, which made him squirm, as if he felt guilty for actually carrying this enormous dildo in his bag."

The woman leaned forward.

"So, tell us more. Who else did you prank?"

Smalley rolled his eyes and smiled.

"If you insist. Okay. Rumor has it that I once had a first-year lawyer working for me who was supposed to cover a hearing right here in New York City. I told him I would cover all his expenses, that I would reimburse his hotel and his meals, but he either didn't believe me or he was afraid to stay at one of the expensive hotels near the courthouse in Lower Manhattan. I reserved a room for him at a place across the river in Jersey, in the type of motel that is usually rented by the hour, the kind of place that's full of shady people and looks like it could turn into a crime scene at any moment. When my boy got there and saw what it was like, he was scared to pay for a nicer place because he wasn't sure if I would reimburse him. He didn't have the balls to call me and check, so he stayed at the motel and had a sleepless night because it was loud and creepy, and he was in constant fear for his life."

Smalley paused to have a drink and see how we responded.

Those pranks sound like innocent fun, but Smalley was known to be mean-spirited when he wanted to extract some revenge on someone who mistreated him. One time, when he was in New York City for a meeting with some lawyers on a case, he was unhappy about how things were proceeding so he took a pound of nova lox from the firm's lunch buffet and supposedly hid the fish in the firm's filing room. A couple of days later, the odor became unbearable, and they had to fumigate the entire office and have it repainted.

"Let me tell you another one. One time, I became embroiled in a major dispute with one of my law partners. When he arrived at work the next day, he found feces on his desk. Uh, huh, you heard me right. Shit. Right there on top of his fucking desk. No one knew where the feces came from, but I was a big dog lover and owned three at the time. My partner was so upset he didn't show up to work for more than a week."

We were roaring.

"And you know what? I didn't give a shit!"

I knew this was a true story because Smalley told his office staff about the incident, which only added insult to injury. I knew someone who worked there who verified everything.

"I heard about that piece of shit you put on Fred's desk."

"I bet you did. I told everybody!"

A few minutes later, Smalley paid the tab, said goodbye to his new friends, and signaled for me to follow him out. We soon checked out the Mercury Lounge, right next door to Katz's Delicatessen, which Smalley said had the best corned beef sandwiches in the entire world. The club was dead on a weeknight, so we headed out toward another one. We passed by CBGB, the famous club that closed about ten years earlier, where so many top rock bands had played back in the day. Smalley had been a big fan and was still annoyed it had closed down.

He suggested we go to Circle, a Korean night club full of wild characters decked out in outrageous costumes, dancing non-stop to extremely loud electronic music. I couldn't stop gawking at all the weirdos while we knocked back a few more drinks, but Smalley took it all in stride, as if it were a second home.

Then he took me to one of his favorite upscale spots, the King Cole Bar at the St. Regis Hotel, where, not surprisingly, he knew the bartenders. Smalley chatted them up like they were cousins or neighbors. It was uncanny watching him recall names and details of the bartenders and even their kids, especially after all the booze we had ingested. This guy was a freaking animal.

"How's your son doing, you know, the one at uh, Kings College, right?"

The bartender was so impressed that Smalley remembered that stuff.

"Is he still playing football? Gonna be a tough son-of-a-bitch, like his old man?"

Smalley's memory served him well with people, but I had no idea how much he really cared about the difference between right and wrong. But on that night, was I supposed to care about stuff like that? We were out on the town to have fun. Still, I was curious about his moral compass. My plan was to ask him questions about his beliefs without him becoming suspicious. I also wanted to see if he could offer me any advice that could help me in my own practice. It didn't dawn on me at the time that some of his "methods" might be unsavory, meaning he wasn't exactly at liberty to share them with an alcohol-soaked attorney he hardly knew.

"So, Bob, what's your view of being a class-action lawyer where, you know, lawyers make all of the money, and the Class Members get next to nothing?"

Smalley didn't hesitate. His gun was loaded on the subject. He responded to my question right away, as though he had just been waiting for me to ask it, or maybe someone had asked him that question before, maybe even many times. It was like all he had to do was unload a round of bullets to make his point.

"Coleman, listen to me. I do not give a shit about Class Members. You hear me? I am only concerned with the riches that I develop from the practice of law. Boom! That's it."

I nodded, trying to make it look like I agreed, which maybe I did. Honestly, I don't know. I remember thinking at that moment, that if you looked up the word "greed" in a dictionary, you'd find a picture of Robert Smalley right there, smiling with perfect teeth, like the ones only large amounts of money can buy.

I was plenty loaded by then, so my filters were largely shot.

"Don't you feel like there's anything wrong that the Class receives maybe a tire or two, maybe only a tire-and-a-half, and the lawyers get the whole damn car? And I mean, a nice freaking car, too."

"Like I just said. I do not care at all. I just don't, because I am doing such a great service for them so I *should* be paid a lot of fuckin' money."

"Course you should."

I nodded, curious to hear more.

"Look, Coleman, I did *not* grow up with money. Got it? I make a lot of it now, as you know. I was fortunate enough to get my start in the class-action field when Bill Charel gave me an opportunity. There's a famous quote where he claims to have the greatest law practice in the world because he has no clients. I could not agree more with him on that and his whole attitude about it."

"Yeah, Bob, you said it."

"Listen, Coleman, I'm not killing anybody. Right? In fact, did you know that some mob members will kill someone for a lot less money than I make practicing law?"

"Of course. Everybody knows that."

"And you know that if it's not me, it'll be some other ham and egger making all the money. That's just the way it is."

"Ham and egger?"

"Yeah, you know some idiot type, some run of the mill lawyer who can't get out of his own freakin' way."

"Oh yeah, I know some guys like that."

"I bet you do."

Even in my mild stupor, I could see that my questions annoyed Smalley, so I backed off, convinced that the two of us had a different moral compass. I cared about people, and he didn't. I mean, he cared, but then again, he didn't. I cared, but then again, maybe I didn't either. By the time we got back in the limo, I wasn't so sure.

Smalley had solidified my concerns about my role in the field of securities class actions, where up until then, at least, I wasn't affecting any genuine change for people. I was merely grabbing money. His take on the whole process made it clear that my work wasn't benefiting my clients, not in the way they expected or deserved. On the other hand, somebody had to handle these cases, so why not me?

I was no different than Smalley in that I loved the money, too, and that was it. There was nothing else to it for him. That was my dilemma, especially on a night like that. There I was with this guy whose reasons for being a lawyer I detested, while at the same time, I had to admire his skill and genuinely liked him during the time we were together.

We ended up at one of the strip clubs Smalley said we'd skip. He arranged for a few dancers to hop on our laps and sample what they could do. It wasn't the most appropriate time to ask him another question, but I couldn't help myself.

"So, Bob, why did you tell me I got balls?"

He looked at me as one of the dancers did some crazy move over his face and then down his entire body.

"Are you fucking kidding me, asking me that shit right now?"

Smalley was genuinely enjoying his dance. It looked like he was in familiar territory, and he was being treated like a royal regular.

"Hey Coleman, why don't you ask Destiny about your balls? She's humping 'em pretty good right now, isn't she?"

I have to admit that Destiny, or whatever her name was, knew her way around a man's lap, especially mine. She kept grinding and smiling and telling me to relax. I was tempted to let go for a moment, considering all the booze talking to me, but even though my marriage was on the rocks, I was still wearing a wedding ring and that meant something.

"Thanks, Destiny, but you know I'm an old-fashioned guy and I can only handle one woman at a time, and my wife kinda outranks you right now, if you know what I mean."

I had no idea if Destiny had pursued an education beyond high school, but this wasn't the moment to find out.

She rolled her eyes.

"Your loss."

Destiny kissed me on the cheek and took off. About twenty minutes later, Smalley came back to the table after a rendezvous in a private room. He looked refreshed, as if his "date" had given him an IV of coffee along with her other more natural "charms."

"Let's go, Coleman. Looks like it's past your bedtime."

Smalley and I parted ways around three in the morning. I lied awake in bed at the Peninsula Hotel, thinking Robert Smalley was the real deal, a crazy character, larger than life, but authentic, nonetheless. We had such a good time together. When we said goodnight, he said I had balls because I went after what I wanted in that courtroom, despite violating protocols. He promised that we would work on cases together in the future and that he looked forward to the next time we got together to tear up the town.

What a guy. Smalley bought people drinks in every establishment we went to that night. He whipped out his credit card and said, "I got it!" loud enough for everyone to hear, so I guess that was his way of showing me and everyone else that he was filthy rich.

Even so, he represented all the ambivalence I felt about class-action practices. His lavish spending made me dwell on my own greed in that case and that made me squirm a little. On the other hand, my primary concern was getting my fee, which could be seen as greedy, but it could also be viewed as deserved.

Hanging with Smalley, who had made hundreds of millions of dollars for himself as a result of corporate greed, made me understand one central thing. The real problem with securities class actions is not just the huge fees lawyers receive. They may seem perverse, but that's not the root of the problem. The real issue here is that corporate greed will never go away, and since the fraud and corruption continues, why not get filthy rich?

Smalley said he had no trouble sleeping. I figured I would do myself a big favor if I learned how to do that, too. I rolled over in my plush hotel bed and passed out, dreaming about corporate executives in their ivory towers who have no problem paying lawyers like Smalley and me to go away happy and satisfied.

# Eight

## Prosperity and Mistakes:
## The Legacy of Energy Protectors and Dick Dickey

As I drove back to Philadelphia, my head was spinning with a menagerie of images from the previous night—the ridiculously expensive champagne Smalley and I enjoyed in Sparks Steak House, the TSA agent finding a dildo in the metal detector, and the lap dance I received from Destiny, if that is really her name.

Thank God I didn't go too far on our night of debauchery, so I wouldn't have to actually lie to my wife, at least not to the extent that could be prosecuted later in court.

"Oh no, Sweetheart, Mr. Smalley and I didn't uh, you know, we didn't do anything wrong or uh, you know. We ate and drank and uh, he wanted to show me his favorite clubs, so you know, I felt like I had to show my willingness to be 'one of the boys,' so to speak, and demonstrate my appreciation for his support and encouragement. Of course, we met some women, but nothing unusual, except one who had a unique approach to communicating with her clients, which is hard to describe. But uh, even though her name was Destiny, I mean, I knew all along that I was meant to be right here at home, with you."

Sounds convincing, right? Maybe if my wife was gullible I would have dropped a clever spiel on her, but she was no pushover when it came to being bullshitted, so I avoided the subject entirely. In my situation, before I shared any information, I had to consider the consequences. Since I wasn't an expert in the legal maneuverings of divorce proceedings, I figured I should check with one of my friends from law school to make sure

I didn't say anything that could be held against me in the future, just in case, if you know what I mean.

Instead, when it came time to explain to my wife what I had done in New York City and why I needed to stay overnight in a hotel, I focused on the career opportunities that Smalley represented. I was learning a lot from him, even while eating, drinking and "selective socializing," as he liked to call his interactions with strippers, as if it were an acquired skill.

But Smalley did spill the beans about Energy Protectors, Inc. (EPI), the enormous defense contractor we had been up against in court back in the class action in Texas. The company reached its peak levels of performance, profit, and pernicious behavior during the war in Afghanistan, which of course was not the most popular military endeavor our country ever engaged in. In fact, most people, me included, never understood what the fuck we were really doing there in the first place.

Well, as Smalley laid it out, it wasn't too hard to understand. He explained how EPI became so dominant inside America's military industrial complex, which, in a remarkably short time translated into billions of dollars in profit for the company and its shareholders, and a private fortune for Dick Dickey, the company's CEO.

As one of the lead lawyers on the case, Smalley was privy to a boatload of inside information and over the course of our dinner he recounted the story of how EPI began, and the crucial involvement of Dickey, the former Secretary of Defense, who seemed to make wheels turn where there wasn't even a paved road available. Being from Texas, Dickey had a firm grip on the old-time oil cartels, which had invested heavily in winning defense contracts with the U.S. military establishment.

Apparently, when it came time to negotiating agreements, Dickey used his influence in Washington to catapult EPI to the front of the line, where they were awarded a series of suspicious no-bid contracts that made them the number one defense contractor in the world.

Rumors swirled, from the Situation Room in the White House to the corporate boardrooms of EPI's competitors, that Dickey had his claws so tight on the deal-making that there was no room for any rivals to operate. But no one could prove any malfeasance or corruption, mainly because the Pentagon, EPI and Dickey made sure that their paper trails were impenetrable and they didn't disclose any information they didn't want to share, citing national security as their default excuse.

"We can't tell you because that would threaten national security."

"Of course, we can't do that now, can we?"

"No, we certainly cannot."

Case closed. That was it. The media stonewalling included the circumstances surrounding Dickey's eventual resignation from EPI, which he orchestrated, privately, of course, when he decided to run for national office. His departure came complete with a payout in the hundreds of millions of dollars, which, as it turned out, he received as deferred compensation while serving in the government. On top of that, he also finagled additional contracts for EPI in the Middle East, once again as the sole bidder, with some as high as $187 billion, which no corporation should be able to do—national security or not.

According to Smalley, who seemed to have sources way up high in the government, Dickey developed quite an inferiority complex as a child, which first surfaced when he was bullied for being short and stocky, a boy literally named Dick. Dick fucking Dickey.

He quickly became known for repeatedly saying, "Don't call me Dick. My name is Richard." This cycle only grew worse during his adolescence, when he struggled with sports and girls, and his lack of success in these areas may have fueled his obsession with being in control of other men, who we all know are really just boys in bigger clothes.

As Smalley shared this personal part of the back story on Dickey, I kept wiping tears of laughter from my eyes. I couldn't wait to learn more about this running joke and the lifelong effects of being called Dick Dickey continue to have, even in the freaking White House.

This guy must be such a head case, I mean, starting in his childhood, with some weird inferiority complex. That's rough, I guess. Maybe his mother was a witch or something like that, and you know what can happen when kids get bullied by their own parents. The military and the government is probably full of abused boys who become twisted men. Hey, some people think that's why lawyers do what they do, because they were mistreated as children.

Not in my case, thank God. Me? I'm lucky I had such a great mom growing up who taught me to be myself and not to take shit from any other kids. That's why I got stitches on numerous occasions, on the top of my head, under my chin, and along the left side of my butt, where Charlie Maloney tried to stab me with a kitchen knife when we were 14 because I was chatting up Marie Bonnafucio, who Charlie was convinced was about to become his girlfriend. We were sure surprised when Marie told us all to take a hike and ran off with the school guidance counselor, who ended up getting arrested for transporting a minor across state lines. Marie did some time in a Montgomery County juvie detention facility before she moved to Hollywood and embarked on a pretty successful career in porn, not that I've actually seen any of her work, but I hear she's pretty good and even won an award for Best Newcomer.

As I handed a bouquet of flowers to my wife, I explained some of this to her, but not the part about Marie, I couldn't help wondering what more I was gonna pick up from Smalley next time I saw him. He was a never-ending source of hilarious and unbelievable information, which I know was true because, I mean, why would he waste his time to bullshit me?

Dicks like Dick Dickey and these humongous corporations had an insane amount of power, most of which normal folks did not even know about. The money they had floating around in a series of court cases, including the costs of hiring lawyers and the fines and settlements they had to pay, were miniscule when you compared it to the sums of money they were sucking out of the U.S. government. And when it came to sucking, dicks like Dickey were the biggest suckers of all.

# Nine

## Smalley The Bag Man:
## Any Day Is a Good Day in Miami

A few weeks later, I flew to Miami to meet with Smalley. He wanted to introduce me to Randy Hollis, an infamous lawyer in the field of class action law, who originally hired Smalley, took him under his wing, and launched his legal career.

I had no idea what I was getting myself into or whether it would be a worthwhile trip, but I figured I didn't have much to lose by spending a day or two in the sun. After all, I had some crisp new money in the bank; my marriage needed a little fresh air, and I was extremely curious to find out more about how Smalley and his peers had gotten so freaking rich from practicing law. Besides, when a guy like Smalley asks, you say yes.

He arranged for me to stay at The Setai Miami Beach, a five-star hotel on Collins Avenue in the heart of South Beach. I was surprised to be met at the airport by a tall and beautiful female driver, posing perfectly in snug, elegant clothes, her hair and make-up so precise, holding a sign with my name on it. I tried to play it cool, but I think my jaw dropped a little, and she noticed.

"Mr. Coleman, welcome to Miami."

She was stunning, almost in a professional way. I wasn't sure I heard her right.

"Really? You're my driver?"

"Yes, Sir, that is correct. All yours, but it's just part of what I do. As Mr. Smalley probably explained, I'm Melody, and I will be at your disposal during your visit."

"Melody. Nice to meet you. Mr. Smalley didn't mention you. I guess he forgot. I can't imagine how he would do that. I mean, right? How could he forget to mention *you*?"

Melody laughed, seemingly delighted with how flustered I appeared.

"Well, Mr. Coleman, you should know that you can contact me for anything you might need or desire while you are here in Miami."

"Anything?"

The minute that word left my mouth I wished I hadn't said it, and I prepared myself for some kind of rebuke or for Melody to simply ignore me and drop me off with a cold stare at the hotel. So, let's just say I was surprised, no shocked, when she explained what "anything" meant.

"Mr. Coleman, you are obviously a man of great value and interest to Mr. Smalley and Mr. Hollis. Otherwise, I would not be taking care of you."

"Really? I like the way you put that."

Melody laughed as she guided me to a private corner of the parking garage.

"Mr. Hollis takes good care of his guests, and I am his favorite care-taker."

I had no idea what to say. This was a new kind of interaction for me. My mind wandered back to the strip club and the lap dance I had not requested but admittedly enjoyed, at least to a point. Destiny. Melody. Who's next?

A few seconds later, we arrived at a sleek, bright red vehicle, a model I'd never seen before. It looked like a race car, straight out of Formula 1, but elongated in the back, like an SUV. I couldn't figure out what it was as I stood there, staring like a kid in a candy store.

"I see you are enchanted, Mr. Coleman, and for good reason. This is one-of-a-kind, specially made for Mr. Hollis by Lamborghini, to combine the speed of their sports car with the convenience of a sports utility vehicle, just in case there's a need for transporting large objects."

"Like a dead body?"

I laughed at my own stupid joke, which Melody didn't find terribly amusing. Still, she humored me with a wan smile and a mild shrug. To tell the truth, her cool response was chilling for a second, as if I had been correct in my assessment.

"As you know, Mr. Hollis is a close colleague of Mr. Smalley. I'm sure you will meet him soon. Perhaps you could ask him yourself."

"Okay, Melody, I don't mean to pry, but I'm a lawyer. That's what we do, and I'm wondering how you know Hollis. I mean, why are you driving his car if you work for Smalley?"

Melody was smooth as silk.

"I am much more than your driver, Mr. Coleman. Let's just say that things will become clear sooner than you think. For now, let's get you to your hotel. May I?"

She opened the back door of the Lamborghini and waved me inside. The seat felt like one of those massage chairs you can enjoy by the minute inside some airports. Once we pulled out, Melody looked back at me in the rearview mirror.

"Mr. Coleman, I'll drop you off at The Setai and wait for you to make your next move."

"My next move? What am I, a ninja?"

Melody laughed.

"Mr. Smalley didn't tell me you were this funny."

"He didn't? No, of course he didn't. Why would he? Wait. I am?"

"Oh, you definitely are, Mr. Coleman, and it's quite charming."

I kept my mouth shut because I was definitely not thinking straight. I was totally distracted by this spectacular looking woman just inches away, telling me I was uh . . . never mind. There's no way I can describe what she was doing to me without getting in serious trouble.

I closed my eyes and leaned back in the most comfortable leather backseat I had ever felt in my life. I don't know how many minutes passed before Melody roused me from my little nap with her velvet voice.

"Here we are, Mr. Coleman."

"Okay then, here we are. I'll be going to my room now."

"Correct. To your own private room in this exquisite hotel. And I will be waiting right here, at your beck and call."

"My beck and my call? That sounds loaded, I mean, that's quite a way to put it."

Melody opened my door and smiled as I got out of the car. An hour later, after checking in and freshening up, I met her outside the hotel, just as she had promised. I was dazzled by her presence, but anxious to meet Smalley and find out why he wanted me to come to Miami.

Melody drove a short distance up the beach to what I can only call a hacienda, an amazing estate right on the ocean, complete with an ornate and seemingly impenetrable fence and what looked like a serious security fortress, complete with a uniformed pair of sculpted guards and a dog the size of a small horse.

I soon found out that this was just one of several homes Randy Hollis owns in the United States, along with a handful of exotic places he maintains in other parts of the world. As we made our way up the long driveway, Melody pointed out the lush, tropical landscape, lined with palm trees of every shape and size, a menagerie of flamingos, peacocks and other creatures I didn't recognize. I noticed a small flotilla of speed boats on a man-made lake, occupied by what looked like armed and intimidating characters, dressed in some weird Floridian camouflage.

Melody noticed my eyes bulging as I took in the sights.

"Questions, Mr. Coleman?"

"Uh, yeah! I mean, holy shit! Who are those people on the boats and why are they carrying such big guns?"

"Oh, that. It's nothing to worry about. Mr. Hollis has certain possessions he needs to protect. One can never be too careful these days, right?"

"Yeah, of course, never too careful. I'll remember that when I get back to my house in Philadelphia and call in the National Guard to protect my barbecue."

Melody laughed.

"There you go again. You *are* a funny man. I can see why Mr. Smalley likes you."

"Oh yeah? Nice. We had a lot of fun during our night on the town in Manhattan, but I'm not sure why he wants to help me. Hey, I'm not complaining, and this is amazing, but why me?"

"Well, Mr. Coleman, I could share my opinion, but let's wait on that. You can ask Mr. Smalley yourself in just a second. He's waiting at the front door."

"Coleman! Welcome to Miami, one of my favorite playgrounds."

Smalley ushered me inside the most enormous mansion I'd ever seen. Since I wasn't expecting a grand tour, especially because I hadn't even met Randy Hollis yet, I wasn't disappointed when Smalley led me into a room that looked like a private library. All the books were perfectly bound and shelved, as if no one actually read them. Everything inside the house seemed perfect and reminded me of the luxury homes I had only admired on television.

Smalley gestured for me to sit myself down in one of two antique chairs, which looked like they belonged in some 18th century French museum. I don't know what Smalley did, but suddenly a young, extremely attractive woman appeared out of nowhere, carrying a tray with what looked like a giant perfume bottle and two crystal glasses, straight out of the same museum.

She set the tray down on a table between us and smiled. As she carefully opened the bottle and slowly poured two drinks, she nodded at Smalley and winked at me before turning to leave. I tried to be cool, but I couldn't take my eyes off her as she left the room without a word.

What was going on? First Melody, if that was even her real name, and now this elegant woman who looked straight out of *Madame Bovary* and her wild world of Parisian indulgence. I wondered if this was just another day at the office in a world of unimaginable wealth.

Smalley lifted his glass in one hand and the bottle in the other. It appeared so expensive I was almost afraid to look at it, like it might crack if a regular dude like me stared at it too long with his ordinary eyes. I mean, it was perfect, the way it reflected the natural light inside the room, with a crescent-shaped bottle top that looked like it was made from priceless crystal and belonged in freaking Tiffany's.

Smalley caught me staring.

"This is no ordinary cognac. It's Hardy L'ete and it goes for $16,000."

"Dollars? I mean, of course, but for one bottle?"

"Welcome to the show, Coleman."

I tried to look nonchalant.

"Thanks, Bob. This is amazing. I mean, first-class all the way. I can't thank you enough."

"You're welcome. So, how's your hotel?"

"Perfect. Top quality, I mean, five-stars, for sure. The bathrobe in the closet probably costs more than I make in a week. Thank you very much."

"My pleasure. I'm glad you could fit in a short visit so I can share some information with you in a private setting. By the way, the reason we are meeting here is that I have some business in Miami and my house up the street is being renovated."

"It's amazing. I mean, I can't thank you enough, from the plane to the hotel to this place and this cognac. Oh my God."

"And Melody?"

I swallowed the cognac a bit too fast, which nearly gassed up through my nose. Smalley smiled and waited for me to answer.

"Oh, Melody, yeah, what a surprise. I never expected to be picked up by anyone like her. She's uh . . . well, you know, she's first-class all the way, right?"

"Oh yes. That's an accurate assessment."

"So, Bob, Melody said I can ask you directly about why you want me to meet Hollis. I mean, I probably shouldn't have said anything to her, being the driver and all, but I couldn't resist. She seems pretty in the know, if you get my drift, like she's no ordinary chauffeur."

"Good observation."

"So, okay then. I don't want to sound unappreciative because you have treated me so well, I mean, in New York City and now here, and I'm amazed by everything, but I mean, I gotta ask you. Why am I here?"

Smalley took a long, slow sip of his cognac.

"As I mentioned, this house belongs to my mentor, colleague and friend, Randy Hollis, who you will meet soon enough."

"I'm looking forward to that."

"In due time, Coleman. In due time."

I nodded. That expression again. "In due time." What did it mean?

"Let me fill you in a little about Randy. It's good if you know how he operates in the legal world, especially among his peers and those who are not quite on his level, or even close. Randy has become notorious for paying referral fees to lawyers to become the lead plaintiff's attorney, and he has repeated his methods in numerous class actions."

"I'd love to know all about that. I mean, his reputation is impeccable as far as I know, so I would be honored if you would tell me as much as you can."

"Of course, Coleman. In due time. You're here because I think you will have real value for us in the future."

I gave myself a silent hi-five.

"That's great to hear, Bob. And if you don't mind me saying, I'm like a sponge, you know? That night with you in Manhattan, I soaked up everything you said, and I've got a steel-trap memory for things like that."

"Good to know, Ryan, good to know."

As soon as Smalley used my first name, I figured I had already moved a step closer to his inner circle. I mean, I was drinking cognac from a $16,000 bottle that came straight from Napoleon's liquor cabinet.

"Of course, Randy has done nothing illegal building his enormous wealth, but one could say, and I'm referring to other jealous lawyers, that he has made a habit of going right to the edge when it comes to ethical behavior, but he never crossed it."

"That would be their petty opinion, right?"

"You're catching on well, Coleman."

I almost winced when he used my last name again, but I figured who cares? I'm in this opulent house, talking about one of the richest men on Earth, so how bad could things be?

"For now, here's what's important for you to know. Since Randy makes a habit of swooping in at the last minute and essentially stealing clients, he has pissed off many of his peers and become a target of their wrath and possible plots to seek revenge."

"Are you kidding me?"

Smalley held up his hand, which I took as a clear signal to shut the fuck up and let him continue. I tend to talk too much sometimes, but I also know when to shut it.

According to Bob, Hollis couldn't care less about these envious pricks. Over the years, the two men have become close friends and confidants. As Smalley shared this with me, I couldn't help but wonder if something similar was happening with me and him.

"Coleman, you should know that I have come to love Randy Hollis like a big brother, but the truth is, he is a crazy partier and a relentless womanizer."

I took another slug of cognac, forgetting that each sip cost more than one of my suits.

"That makes sense, Bob. Look at Melody and that knockout who was here before."

Smalley nodded.

"Here's what I can tell you now, in complete confidence. Obviously, I feel like I can trust you in that regard or else you would definitely not be here. That's for sure."

"Bob, you got it. I mean, I am loyal to a fault."

"Of course, you are. Thank you. Let's drink to that, then."

We held up our glasses and toasted to discretion.

"Coleman, if you're going to work with me and Hollis, you need to know that he has a lot to protect when it comes to his reputation and his property and possessions."

"I hear you."

"That means he has to be extremely vigilant about who enters his inner circle, especially when it comes to women."

"Oh yeah, I can imagine. I mean, I can't really, but you know what I mean."

"Therefore, when it comes to any sexual or romantic encounter or relationship, Randy has decided that in order to protect his fortune and any of his future projects, he will only utilize professional escorts to satisfy his needs. One of his aides, Mona, is responsible for doing the necessary background checks, conducting interviews, and hiring these women."

"Sounds like quite a job, but somebody's gotta do it."

"Precisely, and because Randy has such a voracious appetite, Mona may need your help with some of these interactions, so can we count on you to be at her disposal?"

"What do you mean?"

"That's to be determined, but Randy and I would appreciate not only your complete discretion, but your willingness to do whatever Mona deems necessary and appropriate."

"Okay, I guess so, yeah."

"Very good. Just the answer I was hoping to hear."

"I mean, I've always wanted to be a pimp."

"Good one, Coleman, although I'd suggest keeping your career aspirations to yourself. Just so you know why this is all happening. According to Randy, who brags about always wearing a condom, if he's paying a professional for sexual relations then no drama comes into play, and these women will not chase after his fortune or look to cause any trouble."

"Sounds quite logical if you ask me."

"Yes, it does! Now, let's go enjoy dinner. Melody arranged a wonderful place for us."

As we left the library, I was unsure about what any of this had to do with me, but I was dazzled by all the wealth, glitz, and bravado I had witnessed so far in Miami. I had no idea how I would explain any of this to my wife, but I had a little time to figure it out.

# Ten

## So, This Is How They Do It:
## How The Rich Get Richer

Smalley had more to tell me over dinner in a private dining room inside the Surf Club, one of Miami's finest restaurants. We drove there in a Bentley, the first time I'd ever been in one, and the ride was even smoother than I imagined.

"Melody off tonight?"

"Yes, she is, Coleman. Why? Do you miss her already?"

I laughed, somewhat nervously, as I didn't want Smalley to get the wrong impression, even though any reasonably healthy man would find Melody undeniably gorgeous. I mean, she looked as if she could appear on the cover of *Vogue* and *Playboy* in the same month.

"Well, she's attractive, I mean, crazy hot, but uh, I don't exactly, you know . . ."

"What? You don't exactly what, Coleman? You don't exactly want to fuck her?"

"No, I mean, that's not what I was saying."

"Oh yeah? I think you want to see her again, and I don't blame you. But don't worry, Coleman. You'll have your opportunity."

"Yeah?"

"Of course. In due time."

*In due time. Really?*

As soon as the first round of drinks arrived, Smalley wasted no time giving me some back story on Hollis. He wanted me to understand the current situation and how it had unfolded, in case I became intricately involved in the future, which seemed to be the plan.

I was thrilled to be privy to such inside information, and I quickly understood that what Smalley was about to tell me needed to be done in person, as the stakes were extremely high. I also figured that, even though he seemed to trust me, Smalley, for himself and on behalf of Hollis, was still testing me on a number of fronts, both personally and professionally. I had no idea if I would ultimately pass, but so far, so good.

"Listen, Ryan, I must swear you to secrecy on what I'm about to tell you."

"I'm all ears, Bob. And uh, my lips are sealed."

"Except when it comes to Melody?

I blanked.

"Just kidding, Coleman. Don't be so nervous, even though I've seen every man she comes into contact with react the same way."

"I admit, you got me off my game when it comes to Melody."

"In due time. That's all I can tell you right now. Let's have another drink."

After we toasted again to discretion and beautiful, mysterious women, Smalley launched into what he wanted me to know about Hollis.

"Let me ask you a few things first. You know who Dick Dickey is, right? The prick who essentially ran The White House and used EPI as his private piggy bank."

I nodded.

"And you know that the AFL, the American Football League, has 32 teams and the owners of these franchises basically run small kingdoms of their own, right?"

"Oh yeah, I'm a big football fan. America's sport, baby. You know, some people call them modern plantation owners because they're all crazy wealthy and white and most of the players are, you know . . ."

"Yeah, Coleman, we know all that. No reason to go there right now. We're not trying to change the world. We're just here to run it."

I was speechless. Smalley said that like he meant it.

"Okay, so here we go. After an acrimonious and public bidding war with Dick Dickey and his financial partners, which I gather you heard about, at least to a certain extent, Randy Hollis recently sealed the deal and will be purchasing the Los Angeles Flash for a fee that the media is reporting at $4.8 billion."

"Holy shit."

As the words slipped out of my mouth, I lowered my voice to a whisper. After all, I didn't want Smalley to reconsider sharing this story because I freaked out about any of it. I was thrilled to be one step deeper inside this inner circle and even surprised by how fast I had gained Smalley's trust and confidence.

He went on to explain more about how Hollis became so wealthy, initially through class actions suits, where he made a fortune, including his first $50 million many years ago from the Enron settlement, and then through a series of hedge funds he managed, which don't operate in the public eye and avoid the usual scrutiny that other financial institutions experience.

"It's complicated, Coleman, and most people don't understand how money really works, at least not on this exclusive level, which is beyond what people even identify as elite."

"Yeah, I hear ya, Bob. This is really the big leagues."

"No, no, Ryan. Forget about any of your usual definitions. This is way beyond any kind of a league. This is a totally unique level where only the masters of the universe reside. But each of them are smart enough to know that they cannot maintain that position alone, so they must create an inner circle of people they can trust completely to do anything for them, if necessary."

"Anything?"

Smalley smiled and nodded.

I was hanging on every word because it's not every day that I got to hear details about how a lawyer, or anyone for that matter, comes to be worth reportedly more than $10 billion.

"Randy is an exceptional man, to say the least, and I owe everything to him, except in all honesty, I'm pretty remarkable myself and have made it a habit of proving anyone wrong who thinks that I might be less than I appear to be."

"Oh, for sure, I can imagine. I mean, I can't believe I'm here with you right now, learning so much already. Thank you so much. Thank you."

"Have another drink, Coleman, and relax."

I didn't hesitate to down another glass of Lafite Rothschild, a red wine from 1900 that was valued at nearly ten grand a bottle, which the sommelier had waiting for us when we arrived.

"Hollis has an agreement with the current owners, the Leonidas family, which needs to be approved by a majority of the other teams' owners during an upcoming vote to approve or reject Hollis' offer. Due to Randy's "edgy track record," shall I say, we think some of the owners might need a little convincing to approve the sale."

"Edgy?"

"Yes, Coleman. Do you remember when I explained that some lawyers, and even hedge fund executives, were jealous of Randy's enormous success and have been infecting the rumor mills with indirect accusations that his methods are illegal, or unethical, at best?"

"Yes, of course, you mentioned that, and I'm guessing that some of the lawyers working for these AFL owners have grudges of their own against Mr. Hollis."

"Exactly! Coleman, you're as smart as I thought, and quick, to boot. Keep drinking this ridiculously expensive wine. It seems to be doing wonders for your brain cells."

"It's definitely doing something. If I squint and look closely at the bottle, I think I can see Melody posing on the label."

Smalley laughed.

"In due time."

I took another drink, not sure if I was toasting that possibility or the eventual demise of my marriage . . . or both. I needed to pay attention to Smalley and how he was suggesting I become involved. I figured I should question what was in it for me, but Smalley continued before I had a chance to ask.

"So, here's the upshot of all this, Ryan, and why you are being introduced to the situation and soon to Randy, himself, who will be the ultimate arbiter of whether you will continue on this path or not. Of course, as of now, I will recommend to him that he meet you and find out if you will be a good fit for him."

"It sure sounds like owning an AFL team would be incredible."

"I agree. It should provide a treasure chest of enticing perks."

"Well, I've seen the Eagles play in Philly, but that's about it. What a trip it would be to watch the Flash in Los Angeles."

"In due time, Coleman. In due time. For now, Randy has decided, and I agree with him wholeheartedly, that we will do whatever is necessary to make sure that the vote goes his way."

"Whatever is necessary?"

"Yes, and if Randy approves, you can play an integral role in our scheme and reap significant rewards, personally and professionally."

"Scheme?"

"It's just another word for strategy."

I tried to breathe normally and maintain my cool. My head started to spin, just as it had when I drove home after the all-night binge with Smalley in New York City. I figured I would take Smalley at his word, that in his world, and the one Hollis created, a scheme and a strategy were kissing cousins, and who was I to judge?

"Sound good?"

"Sounds amazing."

# Eleven

## The Lodestar
## Smalley Shares the Skinny on Bill Charel and the Enron Fiasco

After an excellent sleep in The Setai, complete with 900-thread sheets and the best room service breakfast I've ever had, Melody came calling, as fetching as she was the day before, ready to bring me to meet Smalley aboard a yacht that belonged to one of his colleagues.

What a way to start another day in Miami. I still had a lot to digest, from the beautiful and mysterious Melody picking me up to everything Smalley shared with me over drinks and dinner. I was thankful, really, that we hadn't spent the rest of the night in Miami's coolest clubs, as I wasn't sure I could deal with all those temptations, from an endless supply of alcohol and drugs to a slew of eccentric characters and mesmerizing women.

Luckily, as Smalley explained, he had a "commitment," which he didn't elaborate upon, but I figured some things were private and sacred, and I wasn't about to pry into anything too personal. Then again, I had to wonder, as I knew nothing about his personal life.

*In due time?*

Once I bid farewell to the lovely Melody and boarded the yacht for a cruise around Biscayne Bay, my discretion took a back seat to my detective skills. I had hot pants to find out how much this boat cost, as if I could afford one, but seriously, I was overwhelmed by all the luxury and curious to know more about the details of this seemingly unattainable universe.

Apparently, as one of the captain's staff told me, a small, 40-foot yacht can go for around 300 grand while the bigger models can cost upwards of a half a billion. The one we were on was about 120 feet, built by a German shipbuilding conglomerate, called Lurssen, one of the world's most prestigious companies that built yachts for Saudi Arabian princes, Russian oligarchs and "unknown" international tycoons, also known as gangsters. Many of them ranged from 300 to 500 feet long and could probably turn into battleships overnight. Their owners, private individuals and cartels, would pay whatever it cost for these creations.

The yacht I boarded, called *The Esquire*, was one of their smaller models, and cost around $75 million, and it was impeccable everywhere you looked, outfitted like a freaking pointillist painting like the one I once saw in the Philadelphia Museum of Art or somewhere like that, where the artist made these amazing paintings using only millions of tiny dots. Like, they didn't paint. They dotted. Only all those dots turned into amazing paintings. On the yacht, everything was perfectly detailed like that, and I thought for a second that little robots were going to appear and do perfect little things, like fix me a drink and massage my feet.

One of Melody's "associates," a freaking bombshell by the name of Futura, took me on a little tour of the amenities, which included a sauna, a tanning salon (in case it got cloudy), a fully equipped beauty salon for men and women, a movie theatre and seven or eight of what she called "living and loving entertainment suites."

It didn't require a rocket scientist to figure out what she meant, but I couldn't resist asking Futura to spell it out for me.

"Mr. Coleman, Melody said that you might be a bit naïve, but really? I need to explain?"

I nodded sheepishly.

"If you don't mind. I don't like to take things for granted."

"Well, if you insist. Where I come from in Central America, living and loving go hand-in-hand. If you are truly living, we always say, you are also loving, and if you are loving well enough, then you are certainly living!"

"I like your logic. Hard to argue with that."

"Of course, Mr. Coleman, it's a simple formula for enjoyment, and perhaps one day you will experience this equation in the flesh."

"Whose flesh are you referring to?"

The minute those words escaped my mouth, I knew they sounded stupid and would inevitably make their way back to Melody, who I was still thinking about and didn't want to risk un-impressing, if that was even a word. Then again, all the women I had met so far in Miami were total head-turners, but something about Melody was on a whole other level.

Fortunately, Futura chose not to embarrass me. She smiled, as if she knew how far she could go with a guest.

"In due time, Mr. Coleman."

Her words stopped me cold. They were exactly what Smalley had kept saying to me a day earlier, so I had to wonder if she had picked that phrase up from him or made it up herself. Before I had a chance to investigate, Futura guided me onto a back deck, where Smalley was sitting alone, nursing a drink, and talking on his phone. He motioned for me to sit as I watched Futura gracefully glide out of my sight. Within seconds, he ended his call and turned to me.

"So, you've met Futura, I see."

"Oh yeah. I gotta say, whoever is hiring these women has excellent taste. I can't wait to see who's next."

"In due time, Coleman."

That phrase again. Was it some kind of password to a secret society I was just beginning to discover? I had no idea, but I was growing more and more intrigued with each passing minute.

Being naturally curious, and ambitious to boot, I couldn't help probing Smalley for more information on how big-time, class action lawyers like him manipulate the system to win cases for their clients and tens, and even hundreds of millions of dollars, for themselves.

I mean, some would say it's a dirty job, but somebody's got to do it, right? I figured, if I was going to go deeper into this work then I needed to know how the experts did their thing, and no one would dispute that Smalley and his cohorts were the very best at this game.

It didn't take long for him to indulge me. I mean, he tutored my ass on one of the largest securities settlements in American history, which involved Enron, and was orchestrated by Randy Hollis and Bill Charel, one of the most feared lawyers in America, who, together, did a masterful job in getting banks to pay a total settlement of more than $7 billion, which resulted in legal fees of $688 million, which was split among the lawyers and their firms.

Let's just say you could buy an enormous fleet of yachts with that kind of cash, including the one I was on. Okay, yeah, the words "luxury yacht" are redundant, I know. I mean, the word yacht pretty much implies luxury without needing to spell it out, but just in case you weren't sure, this boat, if I can call it that without sounding too pedestrian, was fucking luxurious beyond what I ever imagined one of them to be. I felt like I was inside another episode of *Lifestyles of the Rich and Famous,* only I wasn't rich or famous, but I was rubbing elbows pretty good.

"Coleman, let me just say this: what Hollis and Charel did, with my help, too, I must say, may go down as the most incredible legal feat in the history of American jurisprudence."

"Oh my God, you aren't kidding."

"No, I'm not kidding at all. We don't kid about this shit. Ever. Except, of course, for when we enjoy a joke or two at the expense of one of the judges we take for a ride. But when we laugh our asses off at one of them, we do it in private."

"That must be quite a conversation. I'd love to hear those backroom jokes sometime."

"In due time, Coleman."

"Whenever you're ready, I'm all ears. And eyes, too. I mean, I'm taking in everything, and there's lots of eye candy here in Miami. But meanwhile, tell me more about Bill Charel. I mean, he's a legend, I know, but I'd love to hear from you why we still view him that way."

"Some do. Some don't. Coleman, it pains me to talk about him, but for you, here we go. If you're going to learn more about this universe, then pay attention. Here we go. The epic story of the rise and fall of one William "Bill" Shannon Charel, the infamous super-lawyer, who was once the leading class action lawyer in America and then became a convicted felon."

"That stings, just hearing you say that."

"The truth hurts, sometimes, doesn't it? Look, Charel was a beast. A brilliant, conniving, manipulative motherfucker who threatened, bribed, and sued a shitload of Fortune 500 companies over a period of more than twenty years."

"Right. Disney, Apple, Time Warner, and of course, Enron."

"You said it. He brought those corporate windbags to their knees, but I guess he succumbed to the same corrupt impulses he saw and manipulated in his enemies. Only thing is, he got caught, too, and as you know, he served a couple years in a federal white-collar vacation camp. Even worse, he lost his license to practice law anywhere inside this country."

"Which means nowhere, right?"

"Exactly. As Randy Hollis likes to say, Charel was on top of the world one minute and then he was fucked."

"Sounds like a modern Greek tragedy."

"Except it was the Romans doing all the fucking, Coleman."

I laughed. As much as I could remember, the Greeks were definitely not too prudish.

"Wow, Charel really left a legacy."

"No kidding, Coleman, a real role model for young lawyers and his children."

"You know, I read a book about him. I'll never forget it. *Circle of Greed.*"

"Appropriate title."

"So, the authors said it was, listen to this, 'a tale of a man and his times, about corporate arrogance and illusions.'"

"That sounds accurate, Ryan. Except from what I know, Charel charmed the pants off those two journalists, and they never told the whole story."

"I bet, but hold on, let me finish what it said on the back cover: 'the scorched-earth tactics to not only counteract corporate America but to beat it at its own game.'"

"You remember the exact words?"

"Oh yeah, I memorized them. See, my mother bought me that book shortly after I graduated from law school, and she made me promise I would read every word of it. I don't know, maybe like a warning, I guess, because she was worried I might get greedy like Charel."

"Did you?"

"Like that? Are you kidding me? I mean, yeah I want my share of the big paydays, yeah, but I'm not looking to do what he did, if that's what you mean."

"I'm not suggesting anything of the kind, Coleman."

"Okay, I know, of course, you're not. I'm just saying that I'm not going to become another story of a guy who goes from rags to riches and then ends up wearing fucking rags in jail. No way. If for no other reason then I couldn't disgrace my mother like that."

"Holy shit, you love your mother. How quaint. I'm sure Melody will be impressed."

# Twelve

## Ka-ching! Ka-ching!
## The Lawyerly Art of Clocking Billable Hours

Smalley had me puzzled. I mean, it felt like he was testing me there for a second, but he already told me I had balls, so what was he trying to suggest, that I shouldn't have balls, or that they should be bigger, or smaller, or what? I mean, what the fuck with my balls?

I decided to let that shit pass and focus on some legal stuff, like how these class action lawyers, Charel and Hollis, and Smalley, too, figured out how to make and manage money the way they did, and the totally insane dollar amounts they came up with to charge and get the judges and the court systems to agree to and support, whether it was good for the Plaintiffs or not.

Smalley filled me in some more on Bill Charel, the fearsome money wrangler, as he became known to the Plaintiffs' Bar. His ability to wrangle millions of dollars from dozens of corporations and banks made him a legend (and a pariah) in his own time.

As Charel boasted to *Forbes* several years ago, which bears repeating because it speaks to clients getting little and lawyers getting filthy rich, "I have the greatest practice of law in the world. I have no clients."

One could argue that being able to get nine out of eleven defendants to pay $7.227 billion, after the Supreme Court held that the plaintiffs should not recover any money, has to be the most incredible feat ever orchestrated by an attorney, in this case, Charel and his partner, Hollis, with a huge assist from Smalley. And they were going up against the best lawyers money could buy, or at least that's what the big banks thought before Charel and company fucked them.

I figured I would share what I knew with Smalley, first to show him that I had done my homework, and second, to feel him out on his take on the whole affair.

"Okay, I know that Enron shareholders filed a $40 billion lawsuit after the fraud the company committed was revealed. At its height, Enron's stock traded at more than $90 a share, but by the time all the dirt was clear, the value had dropped to less than $1 per share."

Smalley frowned and nodded.

"I gather that there was talk of competitive companies attempting to purchase Enron, which we know did not happen. As a consequence, the company filed bankruptcy a month later, which at the time was the largest in U.S. history."

Smalley sat back and smiled.

"Yeah, and it turned out to be a groundbreaking Christmas present. All the lawyers working for the plaintiffs on this case, including me, combined their billable time, based on different hourly rates."

"Wow! The cash register was working overtime, huh?"

"You got it, Ryan. Ka-ching! Ka-ching!"

"You're talking 'lodestar,' right?"

"Exactly. You know this shit. It's what happens when you add up all the time spent by lawyers for the plaintiffs and multiply it by the different hourly rates. That's the lodestar."

"I did my homework on that one. The plaintiffs' lawyers in the Enron litigation, which of course included you and Mr. Hollis, submitted a total lodestar of $131,971,588."

"You got some fucking memory, Coleman."

"Thank you. I like to think so."

"Are you on some Autism Spectrum? If that's the case, I need to know that right now."

"No, no, I mean, I just try to remember the important stuff and forget all the stupid shit."

"Okay, yeah, except that one man's stupid shit may turn out to be another's treasure chest."

"That's a good one, Bob."

"Yeah, we should make a T-shirt with that and sell them up and down the beach."

"I don't know who would buy them."

"Hey, if Melody was offering them, they'd sell out in an hour."

"You're probably right."

"I know I am."

"So, Bob, you know the word lodestar means a star that leads or guides, or it could refer to a person who serves as an inspiration or a role model."

"Okay, well, that's very interesting, Ryan, but last time I checked none of us are auditioning for the Boy Scouts."

"I guess not. I mean, I'd like to think I could be a role model, but I don't know."

"Listen, Coleman, the judge on the Enron case ended up awarding a legal fee of $688 million, which was a multiplier of 5.2. In essence, we petitioned the court for 9.52 percent of the $7.2 billion settlement fund. For a mega settlement like that, a fee which represents 9.52 percent of the settlement fund was consistent with other cases."

"Yeah, maybe, except to be honest, this was the biggest securities case ever."

Smalley nodded.

"No one knows for sure, not even me, but Hollis was rumored to have received $75 million from the Enron fee, which he considered 'just another day at the office.'"

"Really? That's what he said?"

"Exactly what he told me and Charel over a celebratory dinner. I'd say he was a fantastic fucking role model."

"You got a point. Tell me more about Charel. I mean, I know he pissed off a lot of people with how he racked up all this money and left his clients high and dry."

"Supposedly, according to an old rumor mill in Washington, DC, Charel spent an evening at the White House as a guest of President Clinton. Soon after, in 1995, Congress passed the Private Securities Litigation Reform Act, which some said was aimed directly at stifling the way Charel practiced law. It was designed to take control away from the attorneys and raise standards to make it more difficult for lawyers to recover ridiculous sums of money in lawsuits."

"I suppose that some of the legislators in Congress who were not lawyers might have been a little suspect about these attorneys making hundreds of millions while the class of individuals they represented received so little."

Smalley laughed.

"You have to understand that lawyers constantly leverage their positions against each other, especially when there are so many corporate dollars to win. I've been fortunate to have a front-row seat to a battle of these gladiators. I'm talking about Bill Charel, the 800-pound gorilla in the class action bar, and David Gurls, one of the most successful litigators in the country. For example, in one case involving Halliburton, I saw them playing games all the time with each other because Charel did not want to cede control of that lawsuit because he knew the case was worth billions."

"Did he have some inside information?"

"Don't be naïve, Coleman. Every lawyer worth his license has inside information. It's all a question of how you use it."

"Like to leverage a settlement?"

"Exactly. When the basis of a lawsuit is internal mistakes and an attempted cover-up, then any top-notch lawyer can play that out to put their collective balls in a vice and squeeze them until they cry uncle and agree to an outrageous settlement. But sometimes, a judge smells foul play and decides to protect the rumored criminals from a team of insatiable lawyers who smell blood and will stop at nothing to suck it all up and drink it down like Kool Aid."

"Enter Bill Charel."

"You're a fast learner, Coleman. To make a long story short, after years of litigation, Gurls was able to settle the Halliburton Case not so long ago for $100 million. If you add the $5.1 billion plus interest it paid in 2005, along with the $559 million it paid in 2009, and the $1.1 billion Halliburton paid in 2014, the total number would be in excess of $6.8 billion."

"Fuck!"

"Exactly. People got fucked and we won."

"But it seems to me that $100 million for Halliburton was a tiny slap on the wrist."

"Okay, Ryan, let's not shed any tears for Gurls. The judge awarded him $33 million."

"I know, but he claimed that his firm spent $43 million litigating the case."

"Gurls claimed that he received only seventy-seven percent of his firm's lodestar and it was not financially productive. Lots of other attorneys fell short on that case, too. But we can't worry about them, can we?"

"All is fair in love and war."

"Something like that, yeah. Look, there are problems with the class action system. I could spend all day sorting through this shit, but what fun is that? You got winners and you got losers, and as long as I'm winning, I don't really give a shit."

I took a moment to process Smalley's opinion. While I was proud to receive my nice big fee, which I had secured in that Texas courtroom, I felt that the case was dominated by lawyers, including me, looking to make millions for themselves, which ended up reaping no benefits for the shareholders of the company that settled and next to nothing for the Plaintiffs.

"I guess Charel was right."

"That flamboyant son-of-a-bitch was amazing, Coleman. During the Enron case, he showed up to court carrying a big box of shredded documents because Enron was accused of shredding everything. Charel was a showman through and through. He played up being in the middle of that media sensation. I have no doubt that the work he did was the most incredible thing a lawyer has ever done."

"Why were his actions so incredible?"

"Charel was able to get some of the most well-established and successful banks and professional service firms to pay $7.2 billion when the U.S. Supreme Court ruled that the two defendants had no liability. The settlement was the largest to date in the securities class action arena, so it has to be considered the best."

"You're right, I guess. I mean, all the defendants were sued because it was alleged that they were complicit in the fraud when the Supreme Court ultimately decided that those defendants were not liable. Merrill Lynch and Barclay's refused to settle and fought strenuously against Charel."

"It's ironic, though, because if they had chosen to settle, the total amount would have easily been over $10 billion, which may have resulted in a legal fee in excess of $1 billion."

"Now *that* would have been a magic act!"

"Yeah, and Charel would have been fucking Houdini!"

I laughed.

"What a fucking lodestar, right? I mean, Charel as a role model. What a concept."

"Listen, Ryan, let his resume become a cautionary tale for any young men and women entering the legal profession who have a deep and abiding wish to retain their soul and better angels, while preserving their long-term self-respect."

"Well said, but then again, self-respect is not a priority for all lawyers."

"You're catching on, Coleman. You're a quick learner, and I like that."

# Thirteen

## On the Edge:
## When Crazy Becomes a Compliment

By the end of the afternoon, having spent a few hours aboard the *The Esquire*, I figured I had passed the litmus test with Smalley and was ready to head ashore and back to the hotel, where I could spend a quiet night to reflect, pack, and catch an early flight back to Philadelphia. So, I was surprised when Smalley hit me with a reason to stay and enjoy the sunset.

"There's someone I want you to meet, Ryan. Not exactly my twin brother, but close. More like an older sister. I know I told you that Randy Hollis is my mentor and a great friend, and anything really big I've ever accomplished in the legal field is a result of his advice and support, but none of that would have been possible if I hadn't had one special friend while growing up in Arkansas. In that respect, I owe everything to the one and only Eugenia Cauley."

"Eugenia?"

"It's Greek for a 'well-born woman' and if there's one thing I can say about Gene Cauley, she was born well."

As Smalley laughed, my memory snapped into place.

"Wait a minute, Bob. Gene Cauley? The lawyer they call 'The Castrator?' That Gene Cauley? Holy shit! You know her?"

"The one and only, Coleman. Of course, I know her. My mother was the nurse who brought her into this world about five years before me. We were neighbors."

"She's a legend, right? I mean, I heard about her when I was in law school from a professor of mine who ran into her in court and got his ass handed to him so bad that he stopped practicing and became a teacher. I hear she has some presence and knows how to use it."

"Ha! That's an understatement, Coleman. For starters, Gene is six feet tall. When she gets decked out in heels, lookout! She loves to menace shorter lawyers just by staring down at them, as if they're children trying to play on the big kids' playground."

"Especially with men, I bet."

"Oh no, Gene is an equal opportunity intimidator. I've seen her bully plenty of women, too. She doesn't care. If someone gets in her way, she's not shy about scaring them off, and if that doesn't work fast enough, she'll mow them down any way she has to. But she takes a little extra pleasure in putting men in their place."

"'The Castrator.'"

Smalley laughed and jumped in the air.

"Did you know that Gene played basketball at Harvard for one season before she got kicked out of the Ivy League for excessive elbows?"

"Fuck, really?"

"Absolutely. Then she sued the NCAA, citing a bias against female players who rebound 'like a man' and no surprise, she won the case."

"A real pioneer for women's rights."

"No, Coleman. A real pioneer for Gene Cauley and her right to do whatever the fuck she wants. That's how she rolls, so best you don't forget it."

I nodded and took another drink.

"You know why she uses the name Gene? She likes it when people don't know her gender. She likes to keep women guessing and have men unsteady on their toes."

"I'd say it's worked wonders for her."

"You're damn right, Coleman. You know Gene's favorite saying, one I'll never forget?"

"I got no idea, Bob."

"Oh, you'll love this, Ryan. She always says, 'Men have dicks for two reasons. To please me when I need to be pleased, and to be fucked when I want to win a case.'"

Smalley laughed loudly and I tried to join in, even as I winced inside.

"So, you both come from Little Rock."

"We certainly do. And you know what they say? You can take a man out of the South, but you can never take the South out of a man. Same shit for a woman like Gene."

"I'm not sure about that, Bob, but I guess they could say the same thing about us dudes from Philly. We have our own, uh, reputation, if you know what I mean."

"Well, Coleman, one day you'll have to fill me in on that. But you're a Philadelphia kid, so you must know what Benjamin Franklin once said."

"Maybe so, I mean, he's a hometown hero with a freaking museum named after him."

"Franklin famously said, 'When you lay down with dogs, you get fleas.'"

"Oh yeah, I know that one. I got it tattooed on my ass."

Smalley laughed.

"I bought stock in an exterminator service years ago. What a great investment."

"Thanks for the tip, Bob."

"You're quite a character, Coleman. I see quite a future for you."

I almost blushed. A moment later, Eugenia "Gene" Cauley appeared on the deck where we were sitting, seemingly out of nowhere, as if she and Smalley had everything choreographed. She looked like a taller version of Sharon Stone, strutting her way through *Basic Instinct* and I wondered if she was going to take a seat and cross her legs to give us both a show we'd never forget. I couldn't believe that Smalley never tipped me off on how smoking hot Cauley turned out to be.

It turned out she owned the yacht and was hosting an intimate sunset cocktail party, which we would enjoy shortly. I'd been invited without even knowing about it.

Cauley could have passed for Smalley's older sister but not by much. He was forty-something, impeccably dressed, and like he said, she was five years older, but hardly looked it. I mean, she looked like she could moonlight as a dominatrix. Each of them generated an aura of invincibility. Standing together, they created quite a strong force field of testosterone-fueled power, even if she ran on estrogen, or whatever.

"Great to meet you, Coleman."

"Oh my God, you, too. Thank you so much for having me here. This yacht is fantastic."

"Of course, it is. Bob has told me a lot about you. I hear you got a real set on you."

I blushed.

"A set? A set of what?"

"Balls! Come on, don't be modest. Bob told me you got right up in Judge Glynn's face down there in Dallas and demanded your fair share of the pie. And a big fucking pie it was, too."

"Well, I spoke out of turn, but so far so good. I mean, I couldn't take any chances risking that kind of payday, and with all due respect, I felt like I was the only one there looking out for me, so I had to uh, you know, speak up or fuck off."

"Speak up or fuck off. I like that."

"I told you, Gene. He's got a brass set on him."

"He sure does. I hear you held your own pretty well in New York City, too, aside from turning Destiny down, which I think you may regret one day."

She winked and looked to Smalley.

"You two look related."

"Yeah, so we've heard. I think that comes from the fact that we share a feral passion for winning at any cost, right, Gene?"

"Yes, my brother from another mother. You see, Coleman, high-powered lawyers like Bob and me need guys like you to refer clients to us, which means we will always make time to speak together and hang out, as necessary."

Since I was still an up-and-coming lawyer, a rookie really, in the class action field, this kind of talk was seductive, especially mingling with a motley crew of outrageous characters, these two, in particular, whose stories were rude, ridiculous and even reprehensible. But I was hungry for more, as if this was the club I'd always yearned to join.

As I came to comprehend the real goings-on in this high-stakes world of corruption and deceit, I began to realize that the deeper I got involved the more complicit I might become in exploiting the class-action arena. But during that afternoon in Miami, I also knew there was no turning back. I was hooked on whatever Smalley and Cauley were offering, and I hadn't even met Randy Hollis yet, who was even more powerful than the two of them combined.

While it's true that I was just starting to enjoy some significant financial rewards, at least for me, which I knew would keep me in the game for quite some time, they paled in comparison to these two made-for-television smoothies from Little Rock, Arkansas, who seemed to be faring quite well in the world without the demands of a moral compass.

Maybe it was time for me to shrug my mother off my shoulder and stop listening to the relentless voices in my head telling me to watch out and remember the ethical code I'd learned while growing up. She had taught me The Golden Rule as a boy and never hesitated to slap me upside the head if I ever seemed to forget it.

For some reason, I felt comfortable enough with my new friends to ask a tough question. I figured if one of them didn't like it, or even if both of them blanched, at least I would know where they stood, and I could adjust accordingly.

"So, uh, if you don't mind, I'd like to ask you a question."

"Fire away, Mr. Balls of Steel."

I laughed.

"You two. Smalley and Cauley. Sounds like a comedy team."

They toasted to my idea.

"So, look, I know you two grew up in the same place, like next door, but how did you connect professionally?"

Smalley looked at Cauley who nodded at him to answer.

"Gene was a real model for me growing up, being as successful as she was in her academic life and with sports. When she got into Harvard, the whole neighborhood was excited, and that inspired me to up my game, so to speak."

Cauley sat down next to me.

"By the time I graduated Yale Law School, which is where I first met Randy Hollis when he visited campus for an alumni event, Bob was an undergrad, doing his pre-law studies and I took him under my wing, just as Hollis was doing with me. I'd say we eventually formed quite a trio, and we still are."

Smalley nodded.

"One more thing, you two, if you don't mind. I'm curious to know something because you've told me a lot about the backroom shit that goes on in this class action world. I'd like to know how you reconcile doing what you do and getting so fabulously rich from it while there are a lot of people, victims, really, who end up with nothing at the end of the day."

Cauley looked at Smalley, who smiled and winked at me.

"Great fucking question, Coleman. You mean, how do we sleep at night on a mattress full of cash while a bunch of miserable fucks are in sleeping bags on the floor?"

"Uh, yeah, Gene. I guess so. I mean, I wouldn't put it exactly like that, but that's essentially my question. Yeah. You nailed it."

I was blown away for a second, kinda taken back with the force of Cauley's reply. She was definitely the type to take no prisoners, and even less inclined to become one herself.

"Of course, no one in polite society wants to put it that way, Coleman, but it's the fucking truth, okay? That's what Gene has so eloquently described, except she left out the part about being a fucking princess sleeping on top of a shitload of mattresses."

"Yeah, and then spitting out a fuckin pea on your head."

Smalley and Cauley laughed, as if the sparring between them was something they had been doing for years, which they confirmed it was.

Cauley leaned in close to me, allowing me a whiff of her expensive perfume. She took a slug on her Martini, flexed her jaw and continued.

"When I have my position, I will go to the end of the Earth with it. I will fight to death."

I didn't know what to say. Smalley nodded. Two peas in a pod.

"You better explain yourself, Gene. Otherwise, you sound like a fucking serial killer."

Cauley laughed.

"Okay, Coleman, this is how it goes. Some fellow lawyers of ours might find me difficult to deal with, which makes me laugh, but in the end, I always get my way."

Smalley laughed and agreed.

"Gene's right, and the same could be said for me, although I'm a little more civilized when it comes to intimidating our opponents. But Randy Hollis, not unlike Bill Charel, can make Gene and I look like rookies."

Cauley nodded and laughed.

"We learned from the best, Bob. So, look Ryan, I made my fortune being ruthless and completely oblivious to who might get hurt in my pursuit of success. That's just how it is. Pretty fucking simple when you break it down."

"Yeah, Gene's right. It's me or you, and in that case, I'm gonna win, no matter what."

"Speak up or fuck off, right?"

Smalley and Cauley laughed, and I readily joined in, thrilled to be in lock step with these two heavyweights. I was impressed and thrilled by their stories. For the time being, I had no doubt about pursuing these new relationships. I wasn't sure about what they had in mind for me, but I was more than ready to roll.

# Fourteen

## Another Family Feud:
## Hollis Takes Advantage and Reaps His Reward

By the time the sun set along the shores of Florida, I knew I wasn't going to make it back home as planned. I thought about calling my wife to let her know that I was going to miss my flight that night to Philadelphia because I was on the brink of a huge breakthrough with Smalley and Cauley, and eventually Randy Hollis, the king of the kingpins.

I tried to imagine the call if it went just right.

"Honey, I'm so sorry. I need to stay overnight."

"Ryan, you promised to be home for our anniversary."

"Oh, Baby, I'll be there."

"When?"

"Tomorrow morning. With flowers and chocolate."

"Oh, Ryan, you're the best."

"I'm trying, Honey."

"I know. Just make sure you don't love your work more than me."

"Never. Not in a million years. Listen, Honey, I gotta go. I got another meeting."

"Okay, Ryan. Good luck and try to enjoy yourself a little. You work so hard."

"I'm doing it for you, Honey. For us."

"For us. Love you, Ryan."

"Yeah, love you, too."

That would have been the ideal conversation, but our reality was different. The marriage had been strained for quite some time, as my ambition and work ethic continued to clash with my wife's desire for us to spend more time together and create a family. Her eggs were talking to her, but I wasn't there yet, and had no idea if I was even cut out to be a father. I mean, my mother wanted a grandchild, but even though I loved my mom, I wasn't in any hurry at all.

So, instead of the warm and fuzzy convo I heard in my head, I opted to text because I didn't want to give Smalley and Cauley any reason to question my focus and reliability.

I told them I needed a minute and stepped aside.

"Honey, I'm so sorry. I need to stay the night."

"Ryan, you promised to be home for our anniversary."

"No, no, I mean yeah. Of course, I will."

"So, when will you be home?"

"Tomorrow. I'm booking a new flight."

"Come first thing."

"I'll try. Don't worry. We can have a nice dinner."

"It's our anniversary, Ryan."

"I know! I'll be there."

"What kind of husband misses his tenth anniversary?"

"The kind that's trying to make it big in this world."

"Really, Ryan? Is that all you got?"

"What? I'm doing it for you."

"I'm supposed to believe that?"

"Of course! You're my freakin' wife!"

"Yeah? For how much longer?"

"Forever, Honey. I'm working to make a better world for you."

"Take your world and shove it, Ryan."

"Really? That's how you want to do this?"

"Fuck you, Ryan. Why the fuck did I ever marry you?"

"Because you love me."

"That was a long time ago."

"Honey, relax. This will be good for us."

"Fuck you, Ryan."

"That's how it is?"

"That's how it is. Just don't get the clap."

"WTF?"

Not my best text exchange with the wife. I mean, she had a right to be pissed, but I thought her reaction was a bit over the top, if you know what I mean. Maybe I should've called her, to tell her in person, but whatever, I mean, I didn't really have a choice. For all I knew, Cauley and Smalley were eavesdropping, and I didn't want them hearing any of my private shit.

I shoved the phone into my pocket and dove right into the bar a few feet away on the deck. Futura was serving up sunset cocktails, and she looked amazing doing so. Having your wife tell you to fuck off kinda makes other women look even better than usual, although Futura already was a knockout and I have to admit, I was getting ideas, only they were mixed up in my mind with images of Melody, which I couldn't shake.

I doubted very much that any of these women had the clap, let alone give it to me. That, of course, would require a bona fide physical interaction, which I wasn't about to initiate. I mean, being a married man and all that would be decidedly uncool, but if Melody or Futura or who knows who else made the first move, could I really be held responsible for my actions?

Of course, my culpability could be debated in a court of law, especially one deciding the outcome of a divorce proceeding, which I didn't put past my wife initiating. In that case, as usual, the prosecution and the defense would present two entirely different perspectives on the case, which might indict me, with no way out, or might give me a reasonable defense.

"Your Honor," the prosecutor says. "Mr. Coleman is a pig. He went to Miami, had an affair with at least one woman, and got the clap, which he nearly gave to his wife, only she refused to have sexual relations with him because he cheated on her. My client wants a divorce, including everything her current husband owns and everything he might accrue in the future. In short, he should pay for his transgressions for the rest of his life."

The judge grimaces and proceeds.

"Your Honor," my defense attorney says. "You've seen the fetching photos of Destiny, Melody and Futura, just to name a few of my client's 'associates.' It's obvious that any man would be unable to resist this temptation. In fact, I'm sure my client's wife would be weak in the knees and succumb to her most basic carnal desire if she were to meet any of these vixens. Therefore, I am asking the court to reject the plaintiff's assertion of cheating and agree that she has demonstrated great mental cruelty toward the defendant and must pay for this transgression."

The judge deliberates quickly and bangs his gavel.

"Not guilty!"

One party leap to their feet in protest.

The judge continues.

"Mr. Coleman has only done what any healthy man would do, and his wife is out of order. I sentence her to 30 days in jail, a monetary fine to be determined, and she must pay for any treatment he requires for the clap. Case closed."

It took me a few minutes to let that fantasy play out in my head before I rejoined Smalley and Cauley, who were leaning against a railing and admiring the sunset.

"Trouble in paradise, Coleman?"

I laughed, trying to appear aloof to my domestic problems.

"It's all under control. So, what's next?"

Over the next few hours, I received a tutorial on AFL ownership and how that white "brotherhood" works. Smalley explained what happened when the Carolina Panthers were purchased for an unprecedented $2.3 billion. The buyer was a hedge fund billionaire, and at the time he was considered by many to be the wealthiest owner in the American Football League.

The other 31 owners were initially ecstatic that Randy Hollis was buying the Los Angeles Flash for $4.8 billion because it would increase the value of their franchises. Alexander Leonidas had purchased the Flash for $72 million back in 1984. When he died, his son, Dino, took over. Then, as it typically does, a fight broke out among siblings over the family fortune and Dino's younger sister filed a lawsuit to sell the team and cash in on the profits.

When the Flash moved the team from San Diego to Los Angeles, they were bleeding cash and the value of the franchise plummeted until they were considered the least valuable member of the AFL family. No one wanted to touch what was perceived to be a dying franchise. That's when Hollis swooped in and bailed everyone out with his generous offer, despite the dubious efforts of Dick Dickey and his underhanded attempts to keep Hollis from sealing the deal. Apparently, Dickey tried every rotten trick in the book, from blackmail to spreading false rumors to supposedly even threatening Hollis through some mercenaries who had worked for him in the Middle East. Hollis held fast and Dickey fell short.

Smalley seemed to be gloating about Hollis and Cauley proposed a toast to the league's newest superstar owner. I joined in, ecstatic to be so close to this world, excited at the prospect of actually meeting Randy Hollis in the flesh at some point in the near future. In fact, I now knew that I would be working with Mona to arrange women for this man, which probably meant I would have to get to know him pretty well. It felt a little creepy, I have to admit, but I figured I had to be open-minded and let things play out, as long as I didn't get the clap!

But for now, the focus was on Hollis and becoming a player inside America's most popular and richest sport.

Smalley spelled it out.

"This is a golden opportunity to propel Randy to the top of the American Football League and to even greater riches. We are lucky to be part of his team."

"Fuckin' A, Bob. You said it. I mean, I can't believe you're creating this opportunity for me, too. I can't thank you enough."

Cauley put her hand on my shoulder.

"Relax, Coleman, It all seems perfect, okay? But it's not, you understand? A few owners, along with the media empires they control, suspect that Hollis may not be a square shooter."

"No. Are you kidding?"

"I don't kid about shit like this. Even worse, that motherfucker Dickey has decided to use his dark money sources and considerable behind-the-scenes power to dig up dirt on Hollis. I don't think he'll succeed, but you never know."

Smalley frowned.

"Dickey will stop at nothing, so we might have to stop him."

"What do you mean?"

This was sounding like some real gangster shit, but I figured Smalley and Cauley were just drinking, enjoying the sea air, and spouting off like geniuses tend to do when anyone poses even the slightest threat to their control of the universe. I wondered what was next for me in this whole affair and couldn't wait to find out more about Randy Hollis.

In the meantime, I headed back to the bar and a little rendezvous with Futura. I had to get my marriage under control so it wouldn't interfere with any of the amazing possibilities that Smalley and Cauley were floating for me. Meanwhile, I had a drink with my name on it, waiting for me with a smile and a perfect little umbrella.

# Fifteen

## Craven Ambition:
## The Legacy of Kingpin Randy Hollis

As Smalley and Cauley explained, Hollis stepped on more than one man's head on his climb to the top. Sometimes, he did it intentionally, like when he elbowed a fellow lawyer out of the way so that he could become top dog in his law school class, but at other times, going back to his youth, he was not always even aware of who or what he left in his arrogant wake.

Smalley spelled it out.

"Look, for Randy Hollis, this approach began early in his life. Since he was born prematurely and remained physically fragile well into his pre-school years, he was pampered by his parents and received special treatment from his teachers, often to the chagrin of many of his classmates. In fact, some of them were annoyed, plain and simple, when Randy got a free pass just because he was unusually short. As far as he was concerned, though, the perks of being physically smaller than everyone were his just reward for the extra struggles his size presented."

But as I found out, Hollis didn't let any part of his disadvantage stop him from dominating his peers. In sixth grade, he ran for class president and spread vicious rumors about a classmate running for the same office, claiming that the boy didn't like girls, that he was somehow "different' and not to be trusted.

Cauley explained the situation further, as if I might not have understood the full context of what had transpired between their mentor and his minions.

"See, Coleman, this was during a time when homosexuality was frowned upon, at best, and even at that age, if a boy was labeled with the 'fairy' tag, his life could be damaged."

"I mean, I hear you. I saw that happen plenty of times when I was growing up in Philly and was just glad it never happened to me."

Young Randy apparently felt no qualms when it came to painting false pictures of his schoolmates. Once he got into his desired junior high school, which being class president helped to ensure, he quickly took over the debating team when he openly accused his older teammates of dealing drugs to young children.

Smalley laughed while he told me this story.

"Can you imagine? The fucking balls on that guy."

Hollis made up the whole story, which was not cool, okay, but I have to give him credit for being so inventive at such a young age. I mean, that shit's impressive. He gained stature, even though he didn't have much to begin with, so kudos to him.

"This kinda sounds like some craven ambition, I mean, right?"

Smalley and Cauley laughed.

"I hope he would be okay with me saying that."

Smalley nodded.

"Coleman, if Randy Hollis wasn't craven, he definitely wouldn't be Randy Fucking Hollis."

"I can't wait to meet him."

"In due time."

Cauley snickered and continued the story.

Apparently, Randy's strategy paved the way for him to essentially take over his high school and make it his personal fiefdom. Before his sophomore year even started, Randy became president of the America's Secret Society (ASS), a group of irreverent students dedicated to rewriting the Constitution so that kids could vote, starting at the age of 13.

According to Cauley, this movement was actually the brainchild of Randy's neighbor, a boy named Henry Rosenfeld, who figured that anyone old enough to have a Bar Mitzvah should be eligible to vote. Randy, who grew up in a family not exactly welcoming to Jews, saw potential in this idea, appreciated the acronym, and used what became *his* ASS to launch what he referred to as "my career in public service."

"Talk about using religion the right way!"

"You said it, Coleman. You sound like a real kindred spirit."

That made me feel good. I mean, hearing Smalley and Cauley share all this shit with me was like a sign that I was being welcomed into their inner sanctum or something.

"Tell me more. This is great shit."

"Okay, so while the campaign eventually failed, Randy gained a fair amount of notoriety and media attention, which pleased him to no end. The local papers and a radio station loved interviewing this kid because he always gave them colorful answers. Readers wrote exasperated or excited letters to the editor and listeners phoned in by the dozens to spout off their opinions, which allowed the newspapers and stations to raise their commercial rates."

As Smalley put it, this was a win-win for everybody, and Hollis didn't miss the obvious lesson: when you say controversial shit, and you don't shy away from it, good things happen.

"You know what really gave those reporters a hard-on?"

"Hollis made a habit of dropping some great one-liners on these guys, like, 'If God didn't want kids to vote, he wouldn't put voting machines inside of schools.' Is that great, or what?"

"Are you kidding me? That's genius. He was in high school when he said that?"

"You better believe it. When Randy spouted off stuff like that, he learned that people pay attention, and you win more followers than you lose."

"In my humble opinion, that was some smart and funny shit he was saying."

"You said it, Coleman. So, just remember that Randy Hollis is always the smartest and funniest guy in the room."

"Got it."

Before long, as they explained further, Randy used his newfound local fame to mount a campaign for school president. This padded his resume even more, along with good grades and a few recommendations he supposedly paid top dollar to secure, all of which combined to open the door for him to apply to a collection of America's most exclusive universities.

Smalley piped up quickly to make a point.

"But let's just clarify one thing. The alleged payments for these recommendations were never proved. So, according to Hollis, everything was kosher, if you know what I'm saying."

"Absolutely! Talk about dedicated entrepreneurship, or what?"

Smalley laughed, as Cauley went on.

"So, by the time Randy went off to Columbia, no competitor was off limits, no matter who they were, what family they came from, or what their potential might be to strike back. Hollis simply didn't care. If he wanted something, or somebody, he was ruthless in his pursuit, and anyone in his way was fair game."

"Yeah, Gene, that's the truth, and that's why we love him so much."

Smalley turned to me.

"Coleman, there's something a bit unusual you should know about Hollis. He has no natural heirs."

"He has no natural hair?"

Cauley laughed.

"Coleman, are you drunk? Heirs, as in family."

"Of course, okay. What was I thinking? Sorry about that."

Smalley patted my shoulder.

"No problem, Ryan. See, Randy doesn't have any brothers or sisters. And both of his parents and grandparents had no siblings. You see, there isn't going be any long-lost cousin shit here down the road."

Cauley held up her hand for a second, as if she were ready to stab somebody.

"That's right, bitches. Randy's billions will be all mine."

Smalley snickered.

"Gene, Randy fucking hates you. He's leaving his billions to charity."

I had to laugh, but I tried to do so without Cauley or Smalley noticing. I didn't want either one of them to misconstrue my intentions. As for Randy Hollis, I couldn't wait to meet the man, the myth, the legend.

# Sixteen

## Virgin Alert:
## Introducing U.S. District Attorney, Mr. Patrick Coyle

Career prosecutor Patrick Coyle, a Yale law school graduate with a multi-generational family history on both sides of policing, was one of the undergraduate students at Columbia University who never quite recovered after being crushed by Randy Hollis.

"It's a long story, Coleman, so let me see if I can sum it up for you."

"Yeah, we've heard it all from Randy and done our due diligence to find out things he needs to know. See, Patrick Coyle's parents were worried about their son when he began his freshman year at age seventeen. From the beginning, he exceled academically but struggled mightily to fit in socially and he had few friends. His father did not want Coyle to go to Columbia, figuring that New York City was too big and too chaotic for his son to manage. He wanted Patrick to become a cop, like everyone else on his side of the family."

Smalley explained more.

"When Coyle was a sophomore, Hollis was a senior and a certified big-shot on campus. Not long after, Coyle, who arrived at this Ivy League institution as a virgin, fell head over heels for Bonnie, a fellow student, who became his very first girlfriend. One night, however, Bonnie told him that she was in love with a senior, named Randall B. Hollis, and no longer wanted to see Coyle. On top of that, Coyle saw the two of them one night having sex in the library. He was so distraught when Bonnie broke up with him that he dropped out of Columbia and became a drummer in a mediocre punk rock band, covering the Sex Pistols."

Cauley just about doubled over in laughter.

"Can you believe that shit? It didn't take long before Coyle became addicted to drugs and hit rock bottom. Luckily, his older brother saved him and got him enrolled at the City College of New York, where Coyle majored in history, got nothing but A's, and ended up at Yale Law School, just a few years behind Hollis."

"Sounds like Coyle had a thing for Hollis."

"In fact, Coyle blamed Hollis for his downfall and never forgave him for 'stealing' his girlfriend. He swore to himself that one day he would be in a position to exact his revenge. But the truth is, Hollis never even knew Coyle existed."

"What? I guess Bonnie never told Hollis about Coyle."

"Yeah, I guess so because she was too busy fucking Randy to cry about Coyle, her whiny little bitch of a dumped boyfriend."

Cauley sure did have a way of expressing herself. Smalley then jumped in to fill me in on more background about Patrick Coyle.

"Years later, when Coyle was appointed First Assistant U.S. Attorney for the Southern District of New York, he assumed a powerful position with potential ramifications for anyone, lawyers like Randy Hollis included, if they so much as approached the line of questionable legal behavior. He was primed and ready to pounce on anyone he didn't like."

It sounded like this became an opportunity for Coyle to right the score with many people he perceived to have slighted him, either intentionally through mere competition, or unknowingly, as Hollis had done in humiliating his younger classmate.

Cauley took another drink and jumped back in.

"Let me explain a little bit more about Patrick Coyle, son of a cop, grandson of a cop, nephew of a prosecutor and cousin of a successful defense attorney, someone who Bob and I respect. This Coyle dude was highly connected and equally insecure about his own abilities and his place in the uh, how should I say, the pantheon of successful officers of the law."

Apparently, after dropping out of Columbia and barely making it through Yale, Coyle began his career in the district attorney's office of Baltimore. After being accused of bribing witnesses to have them testify in his favor, he left in disgrace because even though the charges could not inevitably be proven beyond a reasonable doubt, their mere existence was enough to send him packing.

Luckily, memories are short in Washington, D.C., and he soon began doing policy work for a Congressman, which threw him directly into the maelstrom of national politics. This quickly launched him into the big leagues, where, as we know, few play by the rules, and Coyle was determined to do whatever it took to right the wrongs he perceived had been done to him.

"This guy sounds like a real head case."

"You got it, Coleman. We've checked this out pretty good. Coyle seems to have entered into some kind of an open warfare environment and since he had a shitload of demons in his closet, he had his work cut out for him to repair his reputation. After all, he was starting to work in an influential government position, one he had always coveted and was determined to keep."

"No way he can touch Randy Hollis, though, right?"

"Not that we know of, at least until now."

"Let's be magnanimous and drink to that poor son-of-a-bitch, Patrick Coyle."

Smalley and Cauley filled their glasses and tossed the contents over the side of the yacht.

"To destiny."

"To destiny."

I never thought a toast would remind me of a lap dance, but I was quickly coming to realize that in this new world I was entering, nothing was exactly as it appeared.

## Seventeen

### A Money Tree Grows in Brooklyn:
### Hollis Starts a Hedge Fund

Despite the ample distraction that Futura and a collection of other "employees" managed to produce, I learned a fair amount about how Hollis made his way up the ranks of the class action law ladder. I was equally fascinated by how he leveraged that experience and the money he had made into becoming enormously rich through investments, specifically in the hedge fund world. As we downed more cocktails and feasted on a buffet of lobster and a series of delicacies I didn't recognize and can't even pronounce, Smalley explained how Hollis took the millions he earned from winning or settling those class action suits and started a highly aggressive hedge fund, eventually raising billions from a group of select institutional investors. In fact, some of them were CEOs and board directors from the same companies he manipulated as a lawyer and took for a ride—directly to the front doors of his favorite banks.

"Oh, hello, Mr. Hollis. So nice to see you again. I noticed that you have another armored truck delivery today. How much are you depositing with us this time?"

Hollis laughs and shrugs.

"Too much to keep track of, I'm afraid. Do we need a larger vault?"

Both men laugh and nod to the crew to carry in the cash.

According to Smalley, Hollis quickly turned that money, through investments of his own in Apple, Amazon, Netflix, and Valeant Pharmaceuticals, to name just a few, into an avalanche of profit for his clients and even more for him.

"Coleman, you need to understand something about Hollis. The only thing he craves in life more than sex is money. Don't forget that. Because as Randy says, 'I'll always trust cash more than pussy.'"

"Really? He said that?"

"He sure did. You want me to make you a coffee mug with that inscribed on it so your wife can drink out of it?"

"No, I think I'll pass, but thanks for the offer. I get it, though. If you treat your money right, it will always take good care of you."

"You're learning fast, Coleman."

I was blown away by what I was hearing about Hollis and had to pinch myself that I was receiving all this wisdom first-hand from Robert Smalley and Eugenia Cauley, his two biggest cohorts and most rabid fans. It was obvious how much they admired his accomplishments, even though they were already two of the most successful lawyers in America.

"Coleman, I'm telling you, Randy Hollis is a fucking genius."

Cauley held up her glass for yet another toast to Hollis.

"Okay, so tell me, how did he do it so fast with those investments?"

"It's not rocket science, my boy. It's all about numbers and creative paperwork."

Smalley and Cauley looked at each other and smiled.

"Okay, Coleman, it's time for a little tutorial, especially when it comes to leveraging your reputation into larger and larger profits. This is exactly what Hollis did because he was so impressive in his original field, in and out of the courtroom, so that even people he fucking fleeced wanted to invest with him. And he took quick advantage of their 'monetary lust,' shall we say, to start from the jump racking up huge profits."

Smalley picked up right where Cauley left off. They sounded like some kind of old-fashioned vaudeville team, topping each other with better and better stories, and I was thoroughly enjoying my front row seat to a crazy new education.

For example, while a standard hedge fund charges a two percent management fee and 20 percent of the profits, Hollis produced exorbitant returns for himself because he got away with charging his institutional investors a three percent management fee and 30 percent of their profits. Outrageous? You betcha. This guy had a set of balls like no one else. Based on his cutthroat reputation as a lawyer, investors trusted him and did not care about the higher costs, as they had serious hot pants to have him invest their assets. Hollis knew their motives and never looked back, and in a very short time he reaped millions, like hundreds and hundreds of them.

"He must've got hit with a wicked tax bill."

"No, Coleman, you see this whole operation, I mean the way money comes in under this company and that, you know, it goes down quite well in Delaware, where they essentially invite people to form their own legitimate companies on paper that use these obscure laws of the state to 'protect' their assets.

"Delaware, huh?"

"Yes, which we affectionately like to call 'The State Where Laws Are Made to Make More Money.' Got a ring to it, wouldn't you say?"

"It sure sounds like it."

"Well, then, let's drink to Delaware."

Smalley signaled for Futura to send over a bottle of Dom Perignon, but it was no ordinary version. This was a 1959 edition, valued at more than $42,000 per bottle. It was delivered in a jeweled canister by a young woman who looked as if she'd walked straight off a runway at a Paris fashion show and directly onto the yacht. For all I knew, that's exactly what she had done, and I just tried to enjoy the view without gawking like a horny high school kid.

For the next hour or so, my two mentors gave me another tutorial on how investors like Hollis use strange laws in the state of Delaware to their advantage. For example, after a publicly traded company announces news that it is being acquired, shareholders can buy shares of the stock and challenge the purchase price. This is called "appraisal litigation," and Hollis, like many Americans who have companies incorporated in the state, quickly learned how to take full advantage of the favorable laws. In quite a short time, he raised more than $11 billion through these proceedings.

"Coleman, the state motto is 'Liberty and Independence' and it appears as if they've created ample opportunities for people like us to enjoy those two attributes."

"You're not kidding. So, you both have companies registered there, too?"

Cauley shrugged.

"Doesn't everybody?"

She and Smalley laughed and lifted their glasses once again.

"To 'Liberty and Independence.'"

I found out later that Hollis yielded his largest windfall when Anheuser-Busch In Bev acquired SAB Miller for $104 billion. Hollis figured out a legal way to hold up the transaction until he could manipulate his own cut. He ended up purchasing $2.2 billion of the SAB Miller stock and was paid a billion dollars to go away.

Suffice to say, by the end of the evening I was in awe . . . and three sheets to the wind.

# Eighteen

### Guard My Stash:
### Hollis Employs an Army to Protect His Empire

I found out even more about Randy Hollis before we docked in Miami and I was taken to my hotel, overflowing with stories, booze, and a real hard on for those amazing women on the yacht. My head was spinning as it hit the pillow and I had no idea what was coming next, but I couldn't wait to find out.

According to Smalley, Hollis is one of only a handful of private citizens to own a Boeing 737, which he bought for $75 million from a Saudi Arabian prince. It sleeps ten, with a full-time crew of four pilots and two "stewardesses" and costs millions to maintain. Hollis wants the plane more for status than anything else, even though he uses it to travel between his many homes and a decadent palace on his private Caribbean estate, known to certain VIPs as Hollis Island.

One thing Cauley made sure to describe was the large security team Hollis hired to maintain a 24-hour watch on him, his properties and anyone else in his immediate circle who might need protection on any given day or night. I had seen some of it when Melody drove me up that long, winding driveway to his house. Honestly, those guys on the speedboats waving machine guns were not only exotic looking; they were downright scary. It made me wonder if Melody and Futura were closet ninjas or something, too, ready to knock out anyone who came near their boss with dubious intentions.

"You see, Coleman, when a man like Hollis reaches the pinnacle as he has, you never know who wants a piece of it, or him, so you can never be too careful when it comes to protecting your assets and your ass and whatever piece of ass you want to keep."

"Amazing."

"You better believe it. I've seen some real idiots try to get a piece of the action and they went about it entirely wrong."

"So, what happed to them?"

"Let's just say they stopped being idiots."

I wasn't sure what he meant, but I decided not to ask. Hearing about all this craziness was fascinating, but I admit it also made me a little squeamish. I mean, round-the-clock intense security made Hollis sound kind of paranoid, but I guess if you're worth billions of dollars you got a lot to lose, and God knows he can afford any amount of security he wants.

I had plenty of questions, which Cauley enjoyed answering, as it allowed her to hold court and share some wild stories about Hollis and his excessive behavior. One thing I found out for sure that night—Cauley loved to drink, flirt (with men *and* women), and hold court for anyone who would listen. I had become her biggest fan on the yacht and tried to make sure I didn't drink too much and pass out before she was finished.

The man in charge of this large security team was Harold Jones, who reminded me of a character straight out of WWE. I mean, the guy was huge and had muscles on top of his muscles. He was a retired Navy Seal, who served for ten years in the military before heading to the Middle East, where he led a series of covert operations for an unknown, global paramilitary organization. As far as I knew, these mysterious groups would stop at nothing to execute a mission or a person or even multiple people who needed to be eliminated. It's a different kind of "Don't Ask. Don't Tell" policy, and I didn't feel exactly comfortable asking or being told, at least not all at once on that night.

I was already a bit dizzy from all the stories and booze and women. I wanted to make it home the next day in one piece. After all, I wasn't ready to fuck up so bad that I would throw my marriage away and end up being taken to the cleaners because I went overboard in Miami.

According to Cauley, which Smalley verified, Harold Jones is fearless and fearsome, and not someone to mess with in any shape or form. I witnessed this first-hand when another yacht came too close to ours and Jones had it "removed" from the water. Before you get any crazy ideas in your head, it wasn't what you think. I mean, Jones didn't blow the boat out of the water, but in less than two minutes, or at least it seemed to happen that fast, a Coast Guard boat showed up and impounded the yacht and arrested everyone on it for getting too close to us.

"You see, Coleman? When Jones feels like anyone appears suspicious, he just uses his resources to take care of it without delay. As you can see, Hollis has a well-developed and positive relationship with the authorities, so when there's a problem anywhere nearby they take care of it for him."

"One hand washes the other, huh?"

"Hey, how did you know?"

I laughed. Cauley looked at Smalley and me and frowned.

"It's actually not so funny, Coleman. I must say that I do not like to be in the presence of Jones because he scares the shit out of me."

That gave me a chill. I figured I would learn much more about Jones as I got to know Hollis, especially if I ended up inside his inner circle, as Smalley and Cauley suggested was about to happen.

Smalley leaned in close and whispered, as if he wasn't sure who might overhear him.

"Jones is one bad motherfucker."

"Am I going to meet him? I mean, do I have to?"

Smalley nodded.

"In due time."

# Nineteen

## Missing Lawyer Alert!
## A Cautionary Tale

My head was spinning from all the stories Smalley and Cauley fed me about Hollis—the island, the plane, the houses, the hookers—he had it all, according to his two buddies and convenient co-conspirators. But this level of wealth came at a cost, and anyone who got in the way of Hollis and his desires could face a world of trouble.

That sure got me thinking. Up until then, I had been calculating what it would take for me to reach even a fraction of the success that Hollis had achieved. Or Smalley and Cauley. I had no idea, though, why I should be so careful about Hollis.

About a week after I returned from Miami, the two super lawyers took me for a ride one day down to the Jersey shore. I had no idea why we were going there, but I didn't care. Smalley and Cauley were so much fun to be around, and I was hoping our relationship would keep getting better and better.

As we sped around some windy roads in an open Jeep, I held on tight to the roll bar because I felt like one sharp turn was all it would take to throw me out of the backseat and send me flying off the side of the road and straight to my funeral.

It wasn't like they were trying to scare me, at least I didn't think they were, until we pulled over at a beautiful vista, not too far from Atlantic City. Smalley and Cauley turned around to look at me and stared at my white knuckles, still gripping the roll bar.

"Hey, Coleman, you okay?"

"For sure, I'm fine."

"Pretty fucking gorgeous, huh, Coleman?"

"Oh yeah, I love the Jersey shore. Used to come here with my parents when I was a kid and then, you know, we had some good frat parties here when I was in college."

"I bet they were something," said Cauley. "A real bunch of tough guys."

"No, no, we were pussycats."

"Chasing pussy, you mean, right?"

"Well, yeah, we did our fair share of that."

"I bet you did. Under that schoolboy exterior, you might be a beast." Smalley laughed.

"Our boy here missed his chance with Destiny."

Cauley whistled.

"Which Destiny do you mean?"

"Scores. The one in the VIP room."

"I know, but in Atlanta, Miami or New York City?"

"Wait. There's a Scores in all three cities with a woman named Destiny dancing there?"

"Absolutely. A man's Destiny should be available wherever he goes."

Smalley and Cauley had a good laugh.

"Coleman had his chance with Destiny in the City, and he blew her off. Something about his wife, or whatever."

I didn't know what to say. Smalley was right. I had passed on the chance to experience something "extra" with someone named Destiny. Maybe she was a cyber dancer or a hologram.

"Fucking choir boy, here, huh?"

"Actually, I once sang with my cousin in a church choir in West Phil-adelphia. I enjoyed it, and it was a good way to meet girls."

"Yeah, I bet, but apparently you didn't finger any of them, either."

"Not like you, Bob."

"Yeah, Smalley here was the finger champion of Little Rock. He must've fingered every girl in junior high school."

"Only the loose ones."

We all laughed.

"You know, Bob, all joking aside. I can't thank you enough for bringing me into all of this. I mean, you've opened up a whole new world for me and I want to say I appreciate it."

"Yeah, that's nice, Ryan. Thank you very much."

"You know, Coleman, there's a few things you need to know. That's why we wanted to talk to you today somewhere private, you know, somewhere with a nice breeze blowing to sort of blow shit away after we tell you about it."

"Cauley means you need to keep all of this confidential, understood?"

I nodded.

"Yeah, of course. What are you guys talking about?"

I had no clue what they were up to or what secrets I was about to be told. My heart started picking up its pace and I had to do some quiet deep breathing techniques to calm myself. "Let's take a little walk, Coleman."

I followed Smalley and Cauley onto the beach and zipped up my coat to shield against the wind. It seemed so nice of them that they were taking the time to bring me to the ocean. Anybody can use a good whiff of the salt air and the sound of the waves every now and then.

"So, Coleman, you ever hear of Paul Budman?"

"Who?"

"Paul Budman. You never heard the story of Budman and Hollis?"

I shook my head. I was walking between Smalley and Cauley and looked right and left to let them both know that I didn't know who they were talking about.

"Okay, so anyway, about nine or ten years ago, Hollis got into a real humdinger with another attorney in a class action they were working on together."

"A real twisted conflict."

"Oh yeah. Hundreds of millions of dollars in lawyer's fees were at stake and neither one of them appeared ready to compromise."

"I forget the name of the case. Gene, you remember?"

Cauley shook her head.

"Anyway, the attorney's name was Paul Budman. One day, he just disappeared. No rhyme or reason. One day he was here, and the next day he was gone."

"Crazy, huh?"

"That's messed up. Did he have a heart attack or something?"

"Good question, Coleman. You could be a fuckin detective one day."

We all laughed and kept walking until Smalley and Cauley both stopped.

"Every attorney in the world suspected Hollis."

"At least the ones we knew, including us."

"What? That's impossible."

"What makes you so sure, Coleman?"

"I don't know. I mean, I just figure there's no way that one lawyer would do anything illegal or criminal or whatever to a lawyer he's working with on a case."

"You're right, and most of the time that's true, with most lawyers, that is. But Hollis is not your average attorney."

"So, what happened? Did the authorities find Budman?"

Smalley and Cauley shook their heads.

"No, Coleman, they did not. The police and the FBI investigated for what seemed like forever. But they couldn't make a case against Hollis, no matter how much they suspected him of making Budman disappear."

"That's right. Nothing was found to link Hollis to Budman's disappearance. Not a thing."

"And you know, Paul Budman had a solid, clean career, no enemies, and a wife and five kids. No way he would have left his family high and dry."

"No fucking way."

"Holy shit! This sounds like some mafia movie or something."

Smalley and Cauley were sending a chill down my spine. I couldn't imagine that they were so close with a stone-cold killer. I was a little freaked, but also excited by such a crazy story, like a kid who can't help putting his hand on a hot stove. Even so, I tried to lighten the mood and change the subject.

"There has to be some explanation. Maybe Budman had some secret life with Destiny."

"Good one, Coleman! Very funny, except it's not."

"That's right. We all have our theories, but I'm pretty sure that Jones, that motherfucker, buried Budman in a ditch somewhere."

"You said it, Bob. I don't ever want to get on Hollis' bad side."

I looked at both of them, not sure if I was hearing them right.

"Are you guys fucking with me?"

I watched Smalley and Cauley look at each other and shake their heads, as if both of them were lamenting the fact that I didn't understand the gravity of the moment.

Smalley shrugged.

"Coleman, my boy, let me put it to you this way. It's simple. Here's our only advice. No matter what you do, and no matter how nice Hollis might be to you, never *ever* cross that line with him, no matter what."

# Twenty

## What a Guy!
## Hollis Gives Millions to Charity

I had a lot to consider on the way back to Philadelphia, alone in the back of a brand-new Mercedes Benz S-Class sedan. Smalley and Cauley had sent a driver to take me home while they drove to Washington, D.C. to meet with a federal prosecutor who was rumored to be sniffing around one of their "special" client's business affairs. I had no idea what special meant, but it sounded like they were flirting with something dodgy and nefarious. It all seemed tantalizing to me, to be comingling with two of the most awesome lawyers ever who were living the high life, in and out of the courtroom, on the edge, one I had never been so close to before.

We hadn't gone far when my cellphone rang. Smalley wanted to fill me in on a few more things about Hollis.

"Coleman, we were not kidding around about the seriousness of the situation, but we don't want you to get the wrong idea about Randy. He's a huge philanthropist."

"Oh no, no, no, it's fine. I heard you both and I respect it. I intend to be totally on board with whatever comes down the pike."

"That's the spirit, Coleman, We like that. We like that very much."

"Good to hear. Good to hear."

"Keep the phone close. We'll be in touch."

"When?"

"In due time."

Apparently, as Cauley explained later in a text, Hollis decided early on in his legal career to set up the Hollis Charitable Trust Fund, intended loosely for "those in need." Randy Hollis had grown up in a family with little money, so it was important to him to share his riches once his law firm began to reap millions. It also created public relations gold for him and his firm. Even when he was portrayed as a cutthroat class action lawyer who would stop at nothing to garner an award from the court in the tens and hundreds of millions of dollars for himself, he would respond with a publicity campaign of his own, touting the philanthropic work he was doing in blighted neighborhoods in every city where he made his claim to fame.

I could picture the headlines, from Baltimore to Texas.

LAWYER RANDY HOLLIS REBUILDS ANOTHER NEIGHBORHOOD!

STAR ATTORNEY RESURRECTS ABANDONED DALLAS HOUSING PROJECT.

FOOD BANK SAVED, THANKS TO AMERICA'S TOP CLASS ACTION LAWYER.

I was so excited about everything that was happening with Smalley and Cauley and hopefully Hollis, too, that I couldn't resist calling my mother to tell her all the news. I had recently set her up in a local senior living community, as she had been living alone too long and needed help with the daily basics. Besides that, she had more companionship there than I could personally offer, being so busy and all with my career, and my wife was not exactly chomping at the bit to contribute any extra time to my mother's welfare. The nursing home type place was kind of expensive, to say the least, but it was perfect for Mom, at least so far.

Luckily, she picked up the phone in her room and I launched right into my report on what had happened in Miami, with the yacht and the whole shebang. I even filled her in on more details of the courtroom fiasco in Dallas and how my naked ambition got me chewed out by the judge but impressed Robert Smalley, which I think is way more important than whatever Judge Glynn might think of me. My mother didn't exactly agree with that assessment, as she's not one to challenge authority in any way, shape, or form.

You see, I got my balls from my father, who had no problem standing up for himself and telling people what he thought of them, even if they didn't want to hear it.

"Ryan, my boy, don't be a pussy," he told me when I was like nine or ten. "This is Philadelphia. It's a war out there on the streets, so don't take any shit from nobody. You gotta be tough with everybody, no matter who it is—a bully on the block, a teacher in your school disrespecting you, or who knows who else might be trying to test you. If you want to succeed in life, you have to stand up for yourself and nobody will mess with you. Got it?"

Those were my father's words of wisdom, except he also reminded me to never share them with my mother because they were a little rough and aggressive for her and she would lay down the law on both of us if she ever found out the details of my father's advice.

As I relayed all the amazing news to my mother, she sighed and surprised me with her response. I expected her to be supportive and happy for me, but all she had to say was that I should pay more attention to my wife or else I might lose my marriage and then where would I be in life. I wasn't so sure about that, so I opted to keep my thoughts to myself on that subject. For some reason she never really explained, my mother adored my wife, which proves that one of us must be a lousy judge of character.

As soon as I hung up, my phone rang. Cauley wanted to make sure I got her point.

"Listen, Coleman, some people say that Hollis is a Type-A bully in the courtroom, and I would agree with them, but look what the guy is doing all over the country. You know it's all 'for the children,' right? Come on, now. What are we talking about here? For the children!"

How could I argue with that?

"For the children!"

"You got it, Coleman. For the motherfucking children! But listen. After his first successful year with his hedge fund, Hollis donated $50 million to his charitable trust, and he recently boosted its value with a $250 million contribution."

"Oh my God, that's big time. I mean, wow."

"Randy doesn't mess around, Coleman."

"I hear you."

"Especially when it comes to motherfucking children."

I nodded.

"That's right, Coleman. Bingo!"

"I get it. I love what he's doing in these cities. I mean, how cool would it be to do some legal work for his foundation? I could see for myself how it operates and how it's literally doing miracles in these messed up neighborhoods. Gene, you know I grew up smack in the middle of Philadelphia, so I know a thing or two about messed up neighborhoods."

"That's right. Good to know, Coleman. I like the way you think."

Smalley came on the line and pointed out that the foundation was a bit unusual because even though the organization is in his name, Hollis doesn't decide himself how the money is spent and distributed.

"He hired a full-time specialist who is responsible for allocating the money. Of course, when it's necessary to put a public face out there to promote the fund and maintain or even embellish his reputation, Hollis is not exactly shy about throwing a wild party and making everybody happy, if you know what I mean. He invites every media bastard he knows so he can wine them and dine them to make sure they write something flattering about him."

"I bet it works."

"You better believe it. Randy also appears in public with other investors when it's time to present a check to some boy's club or police league, especially when it seems prudent for his next big hedge fund move."

"It sounds like Hollis is just being modest."

Cauley laughed.

"I wouldn't be too sure about that, Coleman. I never met a lawyer on our level who has ever been described as modest."

Smalley had the last word.

"Remember, Ryan. Keep your phone close. Things are about to get interesting."

# Twenty-One

## Can You Do That?
## The EPI/Dickey Follies: Part Two

I felt compelled to find out more about one of the biggest class action suits to ever rock an American courtroom, the same one that sucked me in and yielded my biggest payday to date. The work I had done on the case, which indirectly linked me to Robert Smalley that day in Dallas, led me to believe that there was plenty of dirt lurking below the surface when it came to Energy Protectors, Inc., the company we were taking to task.

It had become common knowledge that between Dick Dickey and his cronies inside the Defense Department, not to mention other key players high up in all three branches of the federal government, EPI had been able to secure multiple, single-bid contracts, time and time again, until a 20-year career civil servant complained to Army officials that EPI was over-billing and had been unlawfully receiving special treatment from the government.

I mean, can you imagine that kind of corruption going on right here in America? Of course, you can, but you probably have no idea how shit like this goes down. Neither did I until I put on my private dick outfit and started snooping around.

It didn't take me too long to discover that the whistleblower was soon demoted, which led to the whole class-action suit. This action was subsequently expanded to include a flood of other liabilities related to asbestos and the use of toxic chemicals, which, of course, EPI denied knowing anything about. This cynical tactic continued until an atrocious incident in the Middle East, when a convoy of EPI trucks was hijacked and three of the drivers were executed.

The headlines in the news were not pretty. They were all over EPI, looking for a concrete crime to nail them on, but Dickey and his crew of dicks held firm to their position of "We don't know shit." This obfuscation formed an intriguing backdrop for how the legal case proceeded.

For some reason, I smelled something putrid. I knew I had to go back to my connection in Dallas to see if I could revisit some files. Lots of times in these types of cases, there are tons of boxes containing potential evidence that never see the light of day because they are considered unnecessary or redundant. However, they could contain unknown gems that not only make for good gossip; they can end up being the basis for indicting criminal behavior.

I decided to take a day or two to fly back to Texas and see what I could dig up with the help of my colleague, Bill Waterman, who was my local counsel that day in Dallas when we stood before the mercurial Judge Glynn. Bill had mentioned the fact that they had a gigantic storeroom full of unread file boxes, which they had received from the EPI defense lawyers. He also pointed out that these attorneys accumulate millions of pages of who knows what and don't care if they're organized or not, which means in this case, for example, it's up to Waterman to sort through all that paperwork and shit and make sense of whatever they can.

What Waterman does, which was news to me, is to hire a team of licensed lawyers who are not practicing at a firm but are still technically allowed to review legal documents. Since these guys need the work, he can get away with paying them twenty bucks an hour but here's the catch: the courts allow him to bill the class action $500 an hour for these lawyers, which means he and his firm are raking in $480 an hour for eating a fancy lunch while these flunkies do his work for him. On top of that, lawyers like Waterman sometimes get what's known as a "multiplier" from the judge, which is when the court allows them to double or triple their hourly time, which means even more profit at the plaintiff's expense.

Even knowing all of this, I figured I might get lucky if I took some time to join these poor fucks and look through them myself. I didn't think I would find anything, but I had to see for myself what they were dealing with and who knows, I might get lucky.

Smalley and Cauley had no idea what I was doing but I knew they would be ecstatic if I could find anything that would bolster their case against EPI and give them a chance to leverage their position to increase the damages they were seeking.

It sounds like I was doing something questionable, but not really. This was not some hidden collection of mysterious secret files, dropped off the back of a trunk in the dark of night. Like I said, when a company as big as EPI is sucked into the discovery process, you might need a football field to hold all the paperwork they produce, and no one ever looks through all of it.

Waterman greeted me at his law firm with a flask of whiskey, pointed me to the storeroom and wished me luck. That's exactly how it played out, too. Almost. It took nearly all day, but before the sun went down one of those lawyer bozos found exactly what I needed, a collection of documents that showed how Dickey's lack of expertise and bad judgment forced EPI subsidiaries into bankruptcy.

I mean, when it came to making money and hoodwinking people, he was clever, as we all know, but he was an arrogant bastard and sloppy, too. Somehow, even as the class action blew up and he was partially exposed, Dickey was not fired. In fact, he got even richer, thanks to the judge accepting an enormous, unprecedented $789 million settlement, engineered by Smalley and Cauley, who may also be responsible for making the word *chutzpah* so popular.

They eventually reaped an even bigger windfall from the suit, thanks in part to my detective work, so I hoped it would yield a nice reward for me, too. So far, judging from my interactions with Smalley and Cauley, and with a meeting with Hollis in the works, I figured I was well on my way to some genuine success, something my father would be proud of if he were alive to see it. Ever since he died when I was in high school, I've been pushing harder and harder to be "successful."

I've always been chasing his approval and my mother's, too. I guess that's why I'm so ambitious. Looks like my extra efforts might be starting to pay off. She might even appreciate the extra effort I was making to become a big shot. Who knows? Maybe it would even make my wife happy and squash any thoughts she might be having of getting a divorce. I wasn't thrilled at all with the idea of striking it rich and then being forced to split the gold. I'd have to play my cards just right to get in good with these high rollers and keep my wife from messing it all up.

# Twenty-Two

## RSVP:
## Hollis Invites Me to a Party!

Thanksgiving weekend was a sham. I mean the food was pretty good and the football games were decent, but otherwise, it sucked. That's because I spent too much of it with my wife, visiting her family in Dover, a posh suburb of Boston. Apparently, their ancestors were among the original Pilgrims who sailed here from England on the Mayflower, whenever that all happened. Sorry, I'm not an American history expert so the dates elude me, but let's just say they arrived at Plymouth Rock a long time ago.

Like most white folks who claimed to be escaping religious persecution back in England, these immigrants weren't here long at all before they started persecuting anyone who didn't look, act, or speak like them. Considering themselves entitled to do whatever they wanted to the Native American Indians seems like it would fly in the face of religious humility, but I guess they disagreed, claiming that their special relationship with God entitled them to an automatic superiority over everyone else.

The Brewsters reminded me of every WASP family I'd ever seen on television. On top of being White Anglo-Saxon Protestants, they were frigid, pompous, and oozing with moral superiority. But not my wife. She was anything but frigid.

When I first met Beverly Brewster in Philadelphia, she was studying psychology at The University of Pennsylvania while I was "slumming" my way through Temple. Back then, she was anything but snobby. In fact, one could say she traded snobby for slutty because, as she described her own behavior, "I loved to play around" and she wasn't shy about bouncing from one boyfriend to another, sometimes during a single weekend of frat parties, which is where we first met. I think Beverly started dating me because it rankled her parents so badly that she was choosing a boy from the other side of the tracks, who was not only from a working-class family; he was also conveniently half Jewish!

More than ten years later, this little tidbit still pissed them off, even though I was a fairly successful up-and-coming lawyer. The fact that my mother was Jewish, and my father was a descendant of blue-collar workers from the Isle of Man, just did not sit well with them. The truth is, it didn't sit too well with Beverly, either. Once she married me, the ultimate act of defiance toward her family, she slowly but surely began to chip away at my lack of pedigree. First, she largely ignored my mother, who was a widow by the time we wed. Then, she took subtle swipes at my law degree from a university decidedly inferior to her Ivy League institution. Finally, she let no opportunity go to waste to remind me that I hadn't yet won a position at a highly prestigious law firm, opting instead to start my own little partnership with a buddy from Temple.

Suffice to say, the Thanksgiving holiday was a total downer for me. I was so psyched from what had gone down so far with Smalley and Cauley and would have loved to share all that excitement with Beverly and her family, but I knew better. Instead, I kept my mouth shut, ate whatever fancy crap their cook made, and did whatever I could to stay hidden in our guest room, watching the same old team lose, as usual.

By the time we got back home Sunday night, I was exhausted and jumped directly into the shower to wash away all the stuck-up shit I had put up with during the weekend. I mean, Beverly's family came from money, but it was nothing like what Smalley and Cauley had earned, let alone Hollis, who could eat up the Brewsters like a morning snack.

Maybe an hour after I got into bed, just after Beverly had stopped talking about her family and drifted off to sleep, Cauley woke me up.

"Coleman, how you doing?"

"I just spent Thanksgiving weekend with my in-laws. Need I say more?"

Cauley laughed.

"My condolences. We all got a cross to bear, but hey, I have great news for you. I'd like to invite you as my guest to attend Randy Hollis' upcoming Christmas party."

I jumped out of bed and bolted into the bathroom where I could speak freely without waking up Beverly.

"Holy shit! Are you kidding me? His Christmas parties are legendary!"

"He likes you, Coleman, or at least he likes everything Bob and I have been telling him about you, and he wants to meet you in person. We all think it's time."

"Oh, fuck. This is amazing. Sorry, I mean, pardon my French, but I was wondering all weekend about when I would get to meet Hollis."

"Well, Ryan, that time has arrived. Get out your party clothes and get ready to fly first-class to Vegas in my little private plane. My treat."

"Oh my God. When do I leave?"

"In due time."

"Gene, you're not fucking with me, are you?"

"Listen, Coleman, when and if I do fuck with you, you'll know it, and I won't be inviting you to America's best private Christmas party. Stay tuned, my friend, I'll get back to you soon with additional information."

As Cauley hung up, I stared at myself in the mirror with a shit-eating grin from ear to ear. These parties were notorious for sparing no expense or attraction, with bands like the Red Hot Chili Peppers, U2 and Elton John. Cauley mused about the famous people who would be there, some to perform, along with a bevy of the best strippers Vegas has to offer. While that wasn't the most important feature to me, I couldn't help feeling curious about what the "best" strippers in the world actually do to make them earn that distinction.

Apparently, Hollis spends tens of millions of dollars on these shindigs and "anyone who is anyone" goes to great lengths to secure an invite. For these lucky devils, which now included me, it was like receiving a golden ticket from Willie Wonka, except it would not be a G-rated event, not even close.

I slid back into bed, like a kid in a candy store.

"Beverly, wake up! That was Cauley on the phone."

She barely budged.

"Who's Cauley?"

"Waddaya mean, who's Cauley? Gene Cauley. Cauley and Smalley, I told you all about them, at least some things. I explained all this exciting stuff about my new career opportunities. You don't remember?"

"Whatever, Ryan."

"Gene Cauley just invited me to Hollis' Christmas party in Las Vegas! Fuckin' A!"

Beverly rolled over and was snoring in less than a minute.

"Whatever" was right. Based on everything that had transpired so far, I knew that receiving this insider invitation was the key to my future success and a huge step to solidifying my place inside Hollis' inner circle. I'd soon be mingling with his legal colleagues and trusted friends. What could be better than that?

Fucking Vegas, here I come!

# Twenty-Three

## Vengeance, According to Coyle:
## A Lawyer, an Escort and a Private Detective Walk Into a Bar

Patrick Coyle, the federal prosecutor with revenge on his mind, was determined to finally have his way, and settle an old score after years and years of family abuse and humiliation at the hands of his more socially adept and testosterone-happy peers. Case in point: Randy Hollis, stealing his first girlfriend at Columbia University and fucking her in the adolescent psychology section of the library.

Coyle was so out of whack by the time he began his studies at Yale Law School that he started a secret society, called Vindicta Ultio, which is Latin for vengeance and revenge. Apparently, he and everyone else in the "brotherhood" felt as if they had been seriously slighted or downright bullied at some point in their lives, beginning as early as elementary school and as recently as during their undergraduate years. Instead of becoming serial killers, they formed a murderers' row of ruthless, vindictive attack dogs, ready to use the legal system to seek their own private revenge.

For Coyle, the abuse began when he was a young boy. His older brother was a big-time athlete in school and Patrick's father had no empathy for his younger, "sensitive" son and constantly called him a loser.

"You're weak, Patrick. Maybe you're a fag. I don't know. I'll leave that shit to you and your mother to figure out. Just don't come crying to me if you can't cut it in law enforcement. I'm not going to help you. You embarrass me if you want to know the truth. My fellow cops all feel sorry for me, that I got a son like you, who couldn't fight his way out of a soggy paper bag. Would you please do something to make this family proud, for once, or is that asking too much of a fairy like you?"

Fortunately, by the time he was a young adult, Coyle had found a great psychologist, who helped him temper his hatred toward his father and later Hollis, too, at least long enough for the ambitious Patrick to secure his law degree and begin his journey to retaliation.

But Coyle never forgot how his father treated him or what Hollis did by stealing the one and only girl he ever liked and thought he had a chance to be with as a legitimate boyfriend. One of my pals from Temple, who met Coyle during a summer internship in college, told me how freaking determined Coyle was to prove his father wrong and redeem himself by taking Hollis down. Those two were the devils, the thorns in Coyle's side, but since he couldn't really hurt his father in any satisfying way, he focused his attention on Hollis, who represented everything Coyle resented: extreme wealth, unbridled arrogance, and a wicked dose of male entitlement.

For several years, Coyle was distracted by his own problems, which stemmed from his own hubris and lack of self-worth. I mean, this guy supposedly bribed a freaking witness while he was working in the district attorney's office in Baltimore. My friend said that Coyle bragged about that shit, as if it were a badge of honor or something, getting some poor sucker to testify to something that was not true, but would look good for Coyle.

Well, as dumb fucking luck would have it, the dude fessed up right there on the stand under some blistering cross examination and he ratted out Coyle in front of the entire courtroom. No surprise, then, that young Patrick put his head between his legs and skedaddled out of there, lucky as hell that he didn't get disbarred. See, the witness in question had his own issues, with honesty for a start, so Coyle was never deemed technically guilty of anything. Still, he had to leave town ASAP and find some other pathway to exacting revenge on those he perceived to have screwed him, and Hollis remained his primary target.

Nobody quite knows how he did it, and I can't say whether it was through ethical or other means, but Coyle got back in the game through some bizarre chain of connections in Washington, D.C., which rumor has it included Dick Dickey, who was obviously ridiculously influential in Republican and national politics and in the private sector as well, especially in the vast military industrial complex.

According to my own "dark" sources, which means I heard this stuff from somebody in a dark bar somewhere, Dickey helped Coyle climb the ladder in the Justice Department and become a public defender and then a federal prosecutor. Full disclosure: my "dark" source was Smalley, who seemed to know everything, especially things that go on in the dark.

A week before Thanksgiving, Coyle found out about Hollis' purchase of the Los Angeles Flash when it became a national story across the news and social media. The glitzy attention that Hollis was getting drove Coyle nuts. He couldn't help coming across photos of Hollis with beautiful women everywhere, lurking in the background, as if they were there to mess with Coyle. It stirred up his hatred all over again. He decided he was going to get even with Hollis, once and for all, and make him suffer, no matter how far he had to go to do it.

Coyle acted quickly to take Hollis down while he was still hot in the public eye, but he moved a little too quick for his boss up at Justice. He had his full staff working overtime before the holiday break to slap together manufactured charges against Hollis. They showed how he paid referral fees to lawyers who represented hedge funds, which agreed to serve as lead plaintiff in his class action suits. In his mind, Coyle figured it was a criminal action. The whole thing was amateur hour, though, which just showed how desperate Coyle was to take his nemesis down. I mean, Coyle was no slouch attorney, but he was not thinking straight at all.

He got blasted by the top U.S. Attorney in the Southern District of New York (SDNY) for presenting a bogus case against Hollis. Then, during the arraignment, the judge summarily dismissed the case without even completing the initial hearing. He then lit into Coyle.

"You are a disgrace to the judicial system to bring charges that are not even a crime. Not by any definition of the law. You and I both know that while the system is not perfect, and some would say it is flawed, there is nothing legally wrong if a lawyer manipulates the law to his or her advantage to make money for everyone involved. That's just the way it works, Mr. Coyle, whether you like it or not."

It was a total fucking bomb for Coyle. I mean, when a judge cuts you off like that, without even finishing the hearing, it's worse than being a kid in school getting super chewed out by the teacher in front of the whole class. Maybe for Coyle, it also felt like a girl looking at him naked in front of her for the first time and she says, "Really? Is that all you got?"

As a lawyer, I got to tell you the truth. What the judge did that day to Coyle was tantamount to a public castration, and he was lucky that the whole fiasco wasn't broadcast live on C-SPAN. Attorney Coyle was humiliated that day and none of his colleagues stepped up to relitigate the case or even try to get a second hearing with some legit charge against Hollis, that is, if they could even find one. But they couldn't, and Coyle was left out in the cold, a bitter bastard hell-bent on bringing Hollis to his knees.

Young Patrick, who had already gotten into some drug and alcohol shit while he was at Columbia, ended up regressing that night after the botched arraignment. Just like you've probably seen in some run-of-the-mill, mediocre black-and-white movie of some lawyer down on his luck, drowning his pain in a local bar. That was Coyle, in Straylight, a little cocktail bar on Mulberry Street in Chinatown, a short walk from the federal courthouse on Pearl Street in Lower Manhattan. He was plunging into a clear no-no for any recovering addict.

So, the lawyer walks into a bar and then it gets weird. Dick Dickey, who tracks everybody and has been monitoring Coyle's behavior this entire time with his contacts inside the Justice Department, has his own mole inside the prosecutors' office at the Southern District of New York, who were supervising the case, if that's what you want to call rubberstamping it without any real vetting. Anyway, Dickey, knowing Coyle didn't have a prayer with that judge, has quickly arranged to have more than just eyes inside the bar.

That's when a fetching female escort (courtesy of Dickey) walks into a bar to seduce Coyle, who has a history of bad luck with women. According to a friend of mine, who just happened to be inside Straylight at the same time, this woman, who looked like she could have come straight off that yacht I was on in Miami, gets Coyle wasted and has him in the palm of her hand, or wherever, giving her the whole sob story on his busted case.

A few minutes later, a private detective (courtesy of Dickey) walks into the same bar and takes a seat next to the escort and Coyle. Like the smooth professionals they are, he and the escort strike up a casual conversation and suck in Coyle like he's a hungry young boy smack in the middle of the perfect peanut butter and jelly sandwich.

In no time at all, the two of them have enticed Coyle into continuing his efforts to destroy Hollis. The guy actually writes down the whole strategy Coyle will follow in a little notebook that the woman makes sure is secure inside Coyle's pants. They take Coyle back to his place and make sure he's safe and sound in bed, with the notebook in full view on his kitchen counter, ready for him to read in the morning once he can see straight.

Patrick,

It was a pleasure meeting you last night at Straylight.

I so appreciate you opening up to me about your case against Randy Hollis.

I'd love to help you, and I have friends who want to help you, too.

Let's meet soon, and if you're interested, I can help you in other ways, too.

XOXO . . .

Harmony

# Twenty-Four

## Down the Rabbit Hole:
## Coyle's Private Dick Gives Him the Goods to Bust Hollis

I wasn't the only one who had a shitty Thanksgiving. Patrick Coyle did, too. It gets a little complicated, so let me explain. You see, not everyone is who they appear to be, or at least they have mysterious people pulling the strings behind them.

Dick Dickey's mole inside the U.S. attorney's office was a fellow lawyer he knew from their time together at the Defense Department. He was the one who encouraged Coyle to use John Handler, a private detective, to do his dirty work and build a new case against Hollis. Handler could've fit in anywhere. He looked like a regular John Doe, non-descript and boring as fuck. After their meeting in Straylight, nudged along by the fetching Harmony, Coyle decided to seek out Handler, a shady character, to investigate Hollis and conduct surveillance on him.

How did I know this was happening? Come on, now. Think about it. Cauley and Smalley had their fingers in everything, and after Cauley invited me to Hollis' Christmas party she filled me in on a little background information surrounding Dickey.

"Look, Coleman, I don't know everything, but just about. You know, the people working at Justice are not as tight-lipped as we think, and despite their buttoned-up image, these feds like to talk, especially if they are offered 'inducements,' as in cold fucking cash."

Handler responded quite well to that method and Cauley kept him on a short lease. Most, if not all, of his activities, were conducted off-list from the attorney's office. According to Cauley, Handler did not receive money directly from any official sources and any connection between him and Dickey, or anyone inside Justice, were always refuted and denied.

Perhaps the most incredible thing about Handler was that he had full access to all federal and state police records, including every chain of communication that was in their digital cloud files. That became convenient for Coyle, who needed to keep his hands clean, but Handler, even with the unseen backing of Dick Dickey, and working as quickly as possible, could not find anything solid that Coyle could use to implicate Hollis.

The mole attorney who originally referred Coyle to Handler, under Dickey's orders, of course, told Coyle not to question anything Handler did or said because in the end he would find what was needed and make the case for Coyle against Hollis. Since Coyle never questioned Dickey's judgment, he didn't raise any questions about Handler.

Apparently, Harmony did her own thing, too, in encouraging Coyle to follow that path. She used her charms to pressure Coyle, reminding him that if he didn't act fast enough he might lose his chance to arrest Hollis. Dickey was ready to have her offer him cash, millions, if needed, to nail Hollis and put him in jail so that Dickey could swoop in and make his move to buy the Flash. That turned out to be unnecessary because Coyle was all in from the start. If possible, he wanted to ruin the holidays for Hollis, for that year and forever, and he was more than willing to bend the rules to make it happen.

Even though he had nothing solid to go on, Coyle had Hollis arrested a few days after Thanksgiving weekend on some lame charges of racketeering and prostitution. He knew that the chances were slim that the charges would stick but he couldn't help himself. The poor guy was risking his reputation more than ever. I guess he figured that if there was even a slim chance of fucking Hollis, he had to try. Little did he know that Dickey was running the show at Justice and would make sure that Coyle wouldn't get into too much trouble so that he would be free and clear to keep pressing charges and make life miserable for Hollis.

After all, Coyle wasn't the only one who wanted to hurt Hollis. Dickey had his own agenda. Ever since he was a kid, he was obsessed with playing football, first in Pop Warner and then at his high school, but he could never make the starting team anywhere, especially when he tried as a cadet at West Point. He barely got on the field to hold the ball for the kicker, and even got sidelined for a year with tinnitus because he couldn't hear the signals called through his helmet. Due to the ringing in his ears, he had to quit the team.

On top of that, the short and stocky Dick Dickey had his own version of a Napoleon complex, which drove him throughout his life to try and prove something way beyond his capabilities. In this case, it was presenting the kind of profile that other AFL team owners would find desirable. While they mostly agreed with his politics, they were in unison when it came to hating him as a human being. After all, Dick Dickey was just plain unlikeable. Detestable.

As soon as the charges went down, the first thing Hollis did was contact Warren Soffer, the attorney who handled the initial legal transaction when he purchased the AFL team from the Leonidas family. Soffer had mentored Hollis for more than a year on buying a franchise and they had become close friends. He instructed Hollis to call Stanley White, who had a long history of saving corporate criminal defendants. Hollis paid White a $1 million retainer, but he didn't tell him about Smalley calling in a favor with the judge, who postponed the preliminary hearing to give Hollis more time to take care of his affairs. Hollis also neglected to disclose to White that he personally called four U.S. Senators to enlist their help and reduce his charges. While each of the senators took Hollis' call, they hesitated to become directly involved and instead had Smalley act as their messenger to convince the judge to go easy on Hollis.

This is when I figured out that Smalley acted on his own and at the behest of Hollis. He and Cauley had just about everything under their control, including eyes in all the right places and a collection of pliable judges who were more than ready to cooperate . . . for a price.

I found out soon enough that Smalley and Cauley were risking too much of their own reputations, being so big in the public eye and all, so that's why they needed me, which felt like it could become life-changing. I'll explain in a minute.

Meanwhile, Handler, upon Dickey's urging, set up surveillance on me, thinking I was working for Hollis, even though that had not yet happened. Smalley told me I was being followed, for nothing, I thought, even though working for Hollis was a dream I was hoping would come true once I met him in Vegas and we hopefully hit it off and got started.

Smalley assured me that they were keeping eyes on Handler and would not let anything happen to me. I had no reason to question his promise, and even if I had been plagued by any doubts, I definitely would not have let them get to me, not when I was so close to meeting Hollis and joining his inner sanctum.

"In due time" was about to be now.

Even though Coyle's first arrest of Hollis turned out to be bogus, it still damaged his reputation and forced him to resort to what Cauley called desperate measures. See, Handler had discovered that several AFL owners had received bribes from unknown sources, hoping to influence them to approve Hollis' purchase of the Flash.

I gathered that Handler suspected it was me, even though that was impossible, at least up until that point. In fact, I had no idea if any bribes were in the works, and I wasn't about to stick out my neck and ask Smalley or Cauley about any of that shit. For all I knew, somebody was making it all up just to damage Hollis and rattle my cage.

Anyway, the trail to Hollis was quickly established and once Coyle got wind of him talking to those senators, courtesy of Dickey, I guess, he prepared to charge Hollis with obstruction of justice and bribery, both surprisingly approved by the chief U.S. attorney from the Southern

District of New York. Why the guy rubber stamped it I don't know, but let's just say that something fishy was going on and you know the one about the fish rotting from the top. In this case, it seemed like the entire fish was already rotten and nobody cared.

These charges against Hollis were shaky, at best, difficult, if not impossible to ultimately hang on him, especially when he had the best legal team handling his affairs, which included, of course, the judge assigned to the case. I mean, if you were thinking that his or her Honor was above corruption, do yourself a favor and think again. Those black robes can disguise a lot of dubious behavior.

Dickey's thumb print was all over the place and his influence over the SDNY was unmistakable. Hollis was never indicted, thanks to some last-minute wrangling by Smalley and Cauley, who called on a "friendly" judge to dismiss the case against him on a technicality.

I had no idea how lucky I was, that none of the charges mentioned me by name, even though I wasn't involved . . . yet. Handler and Coyle could have pegged me, too, if they wanted, and let the chips fall where they may. It would have been no skin off their back if I had gone down, used as a sacrificial lamb to salvage at least one guilty verdict.

But fuck no! First of all, I wasn't guilty of anything, and second, I wasn't guilty of anything. Maybe I should have stepped back and taken stock of the situation, which was getting stranger by the day, but I didn't hesitate to throw caution to the wind and continue to make plans to attend the party in Vegas and meet Hollis.

# Twenty-Five

## A Real Set of Balls:
## How I Became a Fixer

I wasn't too surprised when Smalley called me the next day. Ever since Coyle had begun to bungle his way through the courts in pursuit of Hollis, Smalley and Cauley had been in a bit of a panic, scrambling to track down exactly how the whole shit was happening. Apparently, they thought I could help, which of course would be a positive development for Hollis. It suddenly sounded like I might be meeting him before the big bash in Vegas.

"Ryan, I hope you had a nice Thanksgiving."

"Thanks, Bob, not exactly, but I appreciate the sentiment."

"Sure. But that's not why I'm calling. Remember what Gene told you about Dick Dickey and the tool he has doing his bidding inside the U.S. attorney's office? Well, it looks like we've got a bigger problem here than we anticipated and I think you can help us."

"Us?"

I know he meant Cauley and Hollis, but I wanted to hear Smalley spell it out.

"Us, yeah. Of course, I mean us. Cauley and I have been keeping tabs on this thing with Coyle for some time now, but we've been forced to go knee-deep over the past few days, digging into all this shit that Hollis is facing right now with this little bastard and the bogus arraignment, and then the stupid, meaningless arrest. The whole thing stinks, and he won't end up in any legal trouble, of course, but this fucking charade could do irreparable harm to his stature and standing with the AFL, especially the other owners who need to approve his purchase of the Flash."

"I know, Bob. It's ridiculous. I told Cauley that I have a friend who knows Coyle and saw him the night after the arraignment went south on him. He was in that bar in Chinatown, drinking his face off and getting all sloppy with some gorgeous hooker and a mysterious guy, who I hear is a real sketchy dude."

"Handler. I know the bastard. He's clever as all get out but he's no good."

"Exactly. And for some reason, he seems to be following me along with whoever else he's tailing, trying to gather evidence and build a case for Coyle."

"Coleman, that's precisely why I'm calling. Your moment in the sun has arrived. Or should I say, these moments may be very much in the dark, undercover, so to speak."

"I'm all ears."

"Perfect. So, look, we need you to get to New York City first thing in the morning. Go straight to the St. Regis Hotel and I'll meet you in the back of the lobby, right next to the shoeshine stand. Cauley will be there, too, and we'll take you to meet Hollis."

"Holy shit! Tomorrow?"

"Nine a.m., sharp. And listen, Coleman, don't wear your Aldens, just in case we need to pass through a metal detector."

I had to laugh, especially because Smalley actually remembered that shit in Dallas with my shoes.

"Okay, sure, but where are we going?"

"In due time, Coleman."

"Like?"

"You'll find out tomorrow."

"Okay, but can you tell me anything at all about what you and Hollis need me to do?"

"Coleman, you're a lawyer, right?"

"Yeah."

"And a damn good one, correct?"

"Yeah, I mean, thanks. Thank you very much for saying so."

"And you're ambitious, am I wrong?"

"Oh no! You're right. I got big ideas for my future."

"That's good, Coleman. We'll get to that in due time."

"Okay, okay, this sounds exciting."

"Keep your cool, Ryan."

"Oh, don't worry. I'm totally fucking cool."

"That's good, Coleman. Let me ask you one thing before I hang up."

"Sure. Fire away."

"You remember when I told you in that Dallas courtroom that you got a real set of balls?"

"Fuck yeah, I remember. Best day of my life. Robert Smalley putting my testicles right up there on Mount Rushmore."

Smalley laughed.

"You ever see *The Fixer*, that movie with Jon Voight? It was like twenty years ago. He played this lawyer who could fix any situation for his wealthy clients."

"Yeah, kinda. Voight was cool. I mean, he was great in *Midnight Cowboy*. But if I remember right, he did some questionable things and then he had some kind of crisis of conscience or something when things got heavy."

"Fuck your conscience. Look at Liev Schreiber in *Ray Donovan*. You think he's got a fucking conscience?"

"Good point, I guess. You know Jon Voight plays his father. Total freak."

"Yeah, whatever, Coleman, but we're not going into all that shit right now. We're not living in a movie, and you're no movie star, like Jon fucking Voight, right? But what I'm trying to tell you here is that we need you to step in and fix a few things for us, things that Hollis of course must steer clear of and even me and Gene, we can't be out there in the public eye, doing some of these things either."

"Okay, but this is starting to sound pretty complicated."

"No doubt. It *is* quite complicated, and that's why we need you to join the team."

"You got it, Bob. I'm all in."

"Perfect. See you tomorrow at nine sharp at the Regis."

"I'm awake at dawn."

"Good. Get a good night's sleep. You'll need it."

# Twenty-Six

## Pimp My Ride:
## My High-Tech Trip to Hollis Island

I was already wide awake when the alarm went off at five a.m. That's just my anxious nature, especially when I'm all psyched for something new and exciting. I'd say an emergency meeting at the freaking St. Regis in Manhattan qualifies for that. I mean, come on! Even though I was in the dark about what was really going on, I felt like I was being initiated into the coolest club ever. If that meant getting up early to drive a couple hours, who cares?

I needed at least an hour of prep before I could leave. This was no ordinary day, when I pop up out of bed, do my coffee routine, some exercise, walk the dog, and then make sure my business attire is looking clean and tight. You never know who might walk into my office on any given day, so I always need to look like a million bucks. For something as deep as walking into the Regis at nine a.m., I felt like I needed to look like a *b*illion bucks, with a *b*.

I mean, this was a whole new level of human existence I was about to enter. Of course, Smalley, Cauley, and Hollis put their pants on one leg at a time and take a shit like everybody else, but come on, their pants are super fucking expensive, probably handmade by the Pope's tailor or something, and I wouldn't be surprised if Hollis at least has someone on his staff to wipe his ass with imported aloe leaves, treated with a rare collection of exotic herbs and spices.

"Only the best for my billion-dollar ass!"

I was careful to not wake up Beverly, who was snoring like a happy moose when I left the bedroom. I took my time to shave just right and almost had a nervous breakdown trying to pick the perfect choice of cologne from my stashbox. I kept my suit jacket on a cedar hangar as I locked the house and headed for my car, trying to contain my excitement so I didn't get into an accident backing out of my driveway. I lived in an up-and-coming urban neighborhood that was gentrified with a lot of young professionals, especially lawyers who would love to sue my ass if my Benz even came within breathing distance of their precious fancy cars.

Smalley sent me an encrypted audio file, which I received just as I started the car and the dashboard lit up. I felt like a brand-new character in *Mission Impossible* for a second, waiting for the media console in my Benz to self-destruct.

"Your mission, Coleman, if you decide to accept it . . ."

"Fuck yeah, I do!"

I started out in Olde Richmond, a suburb just north of Fishtown, an old industrial neighborhood of Philly, which was in the heyday of its revival as an up-and-coming yuppie paradise, with a ton of cool restaurants and clubs. Fortunately, I was blessed with the foresight to buy a house nearby several years ago, when a mortgage in that price range got me a sweet place without giving me ulcers every month to meet the payments. Beverly even liked it, especially the location, less than a mile from one of the biggest and fanciest collection of stores in the Philadelphia area. I hate fucking malls, but if she was happy, who cares?

I drove up the Delaware Expressway and crossed the Betsy Ross Bridge into New Jersey. I'm telling you, Elizabeth Griscom Ross, who was an upholsterer and married three times, by the way, was quite a businesswoman and way ahead of her time. I know this shit because I actually paid attention to my American History teacher in high school, who was an absolute fox.

Anyway, Betsy got a boatload of cash from the Pennsylvania State Navy Board to make a flag, which Congress eventually adopted as the national Stars and Stripes. So, I'd say she deserves a bridge named after her, and luckily, there was no traffic as I drove across it and headed up the New Jersey Turnpike to New York City.

As I put the car in cruise control, I turned up the volume and started Smalley's audio file.

"Good morning, Ryan. If you're listening to this now, I assume you are on the New Jersey Turnpike, heading to New York City to meet us at the Regis at nine. Thank you for making the trip. We all appreciate your willingness to join the team and we feel confident that you will feel the same. As you know, Randy Hollis is in the process of purchasing the Los Angeles Flash and he wants to make sure that nothing . . . I mean nothing, gets in his way. Unfortunately, a few roadblocks have popped up, which we need to remove. That's where you come in, so listen carefully. Some of this information you already know about, and some will be new. There's a federal prosecutor, named Patrick Coyle, who seems to have an old personal grudge against Randy, and he is using the power of his office to harass him. But he is not working alone. He has help inside the Justice department from an individual who has his own motives and agenda, which is in direct conflict with Hollis and his upcoming entry into the elite club of AFL owners. Coyle and his phantom cohort are making things difficult now for Randy and we need you to do your part in fixing this problem. Randy has reached out to a U.S. Attorney he knows well in the Northern District of New York, but since he is a pending defendant in the Southern District, Stanley Walters, the acting U.S. attorney in the Northern District, refuses to take Randy's calls. Understandably, he simply cannot, not now, at least, especially under these circumstances. Hollis thinks he could be in a ton of trouble when it comes to getting his purchase of the Flash approved. He needs a majority of the thirty-one owners to sign off and his arrest could adversely affect the vote. Randy's lawyer, Soffer, has called the Commissioner of the AFL, Roger Hartwell, to discuss the situation, and that outcome is pending. Meanwhile, Coyle's secret partner, the puppet master, Dick Dickey, remains in the shadows, but he is pulling all the strings, lying to suit his goal of purchasing his own AFL team. Our sources have informed us that he has arranged for a private detective, named Handler, to prepare and deliver surprise discovery boxes to all the current AFL owners in a matter of days, complete with a slew of damaging evidence about Hollis and his sordid behavior with escorts and drug trafficking throughout the Caribbean. Naturally, this cannot be allowed to happen. For now, this is all I can share with you, but I'm sure you will find out much more later this morning. Suffice to say, we need your participation in fixing these problems so that Randy Hollis can restore and affirm his well-deserved and spotless reputation so that he can become a bona fide and well-respected AFL owner, to be held in high esteem by his peers and the public. Drive carefully, Coleman, and see you promptly at nine."

"Holy shit! I'm in the game!"

# Twenty-Seven

## WTF?

## Pursuing My Passion in the St. Regis Hotel

I parked in a garage on East 55th Street and entered the St. Regis Hotel at 8:35 a.m., just in time to secure an espresso at the handsome café inside the lobby. I had been here for a second with Smalley before, but it was a blur. This landmark hotel, overlooking Fifth Avenue, just south of Central Park, was founded in 1904 by John Jacob Astor IV, an American business magnate and a lieutenant colonel in the Spanish–American War. He died on the freaking Titanic when it sank on April 15, 1912. Astor also had a huge, bushy handlebar moustache, which I thought maybe I should wear in his honor and as a disguise when I walked into the Regis for my secret meeting.

According to their corporate sales pitch, "The flagship property in the St. Regis Hotel's collection epitomizes timeless luxury, offering an experience beyond all expectations."

I was thinking about that when I ordered, wondering if maybe I should be drinking one of their famed and legendary Red Snapper cocktails. But since it was barely breakfast time, I figured I was too early for that and staying 100 percent sober was probably a good idea.

I looked at the Regis byline on my phone:

"We look forward to helping you pursue your passions with the quintessential five-star hotel experience in the heart of New York City."

I was definitely ready to pursue some quintessential passions, beginning with joining the team right there and then, somewhere inside the hotel. I could hear my future, like this:

"Hollis, Smalley, Cauley & Coleman. How can I direct your call?"

"I'd like to speak with the newest hotshot partner in your firm, Ryan Coleman, please."

"Our pleasure to serve you. Attorney Coleman will be the perfect person to help you pursue your passions with our quintessential five-star legal experience."

I had to laugh at myself, as I was feeling almost dizzy from a triple shot of espresso. I took a deep breath to calm my caffeinated nerves and looked around the lobby, still smiling, trying to see if Smalley or Cauley might be approaching.

"Mr. Coleman?"

I almost spilled my drink as I turned around and saw Melody, looking exactly like she did when she picked me up at the airport in Miami. She smiled mischievously as she took in my surprise, seeing her there in the hotel lobby.

"Miami. Manhattan. Whoa, Melody, you sure do get around."

"Correct, Mr. Coleman. My responsibilities take me far beyond Miami. Today, they've brought me here to Manhattan to escort you upstairs to meet Mr. Hollis."

"All right! Let's do it."

"In due time, Mr. Coleman. We'll go up in a few minutes as soon as I get clearance."

"Sounds like we're about to take off on a flight or something."

"Something. That's right."

"Okay. You want coffee? They make a great espresso here."

"Oh no, no caffeine for me. I'm naturally full of energy."

"Yeah, I get it. I can see that. You have very nice energy, shall we say."

Melody looked at her wristwatch and then at me. She was wearing some kind of fancy digital device that I hadn't seen before, but I figured I was just lagging behind a little on all these contraptions, especially the ones that also had the bling effect of expensive jewelry. I still had no idea who Melody was or what her real job was working for Hollis, but she sure did know how to dress, from the form fitting "uniform" she wore to her perfectly coiffed hair and that futuristic band around her elegant wrist, looking like a femme fatale in the next Bond movie.

"We can go up now."

My heart raced, first from Melody's command and then in anticipation of where we were heading and how it was going to be meeting Randy Hollis for the first time. I followed Melody past the guest elevators and around a corner where we were admitted by a security guard and led to what looked like a special freight elevator. Since I was trying to play it cool, I didn't ask any questions. I figured everything would be made clear soon enough.

"In due time."

That's what they all liked to say, so I figured I would follow their lead.

"Let's do it, Melody."

She nodded, with barely a hint of expression. I decided to ignore my instinctive response, which would have been to keep up the banter and check her out for a playful reply, but I didn't get that vibe from Melody, so I backed off and closed my eyes as the elevator ascended all the way to the Penthouse.

"Here we are, Mr. Coleman, Follow me."

She used a key card to enter the Premiere Suite and ushered me into a lobby area that looked identical to something I'd seen in a movie like *The Great Gatsby*. I was waiting for Nick or Daisy to come prancing out of one of the rooms, but I wasn't surprised at all when Smalley and Cauley greeted me, looking all business-like and serious.

"Coleman, good you're here. Let's get to it."

I followed them into an empty room, except for a single chair and what looked like a super hi-tech projection screen, something I'd never seen.

"Have a seat, Ryan, and we'll see you in a few minutes."

The door shut behind me before I could turn to see Smalley exit the room. I noticed a mirror on one wall and had no idea I was being watched, not until I was told later that I had been observed throughout my visit.

I heard a whirring sound from the console behind me. Before I had a second to look, I was staring right into the face of Randy Hollis. In fact, I was staring at his whole body, from head to toe, fucking right there in front of me, as a freaking hologram!

"Good morning, Ryan. I'm Randy Hollis. Nice to meet you."

What the fuck? I couldn't speak. I couldn't even play it cool enough to nod. I just stared straight ahead and reminded myself to not fall off the chair.

"Sorry I can't be with you today in person. I have urgent business to attend to here on my island, but I wanted to meet you as soon as possible. Thankfully, Bob and Gene were able to arrange for you to be there, and I thank you very much for taking time out of your busy schedule to meet me."

"Uh, sure, yeah, of course, no problem. My pleasure. Mr. Hollis. Sir."

Hollis laughed, or at least his fucking hologram did.

"Call me Randy. Nothing so formal from here on out. Okay?"

I nodded.

"Sure. Nothing formal. Gotcha. I'm a casual guy whenever possible, although I can really tighten it up when the situation demands it."

"I'm sure you can, Ryan, and it's this exact range of abilities that we like so much about you. Bob and Gene have been very impressed, and I can see why."

"Okay, then, thanks. Thank you very much. I appreciate that. I would be honored to work with you, uh, for you, with you, under you, however you want to put it. It would be great."

Hollis nodded. I couldn't really tell how big he was because all I could see behind him was a beach and the ocean, a perfect aqua blue, which looked like my dream vacation spot, only better, so I didn't know if he was short or tall or something in between. For a second, he had this Napoleon kind of look going on, as if he were trying to increase his physical stature by rocking back and forth to make it look like he was going up and down, like he was getting taller and taller by the second.

Maybe I was just too amped up on coffee and adrenaline and wasn't thinking straight, or maybe this was the Hollis effect, in the flesh, or hologram flesh, whatever, playing tricks on my eyes and my mind.

"I'm sorry, Ryan, but that's all the time I have for today. I hear you've been invited to my little gathering in Las Vegas, so I'm sure I'll see you there, and who knows . . . perhaps we will meet again even sooner."

"Okay! I certainly hope so! That would be amazing. And thank you for the invitation. I can't believe it. I'm so excited. Thank you. Thank you so much."

"Have a great day, Ryan."

In a flash, Hollis was gone and the whirring sound behind me suddenly stopped. I turned, half expecting Hollis to be standing there, laughing as he realized how well he had pranked me with some hi-tech projection gimmick.

The door opened and Smalley gestured for me to step out and back into the lobby of the suite, where Cauley was waiting, seated at a beautiful dining room table. She also gestured to me to have a seat, which I kinda collapsed into, still blown away by the encounter I'd just had with Hollis, or at least I thought it was him.

"Sit tight, Coleman. We're just waiting a few minutes. Would you like some coffee?"

"Waiting? For what?"

Cauley leaned forward and smiled.

"Ryan, have you ever had a test for a STD?"

"A what?

"What?"

"Yeah. What?"

"What? Really? You don't know? A sexually transmitted disease. Are you kidding me? You don't know what STD means?"

"Oh. Okay. Yeah, yeah, now I do, yeah."

Cauley shrugged and then nodded. I nodded, too.

"Sure. I know what you yeah mean. I got it. STD. Yeah. Fuck. Okay."

"Coleman. Don't fuck with me."

"No! No way. I would never fuck with you about something like this. Are you kidding? A sexually transmitted disease? That's nothing to fuck around about. I mean, come on!"

Smalley, who was listening to our exchange the entire time with a straight face, moved his chair closer to mine, as if he had something confidential to say. He even lowered his voice.

"No kidding, Coleman. A STD is fucking serious. You're right."

I was kinda pissed by then.

"Okay, Bob, and you, too, Gene. Why are you lecturing me about some STD? What does a STD have to do with anything right now? I don't have a STD if that's what either of you are worried about. Do you? You got something you need to share?"

Cauley laughed.

"You do have a set of balls, Coleman. That's why we like you. So, listen. I'm only saying that when you think you might have a STD you get a test. Right? And then, you wait for the results of that test. Right? Okay. It tells you whether you have the STD and you're positive or you're negative and you don't have the fucking STD. In that case, you want it to always be negative, but now, after you've just met Hollis and been tested by him, you want to test positive. You want to have the STD, only in this case it's a good version."

I was so fucking confused.

"You mean, that whole hologram thing with Hollis was a test?"

"Correct. He wanted to meet you and get his own impression. Of course, Bob and I have been singing your praises and he trusts us, but he wanted to be a hundred percent sure and see for himself if you felt just right for what he needs you to do."

"Which is?"

"Oh, don't worry about that. The important thing is you passed the test!"

"Great! And now?"

"In due time, Coleman. In due time."

# Twenty-Eight

## The Tolls Add Up:
## My First Golden Bucket of Cash

I was driving back to Philadelphia, still jacked up on espresso, when my phone rang.

"Coleman, you made quite an impression today with Hollis."

"Hey, Bob, really? Great! I'm just glad I didn't leave New York with any STDs."

Smalley laughed.

"There's always next time. Let's see what we can arrange."

I wasn't exactly laughing at the prospect of meeting some dicey woman at one of Smalley's favorite clubs, but I did enjoy the banter, as long as that's all it was.

"Listen, Bob, I got to tell you something. That hologram of Hollis was kind of a freak show. I've never seen anything like it, and of course it was amazing but pretty fucking weird, too, if you don't mind me saying so."

"Speak your mind, Coleman. We all like that about you. The technology is relatively new and extremely expensive, so we use it sparingly, just for special occasions."

"Okay, I feel honored, then, to be a special occasion."

"Hollis liked you, which you now know, of course."

"Yeah, I guess he liked me as much as a STD."

Smalley laughed.

"That's Gene's sense of humor. It's a little dark, sometimes, but that's why we love her."

"A little dark, yeah. Hope I never end up knowing any more about the subject."

"That would be advisable."

I had to laugh at that one. Smalley had a biting way about him, edgy at times, and I was never completely sure if he was messing with me or just enjoying the back-and-forth. Once again, I chose not to ask because I wasn't sure I wanted to hear his answer.

"Listen, Coleman, we've got to discuss a few things, including a retainer to begin using your services."

"My services? You mean, as a lawyer?"

"In a manner of speaking, yes. Remember when I told you that we needed some things fixed? Well, that's the point we've now reached, so we need you to fix them. Of course, you'll be compensated nicely for your work, in the way that you should. I'd prefer to do that with you in person, so let's meet tonight back at the Regis at nine p.m. sharp, in the bar inside the lobby. Someone will meet you and bring you up to the penthouse."

"Melody?"

"Maybe."

"Bob, I gotta ask. I was just there with you an hour ago. Why didn't we do this then?"

"Fair question. Gene and I had to rush off to an urgent meeting with a couple of attorneys who are preparing a class action case in Baltimore. I don't quite know how he does it, with everything going on, but Hollis is up to his old tricks. With our help, and soon with yours, too, he has paid referral fees to a couple of colleagues we know to get their clients to serve as lead plaintiffs in a series of securities class actions, which should more than cover White's million-dollar retainer and the monumental fees he will charge Hollis to keep him out of jail."

"Why does Hollis need to do that? He's a freaking billionaire!"

"Well, Ryan, one of the reasons Randy is a distinguished member of the billionaire class is because he operates this way. He raises sufficient funds for these types of emergencies so that he does not need to use any of his own money. Capish?"

"Fucking genius."

"I knew you'd get it. So, in case you didn't know, Hollis still has a license to practice law and he isn't shy about manipulating his way into serving as lead attorney every now and then when it's a juicy case. He has an eagle eye for these things, and most of the time he nails it. That means he ends up reaping all of the legal fees, minus a tidy share for me and Gene and anybody else who needs to be taken care of, like you, for example, as soon as you get started."

"I'm in, baby. I'm all in."

I was almost at my exit on the Jersey Turnpike. I'd have to figure out how to explain all of this to Beverly, at least what I was allowed to say, especially the fact that I had to go back to New York in a matter of hours.

"See you soon, Coleman. Nine sharp in the Regis lobby."

"I'll bring my calculator."

"Don't get ahead of yourself, Ryan. As Gene would tell you, 'There's a golden bucket of cash waiting for you in paradise, but you gotta earn it, my boy.' See you tonight."

# Twenty-Nine

## Extra! Extra! Read All About It:
## Hollis Arrested! Hollis Cleared!

That night at the Regis, just as I was getting up to speed on what Hollis wanted me to do, the shit hit the fan. Coyle, more desperate than ever and under extreme pressure from Dick Dickey, managed to have Hollis arrested—again—on new charges of bribery and obstruction of justice, and the story made front page news and exploded across social media in a matter of minutes.

"Billionaire Hollis Brought to His Knees in Manhattan Courtroom!"

"Legendary Lawyer Randy Hollis Needs One Now!"

"New AFL Owner Faces Federal Corruption Charges!"

"Flash Wannabee Owner Gets Charged!"

The Christmas party in Vegas was less than a week away, so I had to move fast. Hollis already had his all-star legal team assembled, and he seemed confident that he would prevail in court, but he desperately needed to manipulate his public image. It looked terrible to have charges brought against him just before the AFL owners were about to meet and decide if he was to become part of their fraternity, so we had to get this situation fixed immediately.

Smalley wasted no time contacting me.

"Coleman, we're in deep shit here. We've got word out to a few experts in this field, but we're running out of time."

"I know just the right person, Bob. I'll get back to you this afternoon."

I quickly arranged for Hollis to hire a public relations consultant, a woman named Bonnie Spencer, the most expensive and best PR pro in the country. I met her a few years ago when one of my more experienced colleague's clients, who shall remain nameless, got into an ugly scandal when he took his company's executive team (all men I should point out) to what he called a "spiritual retreat" in Thailand. Apparently, their personal "growth" ended up impregnating several minors, who somehow ended up pressing charges and making life hell for my colleague's client, who he soon stopped representing. I mean, who wants to rep a pervert? It's not like I'm related to Allan Dershowitz or anyone like that.

Just as Bonnie Spencer had done for that schmuck, who paid her a gazillion dollars to save his ass, she immediately ran advertisements in newspapers and across multiple media platforms, claiming that Mr. Randall Hollis is a great humanitarian and a saint, and that his arrest was a stunt by his enemies to damage his reputation and thwart his purchase of the Flash.

Ironically, she was exactly right. I mean, I knew that Hollis was a good dude, as Smalley and Cauley had told me over and over, and I also knew that Patrick Coyle was a mean-spirited punk who was not trying to hurt Hollis to keep an actual criminal off the streets, which is what prosecutors are supposed to do. This was pure personal vendetta, spurred by Coyle's bruised ego and his phantom backer, Dick Dickey, who was obsessed with owning his own AFL team and thought he had to "eliminate" Hollis in order to make that happen.

Unfortunately, Coyle and Dickey underestimated Hollis and his unique magic skills. They had no idea that he was well on his way to "handling" the judge and drinking to his freedom from a remote location on his private island.

They also had no idea that Smalley had tipped me off about the pending arrest warrant and had contacted Stanley White, who was representing Hollis, to get him and his team up to speed. He called in a favor of his own, as this is how shrewd, top-of-their-game lawyers operate in this exclusive territory. One hand washes the other, so to speak, even if one set of them may not be exactly clean. But who am I to say whether one person's sanitary habits are better than someone else's?

Anyway, White reviewed the Criminal Complaint, which spelled out the charges, and also received the discovery as a special favor from the SDNY. Whoever passed all that info to him must have done so without Coyle's knowledge.

Within a few hours, the heat began to ease up. We assured Hollis that due to his celebrity status his preliminary hearing would be before a no-nonsense judge who would have no trouble recognizing that Hollis had committed no crime, which was a fucking fact!

I was on the conference call with the judge's clerk when White provided some essential background information in an effort to "educate" the judge on this whole bogus affair. He simply pointed out that Coyle, the U.S. attorney, was coming after Hollis *again* on trumped up charges, that he was attempting to use the fact that Hollis was about to purchase an AFL team and was lobbying the owners, as prospective buyers usually do, to gain their approval. White reminded the clerk that there was nothing wrong with this practice, that high-powered people in the world of sports do this all the time.

White reminded Hollis on an encrypted call that there was no technical crime to speak of and that he was 100 percent certain that he would get the Complaint dismissed with prejudice.

"In a New York minute, Randy. Not to worry. I got this."

I could see Hollis beam with a big sigh of relief. He reminded White about coming to his shindig in Vegas.

Less than 24 hours later, the preliminary hearing went as smooth as a baby's ass.

White and Soffer, his partner, arrived early at the courthouse in Lower Manhattan. Judge Brady, who had been well primed, took the bench at the appointed hour and the charges were read in open court.

Conspiracy to do this. Conspiracy to do that. It was total bullshit. I looked at Coyle as they were read to see if he even believed them.

When it came time for White to address the court, he first explained that Randy Hollis was not able to be in court that day, but would appear remotely from his island, where he was being quarantined, due to his exposure to a rare virus while on a recent African safari.

The judge barely blinked as White laid out this ridiculous excuse. It fucking worked so easily I could barely believe it. I mean, Smalley told me I had balls? This move took the cake. White then took an unusual approach while arguing the merits of the case. He informed the judge that he was filing a motion to have all the charges dismissed because the whole matter was baseless. That was all he said. He didn't even explain why, as if it was obvious.

Judge Brady rolled her eyes as we watched Hollis, a bit out of focus, lower his head and chuckle. Five minutes later, we left the courthouse. At least for the moment, Hollis was liberated, free to continue his charm offensive on the AFL to approve him as a new owner.

I could already see the headlines:

"Billionaire Hollis Triumphs in Manhattan Courtroom!"

"Lawyer Randy Hollis Shows Why He's a Legend!"

"New AFL Owner Beats Federal Corruption Charges!"

"Flash Wannabee Owner Charges Out of Court!"

# Thirty

## From Agent Orange to the Burn Pits:
## Follow the Money and Start the Party

Hollis wasn't the only one hitting the front pages. *The New York Times* ran a huge piece about Dick Dickey and his former company, Energy Protectors, Inc., and the scandal they had originally engineered surrounding the burn pits in Afghanistan.

I mean, who was corrupting who with this shit? Just to remind you what happened, the whole fiasco essentially boiled down to a single headline: Disabled and Burned. Let me put it to you this way. If you are running a military base in a war zone, which was exactly what EPI was doing throughout the Middle East and Iraq and Afghanistan, how do you get rid of all of the trash and human waste? How do you dispose of rubber products and petroleum?

If you're a company like Energy Protectors, it's simple: Burn it.

Basically, one of their subsidiaries did exactly that. They used open fire pits to dispose of all types of trash on their bases in each of those areas, especially Afghanistan. As a result, soldiers and civilians stationed there were exposed to toxic fumes. This was common knowledge inside their boardrooms, but they were making so much money they didn't care. I mean, who cares about the health and future of thousands and thousands of damaged soldiers and civilians when you're making so much cash you can't even count it?

According to the article in the *Times,* "The Burn Pits Atrocity" is this era's Agent Orange, which maimed and killed countless soldiers and civilians in Vietnam and took the American government years to acknowledge. Major defense contractors tried to hide their bad behavior, but once a handful of lawyers got wind of the issue, it was only a matter of time before a number of class action suits worked their way into the courts.

Hollis, Cauley and Smalley organized lead plaintiffs in each of them. The complaint stated that everything was burned using jet fuel as the accelerant. Plastics, batteries, appliances, dead animals, and even human body parts went up in flames. Clouds of black smoke hovered over large swaths of the country.

At the time, it was even reported by the Air Force that burn pits generated numerous pollutants, but they were difficult to determine. For Hollis, Cauley and Smalley, this seemed like a goldmine until they realized what they were up against: a military industrial complex that would never admit their guilt and could manipulate the court to remain in hiding. The three all-star attorneys also figure that this posture by the Feds would also apply to any awarding of funds, so they decided to call it a day and pulled their initial class action suit, as they determined it to be a loser and not worth all the time it would take to litigate. In fact, they were proven right when the class action against the defense contractors, brought by other lawyers, was ultimately dismissed by the appellate courts.

But years later, the situation looked different to Cauley. Under the current circumstances, with Hollis being dragged through the mud, she saw this as an opportunity to strike again with a new class action suit. PR expert Spencer also thought it would be a great idea, one she could run with to inflate Hollis' image even more in the public eye. She was sure she could make him look like the ultimate humanitarian, ready to take on the federal government to preserve the dignity of America's damaged soldiers.

Soon after the expose appeared in the *Times*, Cauley enlisted me to find a lead plaintiff to get the ball rolling. I was knee-deep in fixing things for Hollis, but I promised her I would begin to search among the many men and woman who served in the military after 9/11. She assured me I would have whatever funds I deemed necessary to do this research, so I contacted a few of my colleagues and put the wheels in motion.

Then I had what I modestly call a eureka moment. The fucking light bulb went off one night after I had sex with Beverly for the first time in God knows how long. Except God doesn't know because I don't let him in my bedroom when I'm getting busy. Anyway, I must've gotten inspired or something because that night I got this great idea.

I could ease the spotlight on Hollis' AFL scandal by co-mingling his situation with the tragic story of former all-star football player Pat Tillman, who left a multimillion-dollar deal with the Cardinals to join the Army shortly after 9/11 and got killed in action by friendly fire. How could anyone argue with a story like that? Spencer, Cauley, and Smalley agreed, and thought it was a fantastic idea and would be a great distraction. To top it off, Hollis was thrilled.

We all figured that Dickey was so distracted by the bad media coverage of him and his company that he would stop trying to act behind the scenes to discredit Hollis and pave his own way toward purchasing the Flash. Cauley and Smalley discovered a link to Dickey and his connection to the Hollis case. They tried to stir up trouble for him and his liability in the Burn Pits case, all in an effort to sabotage any possibility of him undermining Hollis and his bid to buy the Flash.

As the one who orchestrated this new strategy, I was sitting pretty, at least for the moment. I had no idea, though, of what was coming, and it wasn't pretty at all.

# Thirty-One

## Leverage or Lunacy:
## A Battle of Gladiators

I'm telling you, that night in the Regis made my head spin. I'm not used to absorbing so many new things on the fly, and between what Hollis wanted and Smalley's agenda, along with a favor Cauley needed done *and* a nice dose of Melody, I wasn't sure what I was doing.

As soon as I drove back to New York City and walked in the lobby at nine sharp, all bets were off. I was met by one of Melody's "assistants," as she referred to herself, a waifish and mysterious looking creature who looked like she might be in Manhattan to audition for a remake of *Cat-woman*, but then again, why would anybody think they could make that movie again and have anyone better than Halle Berry? That would just be stupid.

Anyway, I was standing at the bar by 8:45, sorting out some shit in my head. I was about to get knee-deep in the mud of the EPI class action case, which Smalley and Cauley had asked me to supervise. We needed to move it fast so that we could make Hollis look like an epic savior of the plaintiffs. The plan was to get positive publicity for him to overwhelm any lingering bad press because of Coyle's boneheaded attempt at busting Hollis. I was also trying to attract bad publicity for Young Patrick while blowing up Hollis in the media as the legal knight on a white horse, riding in to save the oppressed from the big, bad, multi-national, corporate war machine.

Hollis had been appointed the lead plaintiff's attorney, and as his fixer, I received every pleading filed in the case. It was going to boil down to a fight between legal gladiators on both sides, often behind the scenes, and

I had a front-row seat to see how the two teams would leverage their positions to win the most money—primarily for themselves. As you may have figured out by now, that's just the way it is in the exclusive world of elite class actions. But as I said, it was equally important to do whatever I could to clean up Hollis' reputation in the eyes of the AFL owners who were about to decide his fate.

This was all bouncing around in my brain when Siesta approached me at the bar and asked me to follow her upstairs to the penthouse, where I was to meet with Smalley, Cauley, Spencer, and the man, himself, Randy Hollis. I had no idea if he would be appearing as a hologram or in the flesh, but I would soon find out.

Siesta was even dressed in black leather pants and some fancy waistcoat, which highlighted her figure and reminded me all over again of Halle Berry, who you might have realized by now is someone I very much enjoy as an actress and wouldn't turn down if she ever asked me to leave my wife immediately and fly off into the sunset.

By the time the elevator reached the top floor of the Regis, my fantasy life had receded to its appropriate location deep inside the confines of my private lockbox and I was ready to make a deep dive into a whole new world of power and wealth. That was turning me on even more than any thoughts of running away with you know who. Besides, no one is named Siesta, I mean, come on, and I doubted if any normal man could get any "rest" if they spent time with her.

All this made me curious to know more about Hollis and his supposed habits with women. Apparently, he has escorts on his payroll whose sole job is to accompany him on his private plane to and from wherever he goes. As Cauley put it with a wink, these women are Randy's personal "consultants," and he considers them indispensable to his success. I could imagine they might be just that. These women are separate from any others he meets in one destination or another. Smalley said they are hired strictly for "inflight entertainment."

The women Hollis meets in whatever city he is in are either local residents or flown separately to his desired destination so that he meets them after a buildup of anticipation, which he favors, as it adds to the excitement and spontaneity of his encounters. For Hollis, it's all about keeping things fresh, from his women to his sushi. His own 737 and a fleet of smaller planes makes this all work well for him. Cauley and Smalley had hinted that I might even get to fly with Hollis one day soon on what they like to call "Randy's flying pleasure mobile."

I spent the next two hours reviewing class action details with Smalley and prepping for a crucial appearance the next day at the offices of the American Football League, which were within walking distance, just a few blocks south and a couple blocks over on Park Avenue. As a longtime football fan, I was so excited at the prospect of visiting there in person and hoped and prayed I would be included.

Hollis was hovering over us the entire time via some remote connection on an enormous computer screen in the conference room of the penthouse. He made it clear that he wanted me to be there, along with him and his top two lawyers, Warren Soffer and Stanley White.

"Absolutely, yes, of course. I will be there. It would be an honor . . ."

That's when Cauley made a subtle sign to me of slitting her own throat to tell me in no uncertain terms to stop talking. I sensed right away that my enthusiasm was a little over the top and not exactly welcome in the moment, so I shut the fuck up in mid-sentence. I was learning that having balls was great, but there was definitely a time and a place for waving them around the room and this was not one of them.

Hollis didn't say another word. Even though I hardly knew him, I could tell he was stressed, and everyone else could feel it, too. He nodded and the screen went black.

## Thirty-Two

### Say Hello to the AFL:
### Fifteen Minutes of Potential Fame

I slept alone that night at the hotel. No Melody. No Siesta. Nobody. I thought I was going to have a hard time with Beverly, explaining the last-minute turnaround and spending the night in the city, but she was surprisingly nonchalant about the whole thing. Maybe it was the sex we recently had, or at least I did, as she didn't seem too thrilled. But it was probably the fact that she'd seen Randy Hollis in the news, just like everyone else, and that's when she realized that her husband was playing with the big boys. I guess she figured I wasn't lying, and if I was, I'd been in a shitload of trouble. I think she was secretly excited that I was on the verge of hitting it out of the park with the kind of money I could bring in. Beverly had a calculator for a brain, and she probably had a whole new shopping list in development. That didn't exactly thrill me, but whatever kept her amused was fine with me.

So far, so good. I slept like a baby on what must have been something like five-million-thread sheets, if those even exist. I mean, it was like someone was softly massaging my skin all night with those sheets! I woke up thinking maybe someone had. Could I have been drugged with one of those date rape concoctions and someone took advantage of me? I had no idea, but I had no time to figure it out. My phone buzzed with a reminder to be in the lobby at 9:30 a.m. to head over to the AFL offices with Hollis and his team.

Fuck! This is really happening!

Two espressos later, I greeted attorneys Soffer and White, who rushed me out of the lobby and into a waiting limousine on Fifth Avenue. It was only a five-minute walk, but I guess people like them don't like to scuff up the bottom of their shoes if they don't have to. Or maybe they didn't want to run into any paparazzi. That was probably it, especially now, with this bullshit in the press.

Hollis was already in the limo, seated alone in what looked like a custom-made jump seat in the corner.

"Ryan, nice to finally meet you."

When he extended his hand, I noticed that he had short arms. He also had short legs, which didn't extend too far at all from his seat, unlike mine, on a six-foot tall body, and White and Soffer, too, who were a similar height. I'm guessing Hollis was five-five, on a good day.

Okay, so the man is short. Maybe he has a Napoleon complex, like when guys who grow up short feel as if the whole world is persecuting them and they're going to spend their entire lives getting back at their perceived enemies, the bullies who made their life hell since they were kids on the playground or choosing them last for pick-up games in the park. Maybe this was the story of Hollis, and if so, join the club, I guess. There are tons of dudes like this who grow up with some fucked up persecution complex and then make everyone else suffer for their shit. I know a bunch of guys like this who grew up all bullied and they still are trying to right those wrongs. I guess Dick Dickey and Patrick Coyle must be charter members of that club. If they only knew Randy Hollis might be just like them maybe they would all just get along.

No way. I knew that. But it was fun for a second thinking I had it figured out. Somehow, I knew enough to let that shit go and not make any predictions or conclusions about Randy Hollis. Not on this day, that's for sure. Not when so much was at stake for him, and me, too.

He looked at all of us and made a fist.

"Let's do this, boys. The charm offensive begins right here and now."

We quickly entered the lush American Football League Offices on Park Avenue before any photographers could gather and block our way.

We were escorted to sit on one side of an enormous conference room table while Roger Hartwell, the commissioner of the AFL, was seated across from us, along with their top attorney, Holly Rosen, her team, and the COO of the AFL, Robert Vincent.

Hollis, who was probably used to being at the head of any table, if he even bothered to be present in person, appeared to be trying to look humble, maybe, although he sat quite confidently, ramrod straight in his chair, with a powerful air of entitlement.

"I belong here, boys, so let's just get the show on the road."

Of course, he couldn't say that, but he sure looked like he felt that way. Anxious, impatient, and at the mercy of a bunch of people he may have even despised. Hollis was notorious for having a short fuse with people he thought were posers, and this power play, which required him to show up on bended knee, so to speak, appeared to infuriate him.

Seemingly always in control, Hollis deferred to his trusted counsel. White let the entire room know that the recent charges against Hollis were ridiculous and would be dropped in no time, just as the previous bogus case had been thrown out of court by a judge who had no time for the prosecutor's shenanigans. He stressed that Randall Hollis is a model citizen and that the other owners would be fortunate to have him join their esteemed club.

Hartwell thanked us all for coming and the entire meeting lasted barely ten minutes.

Outside, we quickly gathered in the limo and headed to Tavern on the Green, a restaurant inside Central Park, where Spencer had arranged a private room for us to have a late breakfast and discuss the meeting. Hollis avoided all of the fancy menu offerings and only drank water. Apparently, he had not eaten much since his first brush with Coyle's manufactured charges, and his upset stomach had only worsened as his nerves were wound even higher, worrying about his purchase being approved.

White and Spencer voiced their concern about him not eating, but Hollis waved them off.

"I need some personal care before I can do that comfortably. Let me buzz Mona to arrange it."

White laughed.

"She can handle anything."

Hollis winked.

"We'll be done within the hour, correct?"

Soffer nodded and told Hollis he had nothing to worry about, but Hollis was not so sure. He looked pale as a ghost and as soon as Soffer explained himself, saying that the owners would fall in line, Hollis excused himself to go to his nearby condo, overlooking the park.

"I need to be alone right now, at least spiritually."

No one blinked. We all knew what he meant. His preferred escort for the morning encounter would know well enough not to ask any questions or even comment on his stress level. Her job was merely to distract him, please him, and disappear.

"Everything I have worked so hard for seems to be slipping away right now. I leave the question of my AFL ownership in your good hands. I trust you will get it right because let's just say it's your only option. Is that understood?"

Everyone nodded and immediately voiced their understanding. As Hollis stood up, I also rose to salute him and gave him a hint of a smile and a slight bow. I didn't want to miss my chance to let him know that I was fully on his side.

If I'm not mistaken, I think he winked at me on his way out, but that might have been wishful thinking. One guy who did not wink at all was Hollis' private bodyguard, a hulking figure who looked like he could turn anyone's coffee cold with just a glance.

As soon as they were gone, Soffer and Spencer continued to describe their strategy for the charm offensive they wanted to use on the other owners and their cohorts.

"I've already begun numerous conversations with the other 31 AFL teams' attorneys. I've informed them about the bullshit charges and the meeting with Hartwell. Today, I will reach out to the attorney for the Leonidas family, who are selling the Flash. They have been approached again by representatives for Dick Dickey, and in lieu of the charges against Hollis, they are considering a different path without him. Obviously, this cannot proceed, and we will be working furiously to devise a new way to convince the Leonidas family to change their tune."

I broke in to clarify a central point on that and to show off a little, too. Although I was brand new on the scene, I was privy to inside information and wanted to be seen as a valuable member of Hollis' inner circle. This was probably an example of my own anxiety getting the better of me, but I was excited and couldn't help myself.

"So, FYI, Hollis' offer was at least a billion dollars higher than Dickey's. Plus, as you probably know, but maybe not, Hollis is paying for the team in cash without any financing. Obviously, the Leonidas family wants the Hollis deal to be approved by the AFL owners, but they are having serious second thoughts."

Soffer held up a hand to stop me.

"Look, Coleman, you're right. It may sound like a slam dunk for the current owner of the Flash to just get the cash from Hollis and call it a day, but I'm not so sure. They have a long-time relationship with the community and Hollis has no previous connection with the old team in San Diego or that community or with the new organization in Los Angeles and the neighborhoods surrounding the stadium. We all know how this shit is important to an owner's legacy and all that crap. Hollis really wants to start off on the right foot and be seen as a stand-up guy who will set the Flash straight and be a positive force in the community."

Spencer looked impressed. She complimented Soffer on his PR smarts and offered to follow his lead, as he knew Hollis better than she did. Soffer thanked her and continued.

"Listen, I don't know if we should share this information with Hollis. He's very worried right now and we shouldn't get him riled up for no good reason. Let's compose a letter to all the owners explaining the situation. I'm sure that Randy will agree and that this will be a positive step toward smoothing any ruffled feathers and letting the sale go through."

Smalley and Cauley, who had been unusually silent the entire time, nodded and signaled their approval. White and Spencer did, too. I wasn't sure what to say so I was relieved when Smalley took me off the hook.

"Coleman here is the perfect person to draft the letter. Right, Ryan?"

"Uh, yeah, of course. No problem. Sure, I'll get on it right away."

"Perfect! We'll need it by lunchtime so let's get you back to the Regis ASAP and set you up with a desk and whatever else you may need."

"Okay, another espresso, and maybe a cocktail for inspiration."

I was kidding, but Cauley wasn't.

"Whatever you want, Coleman. Just get the letter done and your wish is my command."

"Really?"

"No! Are you kidding me? Fuck off, Ryan. Write the letter and you can have a cookie."

## Thirty-Three

### The Letter:
### What I Wish I Wrote and the One We Sent

Back at the Regis, they set me up with a workspace and a computer. Ten minutes later, room service showed up with an espresso and a single chocolate chip cookie on a little plate. Cauley wasn't around, but I knew she had arranged it. Soffer popped his head inside and reminded me of a few key points I should include in the letter. I was a little pissed about the Leonidas family and how they had been responding to the pickle Hollis was in, seeing as they had been reluctant to finalize the sale until the AFL and the owners signed off on it.

I thought they could have told the other owners that they were ready to sell, and to please back them up and let it happen. On the other hand, I was fed up with the AFL and the owners for making Hollis jump through extra hoops to join their fucking fraternity. But how cool would it be for him to become an official owner? I had a lot to balance in the letter.

First, with all that espresso running through me, and with my temper almost out of whack, I chose to write the letter I *really* wanted to write, just to get that shit out of my system. Here's how that one looked:

Dear Sirs, (we know you don't let women in the club, or non-whites or gays, for that matter). Am I right? You bet I am. Now, let's get to it. Are you even considering the idea of not approving Randy Hollis as a new owner? Really? Are you fucking kidding me?

First of all, he has not done anything illegal. If you think he has, come forward and fucking prove it. I'll wait. Oh, okay, just what I thought. You got nothing, so shut the fuck up and vote to approve. Then, move over and get ready to kiss his ass because you bunch of hypocritical, sanctimonious bastards can't hold a candle to Mr. Hollis. He's smarter, cooler, and richer than any of you pompous assholes.

Okay, I'm done here. I think I made my point. Don't vote your conscience because we all know you don't have one. Just vote YES and save yourself the agony of me and my boys coming after you and making you suffer till you cry for mercy, which we will not give you. No way. I love the AFL, but we will torture you first, slowly, and then bury you alive (what's left of you) right underneath your team's end zone, where you will meet the untimely end of your fucking life.

Sincerely,

Ryan Coleman, Esquire (Fixer Extraordinaire)

Okay, so I had to blow off some steam. I never intended to send that version, but it was fun to vomit my sick mind into the computer before I sat down to write the real one. In fact, I called Cauley and read it to her out loud, just to see if her sense of humor was as good as I thought. I was right, too, because she sounded like she was spitting up from laughing so hard. Then, I assured her that I would have the usable version done within the hour, as requested, which is a nice way of saying demanded.

Dear Sirs,

As a legal representative of Randy Hollis, let me begin by reiterating his genuine and deep desire to become the newest member of America's most elite fraternity, the esteemed franchise owners of the American Football League. Each of you bring the highest standards imaginable to this exclusive club, and the addition of Randy Hollis will only enrich your collective legacy.

As you know from the recent rash of unwelcome news, a prosecutor inside the Justice Department seems to have a vendetta against Mr. Hollis and has ventured far beyond what anyone would deem reasonable in manufacturing false and bogus charges against Mr. Hollis. While it seems clear that this is a thinly veiled attempt to publicly embarrass Mr. Hollis, it has also come to my attention that more sinister forces are also at play here and we can ill afford to ignore this behavior and its potential ramifications for the American Football League as an entity and for any of you as individual owners.

To be blunt gentlemen, I have become privy to some troubling information. There is a former government official who had made his own private fortune within the military industrial complex who is hell-bent on owning his own AFL franchise and we fear he will stop at nothing in order to accomplish his goal. That includes using the wheels of justice to try and tarnish Mr. Hollis' reputation.

Thankfully, that seems to have failed, at least we hope so, especially if all of you use your better judgment and see this farce for exactly what it is.

But let me remind you that this person will not stop if his attempt at disqualifying Randy Hollis were to fail. He is known to be diabolically persistent, so that any of you might end up in his crosshairs, and if you do, lookout. He will stop at nothing, and he has enormous resources that may rival yours, if they don't just top them. This may be hard to believe, gentlemen, as wealthy as you are, but as we all know, there is always someone taller or stronger or faster . . . or richer.

This means that no matter what course you take, your current ownership of your respective team will be threatened. That's because even if you reject Hollis as a new owner, the Leonidas family can opt to keep the team or bring in another candidate for your approval and the man I am talking about will still be left out in the cold.

Trust me. Mr. Hollis does not like being left out in the cold. So, once you approve him as a new owner, which I'm sure you will do, as he is a marvelous candidate and more than qualified, the terror he has experienced may soon come to you as this mysterious and terrible excuse for a man sets his sights on you and your franchise.

It looks like you are in trouble either way. But let me offer you a deal that can save each and every one of you. If you approve Randy Hollis as the AFL's newest owner, he and I and our entire team can guarantee you that we will not allow this man in the shadows to give you any trouble. None at all.

We will virtually eliminate any chance of that happening and even put that commitment in writing, if that is what you prefer.

The choice is yours, gentlemen. Approve Randy Hollis, improve the AFL, and do yourself a gigantic favor by ensuring that this dark and menacing monster will never come after you or your team. Judging from your history of success as a business magnate, I'm sure you will make the right decision.

Sincerely,

Ryan Coleman, Esquire (General Counsel to Randy Hollis)

# Thirty-Four

## Warning, to Whom This May Concern:
## Hit "Send" At Your Own Risk

As soon as I finished the second draft and made sure it was just right, I dashed it off to Cauley, reminding her that it was the legit, official letter to the owners but that I was also attaching the joke version, just for fun. I figured she would enjoy reading it, as she seemed to have a similar sense of humor to mine. In fact, hers may have been way darker.

Smalley had told me that Gene grew up in a terrible situation with her father, so she had a pretty serious chip on her shoulder when it came to any kind of power tripping with men. This obviously served her well as a legal professional, especially in courtroom battles and while leveraging settlement agreements, but it wasn't always her best armor in social situations. That's when her acidic humor came into play, and as Smalley described it to me, Gene Cauley took no prisoners and enjoyed a good laugh at any time, especially if it came at a man's expense. So, I figured she would appreciate seeing the prank letter in print.

I had no idea she would forward both versions to Warren Soffer, who was responsible for sending out the letter to all the owners, trying to make things right for Hollis and get things back on track for his pending purchase of the Flash.

I also didn't realize she was sending the letters directly to Hollis. At first, I was horrified that he would see the prank letter I wrote, but Cauley assured me that he would love it, and that he would probably relish the opportunity to threaten them himself, if only he could get away with that kind of sordid behavior.

Well, when Hollis became aware of the chain of command, beginning with me as the one who wrote the letter, and then to Cauley, who supervised it, and finally to Soffer, who added his credentials and sent it out, he decided to send each of us a thank-you gift for our role in bringing that letter so quickly to the attention of the owners.

Within the hour, I received a text, inviting me for a weekend stay at the Regis for myself and a guest (funny he didn't specify my wife), Cauley got a new Rolex she'd had her eye on, and Soffer ended up with quite an unexpected surprise, at least in my opinion.

According to one of the secretaries at his law firm, who was coincidentally a former college friend of mine, Soffer received a visit from an unusual female guest, who claimed she was there to deliver a singing telegram on the occasion of his wedding anniversary to his wife of many years, who was out of town on a shopping spree but wanted to send her special greetings to her cherished husband on such a momentous day.

My friend, Veronica, who was actually filling in for Soffer's personal secretary, thought something was odd when the "singer" showed up wearing fishnet stockings and a full-length mink coat and dropped a small bottle of mysterious lubricant on her way into Soffer's office. Apparently, when Veronica picked up the bottle and handed it to the woman, she winked at my friend and went inside, only Veronica never heard her sing, not a single note.

What she did hear, according to a series of texts she sent me, was furniture moving, a few sudden loud gasps and the sounds of an aging attorney enjoying some unique attention. Veronica then admitted to me that she observed the entire rendezvous when she peaked through a gap in the door and saw the whole tryst happen in real time. When the woman dropped her fur coat, she was butt naked, aside from her stilettos, and she proceeded to have Soffer lean back in his office chair as she got down on her knees underneath his desk and did her thing in between his legs.

The surprise guest told Soffer that she was a gift from Mr. Hollis to show his appreciation for doing such outstanding legal work. At first, Soffer tried to resist, claiming that he had a highly important email to send on Mr. Hollis' behalf. The naked "singer" encouraged him to finish his work as she pulled down his pants and began to express Hollis' thanks by using her unique sexual abilities, which seemed to impress Veronica, who thought the woman was highly adept at performing, especially while on her knees under a desk.

Soffer, who had received the email from Cauley just minutes before his gift arrived, was still laughing at the first letter I wrote. Cauley emailed me that Soffer had read the letters and hadn't laughed that hard in ages and was about to send off the official version. I breathed a little easier when I heard that but got nervous all over again as Veronica barraged me with her texts and a "blow-by-blow" account of the "singer" being on her knees in Soffer's office.

This animated human gift would've been just another frivolous moment in Soffer's day, that is, if we were just talking about a relatively harmless prank. But that's not exactly what happened. As the escort began to perform her particular magic on Soffer, he became distracted, no great surprise, and attached the wrong letter to the owner's emails. I found this out right away because Smalley was copied on each one and contacted me immediately to find out what the fuck was going on. I assured him that I had no idea how it all happened, which I kinda didn't, because, I mean, what the fuck, couldn't Soffer walk and chew gum at the same time?

Within minutes, the email had caused an uproar in the offices of the 31 other AFL franchises. Phones began to ring everywhere as the owners conferred with each other to see if they had also received the same letter. Most of them, we found out soon enough, thought it was a giant prank from Hollis' legal team and considered it brazen but quite funny. Only two owners were offended and threatened to contact their lawyers, but Smalley convinced them not to.

Naturally, Soffer was horrified when he realized what he had done, but his reaction turned out to be quite temporary. When Cauley found out, she was not upset at all. She thought it was hysterically funny and assured Soffer that nothing bad would happen. She tried to assure me, too, but I was hearing none of it. I figured I was doomed, that my life was over, right then and there, as soon as Hollis found out. I figured he would probably have me strung up by my toenails and beheaded in front of my very own mother.

But as it turned out, Soffer sent the correct second version right away, that is, as soon as he could get the escort's head out of his lap. All the owners, including the two Smalley had to massage, realized that it was just a crazy joke, and they all appreciated the sentiment and intent of the legit version.

One of them even joked with Soffer, asking him how someone so experienced and professional could screw up like that, as if he was doing something outrageous, like getting a blow job under his desk while he was working, which made him send the wrong letter. Veronica said the two men had a nice laugh over that one.

When Soffer sent out the second email with the right letter, he added some vital news that had just broken that morning. Judge Brady had dropped the criminal complaint against Hollis in a fashion known in the legal community as sua sponte. That means she did it herself, without any motion filed by White or Soffer. Anyone in the business knows that it is extremely rare for a judge to do anything sua sponte, so we were all unsure about how it actually happened like that.

Soffer explained that White's initial argument before Judge Brady led her to dismiss the Complaint, but we knew, we, being me and Cauley and Smalley, that someone else was acting on Hollis' behalf, but we were not sure who it was.

Soffer told the 31 team owners that the charges were so ridiculous that Judge Brady took the liberty to dismiss the Complaint herself, which never happens unless it is so unfounded that it doesn't merit any court time. So, that's the angle he took, and they seemed to buy it.

Case closed, or so I thought.

The following morning, the media campaign to celebrate Hollis exploded. Spencer had a history of handling troubled clients, such as Bernard Madoff, Harvey Weinstein, Jeffrey Epstein, and that evil schmuck of a client I had suffered through, once upon a time.

Spencer was a champion. She joked to me that Hollis would be as easy as a walk in the park because her past clients had been real scumbags whereas Hollis was actually a great human being. The campaign painted Hollis as a tireless philanthropist whose entire life had been driven by his passionate generosity for those less fortunate.

Later that week, I delivered a check to Spencer in the amount of $2.5 million, a little gift from Hollis to thank her for resurrecting his reputation, which coincided with Soffer's campaign to convince the AFL owners of how badly they needed Hollis.

It seemed like all of us needed Hollis. The question I wondered about was if all of us were willing to "sing" for our supper.

## Thirty-Five

## Humiliated!
## Coyle's in the Hot Seat (Again)

Okay, it's not kosher to bug somebody's office. I know that, but what can I tell you? In the words of the legendary actor, Denzel Washington, in the film, *Training Day*, "Do what you gotta do so you can do what you wanna do." Actually, it might have been Descartes, the French philosopher, who said it first, or John Steinbeck, in his famous book, *The Grapes of Wrath*, which I read in college mostly because I had to.

Anyway, secretly planting a recording device to enable a little bit of "observation" is relatively harmless and not nearly as intrusive as it sounds. Besides, if I didn't do such things, I wouldn't know half the shit I now know, which means I wouldn't be telling you as much as I am, so let's just say, I don't think anyone is complaining. Basically, I'm doing the dirty work for you. I mean, I'm doing it for Hollis, and Smalley and Cauley, and Soffer and White, among others I shall not yet name, but you get my point. I'm doing what you want me to do, which is get the dirt on all these bad dudes, even if I end up a little soiled, myself.

I mean, what's a little dirt among friends? I thought you'd understand. So, with the greater good in mind, here's what happened with Patrick the Foolhardy, also known as Attorney Coyle, although he may not be enjoying that title for long.

On the same day we found out that the judge in Hollis' case had thrown out the charges, Coyle, the architect of that charade, was summoned to the office of Michael Levin, the acting U.S. Attorney for the Southern District of New York.

Coyle was inside Levin's office for barely five seconds when his boss lit into him with a tirade that should go down as one of the most outstanding riffs of humiliation in modern legal history, at least when it comes to a superior ripping his employee a new asshole and gauging out his eye sockets.

Lucky for me, Levin began right away by yelling at Coyle at the top of his lungs. This was helpful because Smalley's mole inside the prosecutor's office did not install the most sophisticated listening device in Levin's office. Since it was a last-minute request on my part, and urgent, to boot, she had to use the only bug device she had, which was mediocre at best. Even so, we were pleased to hear Levin, in real time, not holding back as he tore into Coyle.

"What the fuck were you thinking, Patrick? Oh. Never mind. You weren't thinking, of course, because if you were, you never would have brought these charges in the first place. Am I right? Huh? Answer me! Answer me, you stupid piece of shit!"

Apparently, Coyle either didn't answer or nodded or might have muttered some sad, compliant agreement that he had fucked up in the worst possible way. In any case, Levin continued at full volume, which must have been quite entertaining for anyone else in the office that afternoon.

"I can't fucking believe that you could be this stupid and arrogant to think that these charges, and the bullshit ones you brought earlier, could pass muster in a courtroom, let alone bring such unnecessary blowback on this office. Nobody can make it through Yale Law School if they're idiotic enough to do something like this! But you did! You fucking did! That means you are either a certifiable idiot or you knew full well what you were doing. So, which is it? Don't answer! I know the fucking answer, goddammit! Don't open your mouth unless I tell you to, you miserable piece of shit. I know you're not a fucking moron so you must have decided that this would be a good idea, to try and take down Randy Hollis on totally manufactured charges, which had no chance at all of succeeding.

But you know what? You succeeded at one thing. You have embarrassed me and this office to a degree I never imagined possible. Judge Brady has already filed a complaint against you and me and the entire S.D.N.Y., alleging malpractice or whatever the fuck she called it. So, let me tell you this, Coyle. There is no way in hell I am going to take the fall for you and the department. I've already informed the court that you acted on your own, without my approval, and so now it's your ass, and your ass only, Coyle, that is on the chopping block, and I guarantee you, your ass is going to be chopped into a million little pieces of bloody suffering and maximum punishment. I'm talking total disbarment, multiple fines, and if I have anything to say about it, incarceration for as long as possible. That's what you fucking deserve and that's what I intend to make happen. And then, when you get out of jail, whenever that is, I will personally make sure that you will only be reinstated to practice law in the farthest reaches of remote Alaska, where you will serve a total population of less than 50 people in a village that is dark 18 hours a day and lives on a diet of fucking seal meat and ice chips. You better just hope that Hollis doesn't have his legal team file a lawsuit against you for abuse of process. I've already assured his lawyers that I had nothing to do with this, that it was all your fucking fault, so if there's revenge to be had, they will be coming directly after you, Coyle, and you, alone. Now, get the fuck out of my office and make sure I never fucking see you again until your sentencing date. Then, I'll be in the front row to watch you cry and whine and make a bunch of entitled fucking excuses for your behavior."

Levin laughed and we heard the sound of a door slamming as Coyle presumably left the office. Apparently, he was smart enough to not reply to Levin's tirade. Smalley's mole, who was observing from her desk outside Levin's office, told me that Coyle was swearing to himself as he wandered away down the hall, repeating over and over that he would still make Hollis pay. She pretended to go to the bathroom so she could eavesdrop on who Coyle called after his encounter with Levin. Apparently, Coyle contacted Handler, the private detective, to see if he could dig up any new dirt on Hollis and then he arranged to meet secretly with Dick Dickey to discuss a new strategy that would benefit both of them.

# Thirty-Six

## The Boys Club:
## AFL Owners Vote on Hollis

With my two letters now thankfully in the rearview mirror, AFL Commissioner Roger Hartwell conducted a conference call with the team owners to cast their votes on Hollis' purchase of the Los Angeles Flash. None of the 31 billionaires would be sending their lawyers after me with accusations of threatening or blackmailing them. So far, that tactic was not necessary, although it had been discussed in a late-night rendezvous I had with Smalley and Cauley. At this point, they sounded fully confident that the sale would go through with the unanimous vote it required. But if it didn't, drastic measures might be needed, and we wanted to be prepared.

Fortunately, "The 31 Wise Men," as Soffer liked to call them, unanimously approved the sale, and a day later, less than 48 hours after I wrote those letters, the AFL issued a press release to make the news public.

"Maverick Billionaire Randy Hollis Purchases Los Angeles Flash!"

"Devout Hedge Fund Icon and Philanthropist Joins the AFL Boys Club!"

"Randy Hollis Trades In His Legal Hat for a Football Helmet!"

Spencer orchestrated the headlines as much as she possibly could to feature Randy Hollis' diverse career and personality. He was overjoyed and promised a special party for his team of lawyers. Of course, he also invited Cauley, Smalley and me, along with a guest of our choice. I figured I'd better invite Beverly, just to make sure she was reminded in person that I wasn't doing anything to compromise our marriage.

On the other hand, it was kind of a foregone conclusion that we would be splitting, but I didn't want to give her any ammunition to make my life miserable later on in the bowels of a state divorce court. It was a tough call. Do I placate her with a show of what I've been doing all this time, or do I keep her at a distance and maintain a discreet personal privacy when it comes to the eyes and ears of Smalley, Cauley, and Hollis? I also had no idea if Hollis would be inviting his usual coterie of escorts, which could be a big ball of fun but would definitely raise Beverly's finely manicured eyebrows.

"Ryan, who *are* these women?"

"Honey, can't you tell? They're represent America's finest legal minds."

"I'm not looking at their minds. Since when do lawyers dress like that?"

"Once they leave the courtroom, I guess. I don't know. I've never spoken to them."

"Oh, really?"

"No, Honey! I'm here strictly to work, not to socialize."

"Hmm."

I wasn't sure I should risk an encounter like this, so I asked Beverly if she wanted to go. She actually turned me down because one of her girlfriends had tickets to a Flyers hockey game that night in Philly. Beverly was a big fan, which came in handy on this occasion.

I drove up to New York City to meet the gang at Jean-Georges, an exclusive restaurant inside the boutique Mark Hotel on East 77th Street. Hollis chose this location because the owner was willing to close the restaurant, for a price, and keep any hotel guests from entering. That meant our team had exclusive access to the facilities without any press or photographers allowed.

Hollis was visibly relieved to be finally celebrating his approval as the new owner of the Los Angeles Flash. He had been through what White called "a living hell" and wanted to thank each of us for our part in making him an official AFL owner.

Okay, I know. First world white guy problems, but whatever.

The celebration was low key and didn't last long. Within an hour, Hollis excused himself, saying that he needed to be on his way to Las Vegas to make final preparations for the "real" party, which would take place over the coming weekend. He promised that it would be a memorable time and that none of us should miss even a moment of it.

"There will be something . . . and someone . . . for everyone there. I think I know each of you pretty well and I will make sure that every one of your personal preferences will be met with the maximum pleasure allowed in the city of Las Vegas, which as you know takes an unlimited approach when it comes this type of indulgence."

Hollis smiled at each of us as he said that and winked at Mona, "my designated head of the indulgence game," as he put it, the one responsible for making sure that each one of us would enjoy a "customized personal pleasure plan."

"See you soon, everyone. Let me leave you again with my sincere thanks for making my dream a reality. I assure you that each and every one of you will eventually be the happy beneficiary of my appreciation. In due time."

He then handed Soffer and White an envelope with a special gift inside for each of them, a thank you for getting the job done despite the horrible odds.

"I know that both of you pulled off a miracle here, and for now, at least, I don't even want to know the details of how you managed it. All I know is, Judge Brady is no pushover or some kind of easy cupcake to convince, so you must have done something remarkably clever to persuade her to throw my case out of court. So, thank you both."

We all broke into applause as Hollis expressed such appreciation. As I looked at White and Soffer, and then scanned Smalley's face and Cauley's demeanor, I had to wonder just what Hollis meant when he referred to them doing something remarkably clever.

At that point, I felt a hand gliding down my back, beginning at the nape of my neck and moving smoothly to the seat of my pants. I glanced over my shoulder and saw Melody's face, slowly breaking into a sensual smile. Her touch triggered something inside me, and I stood up quickly, grabbing my drink and the attention of everyone at the table. Even Hollis turned as he was leaving the dining room.

"I'd like to make a toast to Randy Hollis and everyone else gathered here tonight."

Melody cheered as Cauley pounded her fist on the table.

"Let's hear it, Coleman!"

"Okay, okay, my toast is this: what I don't know can't hurt me."

Everyone laughed, and then Cauley chimed in.

"Are you sure, Ryan?"

I winked at Melody and addressed the room.

"I'm quite sure of it. But never you mind because I already know too much!"

Everyone laughed again, but I didn't enjoy the moment because something disturbing had come to my attention. As Hollis made his way out of the restaurant, I noticed one of the busboys, who looked decidedly suspicious. On closer inspection, I realized it was John Handler, the seedy but brilliant private detective who had been working with Coyle, financed of course by Dickey, who was still hell bent on taking Hollis down. I guess they had gotten wind of the owners' approval and were making one last ditch effort to sabotage the sale.

Handler had been conducting surveillance on all of us and who knows who else had eyes and ears on our proceedings? I was determined to find out and decided to excuse myself from the festivities to do a bit of detective work of my own. I figured that if I could expose Handler, and then Coyle and especially Dickey, I would endear myself to Hollis even more.

# Thirty-Seven

## Crisis at 35,000 Feet:
## I Decide to Hold Tight and Keep It In My Pants

I was not prepared at all for what awaited me in Las Vegas. Actually, the debauchery began in Philadelphia, when I boarded a private chartered plane, which Hollis had booked (and paid for) to thank me for my work on the class action and the letters.

Before Hollis left the restaurant a few nights earlier, he had leaned over and whispered to me that he loved the prank letter and wished we could not have only sent it, but actually carried out the threat, as he said, just for the fun of seeing their faces before we snuffed them out. That shook me up a little, as I never imagined actually "snuffing" anybody. I guess I got a taste of Hollis' dark humor. I don't know. He also told me how much he appreciated the second letter I wrote, the real one, and that he thought it was why the owners unanimously approved the sale of the Flash to him.

I was feeling pretty satisfied with myself as the party weekend approached. Beverly had a family gathering in Massachusetts during that same time, which I sadly had to beg my way out of, although I'm sure that did not disappoint her parents. They still had little tolerance for me, so I figured that my missing out on their reunion was a win-win for everyone.

I was going to promise Beverly a separate trip to Las Vegas whenever she wanted, but I didn't even bother to extend the offer because I knew in my gut that she was done with our marriage, and frankly, so was I. Less than a week ago, as we were having a paint-by-the-numbers sex moment, I realized that it was more of a nostalgic event than a spontaneous act of love. Our divorce was inevitable and there was no sense wasting any tears over that. I only hoped that it could be done as amicably as possible, especially when it came to the drag on my finances.

Just as I was about to book a commercial flight to Vegas, Mona called to let me know that Hollis had arranged a private, chartered plane for me, complete with what she called a "full-service flight." All I had to do was show up on time at a private hangar at the Philadelphia airport with my suitcase and "an open mind."

I knew right away what that probably meant, but I didn't want to assume anything, so I didn't give it too much thought on my way to the airport. Everything was in place when I boarded the Hawker Beechcraft 900XP, a nine-seat private jet, which Mona touted as the most elegant ride of its size in the world. I had no idea if she was right, as I'd never been on a private plane of any kind, but it sure looked pretty fancy.

Perhaps I should say that every*one* was in place. I was the only passenger but there were three female "travel guides" on board when I arrived. Each of them looked magnificent. I mean, I thought I was at a Victoria's Secret convention or something. They weren't wearing lingerie, at least as far as I could see, but they sure looked like they knew how to work it, for professional and/or personal reasons.

I did okay with girls when I was in high school and college. I had plenty of dates and no problem getting some pretty young women to go out with me and get into some fun, but I never *ever* ended up alone with three fucking super models in a private fucking plane. I couldn't believe this was really happening to me. I had to wonder if Hollis was testing me or something. I mean, he knew I was married, so maybe he was checking me out to see if I was a faithful guy or just another philanderer who didn't take marriage too seriously. I had no idea if Hollis knew that my marriage was on the rocks, but in either case, I was determined to stick to my guns and do what I had to do, which on this day, as much as it hurt me, was nothing, absolutely fucking nothing.

"Hi, my name is Ryan. I may not look like it, but I'm the Pope."

I took a wild guess that the three women were escorts, hired to accompany me to Las Vegas and then attend the party. They were full of smiles and little touchy-feely actions, making sure I was comfortable in my plush leather armchair. Each of them took a seat right near me and crossed their legs suggestively. I decided that since we had a long flight ahead of us, I better make my situation clear from the jump, as much for me as for them. In fact, it was all for me because my mind was jumping all over the place, imagining myself joining the infamous mile-high club three times over in a span of four hours. I smiled at each of them and said hello, looking pretty calm and collected, or so I thought, but inside I was a hot mess of lust, curiosity, and a cocktail of testosterone.

I had to make myself clear as soon as possible. As soon as we took off and started to climb to our cruising height, I nipped things in the bud before any of the women even loosened their seat belts.

"So, uh, listen, it's great to meet you all today. I know you're working for Mr. Hollis, and I appreciate you being here to look after me during our trip. I'm sure it's going to be great in Las Vegas. I've heard a lot about these parties, and they sound amazing. Have any of you ever been to one of Mr. Hollis' shindigs?"

They all smiled and nodded. As they did, I kinda felt old, having used the word, shindig. It was an expression I'd always heard my mother say, but I don't think she would have used it in this circumstance, not with three fancy escorts, or hookers, as she would've called them, inviting me to get naked at 35,000 feet. She would have been horrified if she knew my situation and how close I almost came to losing my airborne virginity.

"What would Beverly say? What about you, Ryan? Do you think it's okay for you to have sex with three perfect strangers in the middle of the sky, for Christ's sake? What about God? Do you think God wants you to get a venereal disease from someone you just met?"

Imagining my mother going on like this made me laugh until I started to feel nauseous. Even if I opted to take full advantage of the situation, there was no way I could get into it without hearing my mother's voice every step of the way.

"Ryan, what are they doing to you? Why does that woman keep bending over a chair? Did she drop something? And what is that other one doing with that paddle? Why is she hitting you and making you wear a mask? You didn't do anything wrong, did you? Are you in some kind of cult?"

I had to exorcise the demon right away, which meant setting things straight with these three gorgeous women. I figured if I took myself off the hook right then and there, I could just settle in for the flight, get some work done, and maybe even take a nap before we landed.

"Okay then, let me make something clear for all of you before we go any further and anything happens, which it's not going to, by the way. I don't want to make any boneheaded assumptions, but I wasn't born yesterday and I'm not as naïve as I might look."

They laughed, which was not exactly the effect I desired. I wanted to be taken seriously, so I could say this once and be done with it.

"Look, I'm married. Just sayin'. I mean, I gave my vows to my wife a bunch of years ago,  for better or worse, you know the routine, and so as long as I'm wearing this ring I can't touch any of you, as much as I might like to, if we're being honest here, and I can't be, uh, touched either because you know as well as I do, or probably way better, that one touch leads to another and then another and then you know, little babies are running around and I don't think any of us are ready for that,. But I don't want to make any assumptions about you. I'm just blabbing my mouth off now because this whole situation obviously makes me nervous. I'm sorry if I can't do what you were thinking I would do, but if you want to get into something with each other, I would be willing to watch, as long as none of you start recording anything on your phones."

One of the women leaned in close to make sure that I could hear her perfectly clear.

"Ryan, that was a lovely speech, and we all applaud you for your chivalry and loyalty to your wife, Beverly. Nicely done."

*Huh? How the hell did she know her name?*

The three escorts smiled and applauded, as if I had just performed a little show for their amusement before diving into making a sex video for a bunch of horny lawyers to enjoy. I wanted to make sure that they knew I wasn't kidding.

"Look, it's nothing personal, but where I come from, we value marriage and even though my situation with my wife is not exactly working out too well, I'm still fucking married and as long as I am, and living under the same roof with her, I am not going to mess around with anybody on a fucking airplane and get some kind of disease or whatever it is I could catch. Not that I'm saying you are diseased, but I think you know what I mean. A guy just can't come home from a business trip all itchy and shit and have to make up some lame excuse for his wife. Fuck that. That's a total shit show and I won't do that. No way. No fucking way. Have I made myself clear?"

All of the women smiled and nodded their understanding. Or at least they pretended to because it seemed like they were ready to smile and nod at just about anything. The one who seemed to be in charge put her hand on my knee for a second.

"Ryan, I'm sure Mr. Hollis will be impressed by your faithful approach to marriage. That's very commendable, but let me assure you that you are missing out on something very special here today. You know, just as you are totally dedicated to your work and impeccably professional, so are the three of us. We take our jobs seriously and always aim to please, and when we do please someone, which we always do, they never forget it."

The way she said that took my breath away. I almost felt dizzy and wanted to get some air, but that was not exactly an option. I closed my eyes for a moment and looked back at the three of them.

"I guess we understand each other. You can tell Mr. Hollis that I am a man of his word. Actually, I'll tell him myself when I see him in Vegas."

"Ryan, no worries. We will let him know that you are a man of your word."

I spent the next few hours pretending to get some work done on a few cases I had back home, but who was kidding who? I had to keep my head in my laptop or lean back and close my eyes because looking at these women all day was too challenging. I had to arrive in Vegas in one solid piece, not a shell of myself after a sex fest in a private jet. On the one hand, it would have been cool to have a beer and tell the story to a few guy friends I knew from college, but in the real world, the one I tried to live in as much as possible, fucking these women would have fucked me up for good.

## Thirty-Eight

### Let the Party Begin!
### Hollis Turns Christmas Upside Down

McCarren International Airport is located in Paradise, Nevada, five miles south of downtown Las Vegas and just minutes from The Strip, a four-mile stretch of Las Vegas Boulevard with resort hotels and casinos of every size, shape, and color lining both sides of the street.

Apparently, this was inspired by the Sunset Strip in Los Angeles, which got its famous name from a city employee impressed by the beautiful sunsets in her neighborhood. Eventually, the area grew full of nightclubs and tourist attractions and extended all the way from Hollywood to Beverly Hills. Naturally, it attracted its share of fancy clientele along with an endless stream of waddling idiots, undesirable misfits and downright criminals.

The Strip in Vegas made all that look quaint. You could go blind from all the neon signs and flashy billboards and then have a fucking heart attack from eating all the huge buffets full of every type of fried food and cake concoctions you could imagine. I mean, Las Vegas is famous for indulging everyone's biggest pleasures and their worst habits, which for some people might be one and the same, so it's hard to say if it's good or bad. Nevermind. It's totally both.

As they say in Sin City, "What happens in Vegas, stays in Vegas."

That's debatable. I mean, if you throw away a shitload of cash in a casino, it stays there, but let's say you end up in a hotel bed with a woman you meet at the roulette table and you get a STD. You bring that shit home with you! You might also come home with your head between your legs because you lost all your money and now you have to explain to your wife why you can't go on vacation this summer. Ouch!

Luckily, this never happened to me, but I know some people who fucked up pretty bad in Vegas and I guess you do, too. I was thinking about this as we descended, and I watched what looks like a fictional city appear out of nowhere in the middle of a fucking desert. I mean, who ever thought this was a good idea, creating this dystopian universe where people come from all over the world to indulge in the worst of human behavior before they go home and say they had the best time in their life? Are you kidding me?

Suffice to say, I was kinda conflicted about what I was heading into, as I had no idea how it would play out. I had heard that Randy Hollis spares no expense when it comes to his annual Christmas parties, so I expected a lavish event with crazy decorations, dancing girls, amazing food, a bunch of famous musicians and all the usual "entertainment" that makes Vegas so famous. Boy, did I have it all wrong.

As soon as we landed, I was whisked away to a small helicopter pad. I had barely waved goodbye to the three escorts I had managed to resist when another one, tall and sleek and maybe even better looking than the others, guided me inside a chopper, her hand firmly placed on the small of my back. She made sure I was properly buckled in and fitted with headphones. We were up in the air in a flash and then I heard a voice in my head, hypnotizing in its sensuality, coming from an exquisite creature sitting across from me.

"Hello, Ryan. Welcome to Las Vegas. Or should I say, bye-bye Vegas. Mr. Hollis asked me to chaperone you today so we could get acquainted. So, settle back and relax, and enjoy the ride. Have you ever been on a helicopter?"

I shook my head, mesmerized. I'd always wanted to try it, but I had never had an occasion to do so. I parachuted out of a plane once and nearly passed out from a panic attack. This time, safely within the confines of a four-seat helicopter, I figured I would be okay, especially in the hands of such a caring escort.

"Don't worry. All helicopters are loud. If you feel nauseous at all, there's a little relief bag under your seat. Hopefully, you won't need it."

"Hopefully. Yeah."

"Did you enjoy your flight?"

She didn't exactly wink at me, but I could tell she was probing, trying to find out if I had taken advantage of the opportunities presented to me over the past few hours. I wasn't sure if she knew the answer or if I should tell her anything at all. At least there was no incriminating video for me to worry about.

I was confused. Was Hollis testing me? What would constitute me passing the test? I didn't know if he would be impressed by my self-control and faithfulness to my marriage, or if he might be disappointed that I didn't take advantage of having three incredible beauties ready to bang the shit out of me all the way from Philadelphia to Vegas. And now, on my way to who knows where, was I about to skirt another gorgeous skirt?

"So, uh, what's your name?"

"I'm so sorry, Ryan. I forgot to introduce myself. My name is Gia. It means God's gracious gift, but everyone calls me G."

"Nice to meet you, G. It looks like God did a very good job . . . if you don't mind me saying so. Now where are we going?"

"Thank you, Ryan. You're as sweet as they say."

"Really? Who says so?"

Gia explained that she had received a series of texts from the women on my flight to Vegas, telling her that I wasn't exactly "open" to any of their overtures and should be treated with kid gloves, that I seemed to be a nervous or sensitive type. I appreciated her candor but wasn't sure why they had come to that conclusion just because I opted to keep it in my pants.

"So, Gia . . . G . . . where are we heading? I thought the party was in Vegas."

"It is, or should I say, part of it is. There are two parties this weekend. The usual activities begin tomorrow night inside the newest hotel resort on the Strip, The Purple Angel, which is owned by Mr. Hollis and a consortium of foreign investors. This is where most of his invited guests will gather. That's also where Mr. Hollis will use the opportunity to announce that he is going full steam ahead with his management of the Flash."

"Perfect timing, I'd say."

"Exactly, Ryan. Mr. Hollis has invited AFL personnel from the other 31 teams, along with everyone from the Flash organization, even those he will be firing Monday morning."

"Wait. What? He just bought the team and he's firing people already?"

"Exactly! Mr. Hollis doesn't play around with his possessions. Since the team's record has not been good at all, with three wins and 13 losses this year, Mr. Hollis knows that he has his work cut out for him. In order to win over his fan base, he has to begin by firing the coach, who was hired four years ago and has compiled a mediocre record, to say the least."

"Sounds like you know a lot about football."

Gia smiled.

"I'm not just a pretty face with a rockin' body. I have a MBA in corporate management and a PhD in sports psychology. Besides my long-time personal friendship with Mr. Hollis, I have also been his main consultant, behind the scenes, that is, when it comes to his purchase of the Flash."

"Impressive."

"Thank you, Ryan. Now, since the season is over, Mr. Hollis doesn't want to waste any time letting the rest of the league know that he will be a hands-on owner, invested in every aspect of the team's future success. He is planning to announce a series of changes that will affect most everyone connected to the team."

"Clever."

"Exactly. Tomorrow, thousands of VIPs and other guests, will gather to celebrate Mr. Hollis and his long-awaited purchase of the Flash. Sunday morning, those who are not too hung over may go to church and say their prayers, and first thing Monday morning we will issue a press release announcing a wholesale cleansing of the Flash organization, from top to bottom, from the front office to the players to the equipment managers."

"You mean, they all come to the party and then find out they've lost their jobs?"

Gia nodded and smiled.

"That's the way the cookie crumbles. Welcome to the big leagues, Ryan."

I was shocked by how easily Gia dismissed the idea of people losing their jobs, especially how they were going to blindside them by inviting them to a lavish party and then fucking them over wholesale a day later.

I decided to keep my mouth shut and see how this played out. My own moral code needed to stay on the shelf, at least until I saw how this affected everyone and how the media reacted. I was on Hollis' team, so I felt stuck with going along for the ride, at least for now.

"So, what about the second party?"

"Oh, of course. That's about to happen at the Grand Canyon."

"What? A little sightseeing tour before we circle back and start the party?"

"Not exactly. This is no ordinary excursion we're making, along with dozens of other helicopters and specially outfitted buses. This is not a typical gathering of tourists who come from all over the world every day of the year. This is different. Mr. Hollis has rented out the Grand Canyon for his private party."

"Wo! Excuse me, but did you just say that Randy Hollis has rented out the entire fucking Grand Canyon for his own private party? You gotta be kidding me, right?"

Gia laughed and shook her head.

"I didn't know people could do that. I don't mean regular people. I didn't think even a fucking billionaire could do something like that."

"I understand your reaction. In fact, I only just learned that no one has ever done it until Mr. Hollis made an offer that the National Parks Department could not refuse."

"Holy shit! He rented out one of the eight wonders of the world!"

"That's right. It just goes to show you that everyone, and everything, has a price, and if you're willing and able to meet it, the world can be your oyster. Mr. Hollis, of course, is quite willing and very able, so here we are, on our way to the greatest natural wonder in the entire United States of America. Enjoy the ride, Ryan. We'll be there soon."

I tried to imagine what might come next, if Hollis was going to purchase the whole damn canyon and build some enormous freaking mansion right in the middle of it with his own herd of donkeys and American eagles, flying around on cue while *Eye of the Tiger* played on the biggest sound system the world has ever known.

For all I knew, Hollis was planning to move the Los Angeles Flash to the canyon and build stadium right there! Fuck! Imagine the ticket sales for an outdoor stadium in the Grand Canyon. It could probably hold a million people, and nothing could block your sight lines from anywhere. Okay, it might get a little hot, to say the least, especially early in the season, but then they could make a fortune selling suntan lotion and hats with the Flash logo all over them.

"The Grand Canyon Flash. Got a nice ring to it, right?"

"That's sounds fantastic, Ryan. You've got a flair for marketing, I see. Maybe we can find a special consulting position for you inside the front office."

"Maybe so. That would be a quite a change for me."

I had arrived in Las Vegas with fucking on the brain. Now, I was minutes away from one of the most famous places on the planet with no idea what was coming next. What kind of party do you throw at a giant hole in the ground?

"Relax, Ryan. Keep an open mind and anything can happen."

# Thirty-Nine

## This Is How We Do It:
## Keep On Rockin' in the Free World

For a second, as we descended to the bottom of the Grand Fucking Canyon, I thought I was riding on an alien ship entering an alternate universe or at least flying into the middle of the opening ceremony of the next Olympics, with every light show, sound experience and visual feat you could ever imagine on full display. My insides were churning. My eyes were bugging, and my head was spinning, struggling to believe what I was seeing with my very own eyes.

I don't know how Hollis did it, but he had turned the canyon into the most epic circus you could ever imagine. I never did hallucinogenic drugs like guys I knew in college, but maybe this is what it looks like when you're tripping your brains out. I'd never seen so many colors or heard such banging loud music, bouncing off the interior walls of the canyon, as I did in those moments when our helicopter descended 3,500 feet to the bottom of the Earth.

Fuckin' A! This whole scene was an orgy of the senses. Whoever planned this thing must have been taking some powerful meds. Giant creatures, looking like American eagles and other big birds, were flying all around, using some hi-tech jet packs or something. I kept thinking they were going to crash into our helicopter and the others that were descending to the bottom of the canyon, but somehow no one did. Multiple people were walking on cables from one side of the rock walls to the other, like wire walkers on steroids in a three-ring fucking circus. Donkeys were dressed up like creatures from some crazy Fellini movie, prancing around and humping each other like an ancient Roman bacchanalia.

On a stage bigger than anything I ever imagined, like 10 times more than what they do for a Super Bowl halftime show, I saw Neil Young killing it with "Keep On Rockin' in the Free World." Then, U2 started belting out their greatest hits. Bono's voice echoed off the walls of the canyon and then Beyoncé joined him. Jay Z was playing a trumpet, which I had no idea he could do, and then the craziest thing happened. I swear to God I saw Elvis Presley, Jimi Hendrix and Whitney Houston singing "Joy to the World" together. I had to rub my eyes, figuring I was hallucinating, but then Gia reminded me how amazing holograms are, even how they can recreate dead people right in front of your disbelieving eyes.

As soon as we landed, I was whisked away to a buffet table that must have followed along the entire length of the Colorado River. I'd never seen anything like it. Every type of food you could think of, laid out in complete excess. The whole floor of the canyon was covered in rose petals, too, which must have taken every fucking rose in the whole world.

Gia leaned into my ear.

"This is what's possible when money is no object."

"I guess so. I still can't believe you can have a private party in the Grand Canyon. I mean, come on. Who ever thought of this as even a remote possibility?"

"Ryan, it's time for all of us to think big. B-I-G. Like I said, the world is our oyster."

"I mean, if you say so."

"I do. I definitely do. Do you like oysters, Ryan?"

Gia took my hand and guided me into a rainbow-colored tent where a group of guests were lounging on what looked like beds and being fed oysters and champagne by a bevy of beautiful women and male models.

"This is a fucking orgy."

"What's wrong with that?"

I had no argument for G. I mean . . . if you got it, flaunt it, right? Hollis surely had it, as in having the means *and* the vision. I had to admire that about him. It was one thing to be as supper successful as him, as a lawyer and a hedge fund founder, and crazy wealthy as a result, but his vision to even think of doing something like this was beyond impressive. I mean, Hollis was a fucking rock star!

By the time I was drunk on oysters and the most expensive champagne known to mankind, Gia ushered me back outside, where I was almost shocked to realize that I was still inside the Grand Fucking Canyon, listening now to Sting singing a duet with a hologram of Aretha Franklin, with The Spice Girls back together again as their back-up singers.

Was I dreaming, or was this really happening? Before I could come to a clear conclusion, I was greeted by Bob Smalley and Gene Cauley, who casually dropped out of the sky in two parachute contraptions I'd never seen before. Apparently, these "luxury flying pods," as they were called, were one-of-a-kind, futuristic samples of the wave of the future, when rich people will be able to jet stream around the world in their own private containers.

"Coleman! You made it!"

Smalley put his pod down and grabbed my shoulder.

"Well, fuck me, Coleman. Nice to see you!"

I noticed Cauley needed a minute to adjust her clothing before joining us. I was still shocked by how they had appeared out of nowhere and couldn't figure out where they had come from or how they had landed without crashing and burning. It seemed like science fiction was coming to life in the middle of the desert.

"How the hell? I mean, what are these contraptions?"

Smalley laughed, took a swig from a flask he had and explained.

"Randy is one of the key investors in a company that is producing these transportation modules of the future. Amazing, huh? Maybe you can try one before we leave."

Cauley seemed ecstatic as she spoke.

"Coleman, I guarantee you that within 15 minutes inside one of these pods you will be either peeing in your pants or ejaculating like an over-sexed beast. This is the biggest rush I've felt since I had 'sexual relations' with all the members of my debating team at Harvard."

Smalley laughed.

"'Sexual relations'? Really?"

Cauley winked at both of us.

"Forget the relations. Sex. Pure and simple."

"Gene, what a sheltered life you've led," Smalley said. "I'm sure that if you think about it you can come up with a few thrills you've had since those days."

"Ha!" said Cauley. "Just a few."

She grabbed a cocktail from a waiter walking by in the skimpiest G string I'd ever seen. Cauley slapped his ass and turned back to Smalley and me, looking like she was laughing and crying at the same time. She looked disturbed. I'd never seen her even remotely out of control.

"You don't know shit, Bob."

She sneered at Smalley, who didn't react at all, and then she pulled me aside.

"Come here, Coleman. You want to know about my sheltered life? Come with me. I'll tell you the truth that no one else will. Time for you to get a little education."

She pulled me away from Smalley and took me close to the edge of the canyon. As I looked down onto the abyss, I was glad I hadn't imbibed too much. Otherwise, I might have gotten dizzy and fallen right in.

"Mrs. Coleman, we're sorry to inform you that your son, Ryan, had a few too many drinks at the Grand Canyon and fell over the edge . . . obviously to his death."

So, while my mother hears this news and is ready to jump out of the second story window of her nursing home, my wife, Beverly, gets a similar visit from the authorities and the first thing she does is call my lawyer to make sure that she's number one in my will.

This nonsense is running through my mind as Cauley grabs me and starts going on and on about all these men she's had to put up with her entire life. I had no idea why she was telling me all of that, but I wasn't about to challenge her on it, either. I definitely did not want to get on the bad side of someone like Eugenia Cauley, especially when we were both pretty high and standing on the edge of the Grand fucking Canyon.

"You see, Coleman, no girl should have to endure what I had to put up with from all these men. I thought it was bad enough that I had an uncle and two teachers who started coming on to me when I was in junior high school. I was tall for my age, and as soon as I showed the first sign of tits they wouldn't leave me alone. There was nothing I could do unless I wanted to be accused of lying about my uncle raping me because according to everyone in our family he could do no wrong. And if I had ratted out my teachers, I would have failed French and Current Events, which would've ended any chance I had of getting into a good college and far away from fucking Little Rock. That's all I cared about back then— getting as far away from Arkansas as I could, no matter what shit I had to put up with, and believe me, it was a lot."

"Oh, Gene, I'm really sorry to hear about this. I had no idea."

"Of course, you didn't. Smalley knows about my fucked-up father but not much else. Nobody knows anything about the other abuse I survived. At least I think I survived. Throughout college and then law school, all the guys in my classes, and the teachers, too, goddammit, all they wanted to do was fuck me. None of them took me seriously. Even some of the women treated me like an object. Don't get me wrong. I fucked some of them, and I enjoyed it, too, even though I learned really fast to use sex as a weapon for getting what I wanted. For the most part, I was viewed as a hot piece of meat, and it fucked me up. When I passed the bar and started doing cases in court, I had to put up with a whole new collection of horny judges who were sleazy as shit, those bastards."

"Really? Judges?"

"You bet your ass, Coleman. They're the worst. They think they look dignified in their robes, but a pig's a pig, no matter what he's wearing."

I didn't know what to say. I had no idea that Cauley had been through so much shit, and while it was shocking, it almost made sense. I mean, something had to explain how she had become such a ruthless and powerful hard-ass, who took no prisoners in her career.

"You see, Ryan, I had to become a bigger beast than any of them could ever be, a real maneater, if you know what I mean. They thought they were the 'baddest' men on Earth, but the truth is, they all have tiny dicks and are afraid someone will tell the whole world."

"Gene, I don't know how you could put up with that shit for so long."

Cauley took a deep breath, as if it might be her last.

"It's been too much, Ryan. I'm tired of it. Enough is enough."

"How about we go back and see what Bob is doing."

As soon as we found him, he wasted no time hounding Cauley.

"So, Gene, did you take our new friend here to school?"

Before Cauley could respond, our attention was diverted to an enormous burst of fireworks, which came at just the right time as the sun was setting and the multi-colored hues of the evening sky washed over the canyon. On another stage several hundred yards away, which appeared to be a replica of The Hollywood Bowl, The Los Angeles Philharmonic Orchestra began to play "Bohemian Rhapsody" by the legendary band, Queen. Brian May, the band's lead guitarist was there live, playing along with the orchestra and a hologram of Freddy Mercury.

The overwhelming sound and light show continued for what seemed like forever until they all segued into "We Are the Champions" and Randy Hollis appeared in the sky, suspended over us in a giant floating Flash helmet, hovering over the stage.

Suddenly, the orchestra and the band stopped, and Hollis began to speak.

"Hello, my friends! Welcome to paradise! I hope you are having a good time. Thank you for coming. This is a great day to celebrate the future of The Los Angeles Flash! Enjoy yourselves here tonight and see you tomorrow in Vegas!"

Boom! A second later, Hollis was gone. He vanished as easily as he'd arrived in whatever mysterious capsule he'd arrived in. I was stunned, like everyone else. I looked at Smalley and Cauley, who appeared calm and collected, as if this kind of thing happened every day. They smiled at each other and nodded to me.

"That's it?"

They laughed.

"I mean, what the fuck just happened?"

"Well, Randy said what he had to say and now he's off to do other things."

"Other things? What could possibly be more spectacular than this?"

Smalley took another swig from his flask.

"Coleman, you're a smart guy, but you've got a lot to learn, especially when it comes to Randy Hollis and how he ticks. He's not exactly a social butterfly. In fact, while he knows these events expand his reputation and are vital to his public standing, he actually loathes being around so many people, no matter how beautiful and interesting they might be."

"So, it's all a big show?"

"Of course, it is! What isn't?"

Cauley grabbed Smiley's flask and took a swig.

"Smoke and mirrors, my boy. Don't you know? It's all an illusion, except it isn't!"

She laughed like a devil and danced away into the oyster tent.

"I must feed the beast! Feed the beast!"

Smalley and I laughed and stood there, watching the moon rise over the canyon walls.

"Coleman, I thought I told you that you got balls. It sure sounds like you didn't use them on your flight to Vegas."

"I'm just selective about who gets to play with them."

Smalley laughed.

"So, what are you drinking, Bob?"

"Oh, this old thing? For special occasions like this, I like to indulge in a concoction first made famous by Ken Kesey and The Grateful Dead, back in the day in San Francisco, during the acid tests, when they partied all night long an drank the Kool Aid. Of course, it was spiked with LSD, and you never knew how much you were drinking or how much of the hallucinogenic drugs were actually rushing into your bloodstream. But nobody cared! The whole idea was to rock out and dance all night long. Free love, baby!"

For a minute, I wasn't sure if he was pulling my leg or simply surprising me with a side of him I didn't know existed. These guys were such a mystery, and the more I thought I knew about them, the less I seemed to know.

Smalley held out his flask to me.

"No, thanks. I'm not thirsty."

"Don't be a fucking prude, Coleman. Now is the time to let your hair down and have some fun. Don't worry. Your wife is not here. Your mother is not here. No one will judge you. Just fuck off and get happy!"

I took a deep breath, grabbed the flask and downed a big slug of what kinda tasted like Kool Aid, only not so sweet. Smalley had to stop me from drinking too much.

"Easy, boy. You'll levitate without a battery pack."

Within an hour, I had no idea who I was. I started feeling waves of warmth rushing throughout my body and I was overcome with so many emotions. I laughed. I cried. I sang. I danced. I even thought I could fly at one point, so it was good I was at the bottom of the canyon at that moment and not standing along the edge, looking down to my drugged-out death.

I remember Smalley telling me that Gia would be looking out for me, as she was an experienced "tripper" as he called her. But that's about all I can recollect until the sun came up over the canyon and I was taken back to Vegas on another helicopter, safely tucked into a seat by Gia and held perfectly in her arms during the entire trip. When we arrived, she brought me to The Purple Angel and checked me into my suite, where I would sleep off the effects of my "trip" and rest up before the next party began.

# Forty

## Party Party, Part Two:
## Hollis Upstages the AFL

I woke up with Gia's shoe up my ass. Literally. I could feel it squeezed right between my cheeks. I had no idea how it got there, or where the other stiletto was, but I realized a few seconds later that her foot was not inside it. In fact, she was nowhere to be seen. Then, I rolled over in bed and found her note on the bedside table.

> Ryan, I hope you're feeling well when you read this.
> Don't worry. You didn't do anything that your mother wouldn't approve of,
> that is, if she has a good sense of humor. Just kidding. Or maybe not.
> Your wife called this morning, too, but I didn't pick up. Or maybe I did.
> LOL. You'll find out soon enough. Curious? I bet you are.
> Check your phone for evidence. Just kidding. I think.
> P.S. Did I leave one of my shoes in your room?

I fell out of bed reaching for my phone. No photos, as far as I could tell. Was Gia fucking with me? I had no idea. I stood up, expecting a hangover, at least from the champagne, if not from what was in that flask, but I felt fine, as if I hadn't ingested anything at all besides a bucket of oysters and a spoonful of whatever Alice had when she went down the rabbit hole.

I called room service to order breakfast, only to find out that it was already approaching dinnertime. I had slept the entire day, which probably explained why I felt relatively refreshed.

"I'd like a pot of coffee, please, and what do you recommend after being up all night and then sleeping off an acid trip?"

"I don't know, Mr. Coleman, but I will confer with the chef. Perhaps a bowl of chicken soup? I hear it's good for whatever ails ya. At least that's what my grandmother always says."

"Mine, too. How do you like that? Great, I'll take a bowl of soup and how about you send up the daily newspapers, too? Thank you."

I wanted to see if there was any coverage of what had taken place at the Grand Canyon. I felt like I needed some proof that it had really happened because I wasn't completely sure. First the flight with those escorts, and then Gia and the helicopter ride, and then all that crazy shit at the canyon, and then what? I had no idea how I ended up in bed with one of Gia's shoes up my ass and I needed to look for the other one.

First, though, a shower. As soon as I stepped into the bathroom, I saw handwriting on the mirror in red lipstick. I thought immediately of all the horror flick scenes where the next thing that happens is somebody gets stabbed and the blood runs down the shower drain. Luckily, I hadn't lost my mind, not yet at least, and I stepped closer to read what was written on the mirror.

"In due time."

What the fuck? That's it? "In due time?" Was that some sick motto of Hollis and all the people on his team? Was it just a matter of time before I started saying it, too?

I took a shower and tried to calm down, as the invite for Hollis' party said it was starting in a couple hours. I had a few things to do before then, like a workout in the gym, having something to eat, and finding Gia's other shoe and getting it back to her. Fortunately, I found it under the pillow, which still left me with a huge question: what happened in my hotel room?

I had no way to contact Gia so all I could do was wait. I drank some coffee and headed to the gym, which was the finest fitness center I had ever seen, complete with every machine you could ever want, a buffet of nutritious snacks, a roulette table set up with treadmills around it so you could jog and gamble at the same time, and a team of trainers on call to boost your every lift and stretch before dabbing off your sweat with the softest towels I ever felt in my life. I thought I had to get some of those and bring them back to Philly because Beverly would go nuts about how soft and plush they felt on her skin.

I was wondering if Gia would walk into the gym at any minute. For all I knew, she had planted a tracking device up my ass, too, just to make sure where I was in case I woke up out of my deep sleep, and still high, wandered naked out of the hotel and into the Vegas traffic. Boy, that would have made the news everywhere, even reaching my mother and giving her three or four simultaneous heart attacks. As I pedaled on a stationary bike, I moved my ass around on the seat to see if I could feel anything unusual, but all that did was get one of the trainers to come over and ask if I was okay. That was enough for me. I had to get back to my room and regroup. Whatever was inside that flask felt amazing at the time, but it was now making me feel weird and almost paranoid.

I went upstairs to my room and showered again. Somehow, my overnight bag had been brought to my room, along with a gift bag from Hollis and the Los Angeles Flash. It was full of AFL swag, enough to start my own gift shop on Hollywood Boulevard.

Then the phone rang.

"Ryan? It's Gia. How are you?"

"What a question. To tell you the truth, I have no idea. I mean, what happened when I got to my hotel room here? Do you know why I woke up with one of your shoes up my ass? I mean you must. It's your red stiletto, isn't it?"

Gia laughed.

"Of course, it is. Did you find the other one? I was a bit 'out of this world' too, you know, so I'm not sure how I lost my shoes, but did you find it?"

"Under the pillow."

"Under the pillow? How did it get there?"

"Your guess is as good as mine. Actually, it's probably better. Just tell me one thing. Do I need to call a lawyer?"

Gia laughed again.

"For what, Ryan?"

"To negotiate the terms of my divorce when my wife finds out I was tripping on LSD and having sex with a total stranger."

"Oh, Ryan, really? I think you know me well enough to not consider me a total stranger, don't you?"

"I think I'll pass on answering that. Maybe it's better I don't know what happened and we leave it at that."

"Sure, Ryan. We can do that. Now, you get ready for the party, and I'll pick you up in 20 minutes. I'm right down the hall."

Twenty minutes later, Gia was at my door, about six inches shorter than I remembered her. But she still had command of the room when she entered, and then reasserted her presence once she stepped back into her heels.

"Okay, Handsome. Let's go!"

Gia escorted me through a maze of tunnels and walkways until we entered an enormous tent behind the hotel. I mean, it was like three football fields long and high enough to launch a fucking rocket to the moon.

"Mr. Hollis has invited more than 10,000 people. I'm sure you'll recognize some of the VIPs and celebrity guests. Look! There's Johnny Depp and Matt Damon and Cher. Oh my gosh, look! It's Madonna and Sean Penn. Maybe they're back together."

I looked around and saw a collection of world-class entertainment, a mix of the best of Disney World, Las Vegas and underground characters you can only find in some surreal movie by the Coen Brothers or Quentin Tarantino. Some of my favorite actors and musicians were hanging out, along with a handful of senators and cabinet members, who I figured were there to kiss up to Hollis and see if they could get him to donate to their campaigns.

Hollis had other things in mind when it came to his money. According to Smalley, who joined us at a tequila tasting bar, sponsored by Mike Tyson and his new line of booze, the sole purpose of the party, besides extreme indulgence, was to act as a fundraiser for the many charities Hollis sponsors. Everyone in attendance was there to be seen, of course, and to congratulate him on buying the Flash. About an hour later, Hollis appeared, by hologram, of course, to thank everyone for attending. It was so weird. He hovered over all of us, as if he were some mythical God from outer space. He had a team of assistants onstage in the middle of the tent, and while TV cameras from all over the world were rolling, he presented millions and millions of dollars in gifts to his different charities.

He also announced a new foundation he was creating for the Flash as all 32 AFL franchises sponsor a charity organization. Hollis was funding it with an initial gift of $50 million, twice as much as any of the other owners had done. The purpose of the charity is to help under privileged children, but I had to wonder if some of the owners might suspect that Hollis was trying to upstage them right away. I made a mental note to contact Soffer and have him contact the owners ASAP to assuage any hard feelings that Hollis' generosity may have caused.

Cauley came up to us and sampled the liquor. She seemed a little off, but I couldn't figure out why.

"See all the Flash players and coaches over there? And all the office people and other staff? They're all here, celebrating Hollis and all the big-time cash he brings to the team. Man, are they going to be surprised on Monday morning when they're all fired!"

I had no comment on that one because I still couldn't believe that Hollis would do that. Meanwhile, Handler, the sneaky private dick, was still investigating Hollis and everyone in his inner circle, including Cauley, Smalley and me. How did I know that? I didn't. Not really. I figured men like Coyle and Dickey were not through trying to fuck Hollis, especially now that he was getting all of this positive press and accolades. It had to piss them off to no end, and when conniving little bastards like them can't handle the truth they go apeshit and pound their fists like little boys.

I smiled as I wondered what my next move should be, and when I should make it.

"In due time."

# Forty-One

## A Lawsuit Too Far:
## Cauley Bites the Dust

Eugenia "Gene" Cauley never made it home from Vegas. She blew her brains out across the hall from me in The Purple Angel and left a $10,000 tip for the housekeeper to clean up the mess. For all her ruthless and unconventional behavior, some of which I soon found out was blatantly illegal, Gene was so considerate. I mean, who fucking kills herself and remembers to show her appreciation to the person who has to clean up all that fucking blood and brain matter?

Apparently, Gene bought a Glock at a local gun show. She stuck the barrel in her mouth and shot herself while I was sleeping, hung over from a party menu of tequila, poppers, and some extremely potent marijuana, not to mention whatever it was in that Kool Aid. My body had no idea what to do with that, along with those poppers and the weed, which I hadn't smoked since my law school graduation party. Let's just say I slept like a baby that night, alone, I think, and didn't hear the gunshot.

Maybe Gene was so high she didn't realize what she was doing, or maybe she'd been suffering from some serious mental health crisis. Fuck if I knew. When I found out the next morning, after Hollis' party, I was shocked, like everybody else, but nobody was talking. Police were going around, room to room, banging on our doors and waking us up, investigating whatever they could and getting all us guests to get our shit together and vacate the premises.

I had nothing to say, other than I was sleeping when she apparently did what she did. They wanted me to leave my room and join the other guests in a ballroom, where they would follow up with more questions.

Once again, I had to call Beverly and tell her I might be delayed. I spared her the details, that Gene's skull had been splattered all over her hotel room, and that her bed and the carpet were soaked in blood. Luckily, my wife was still with her family, so she didn't have any complaints or questions, other than why would a super successful lawyer blow her brains out? Naturally, I had no answers for her or anyone else.

I found Smalley near the elevator, wandering around in a daze. Gene was his lifelong friend and mentor. He knew more about her than anybody, but I wasn't about to start bugging him with a barrage of questions. He cornered me, though, and started flapping his lips.

"Gene was 53 years old. Divorced twice, with two children and three step-children. Great kids, even though she didn't see them too much. She owned several houses, you know, a Manhattan brownstone on the East Side, two condos in the Caribbean, three luxury timeshares in Europe, another one in Dubai, and that yacht we were on in Miami."

"Oh man, Bob, I don't even know how to tell you how sorry I am."

Smalley pulled me aside where no one could hear us, not even the cops.

"Listen, Ryan, you need to know a few things because the shit is going to hit the fan real fast, and this will be all over the news and we can't let it fuck up things for me or Hollis. Or you, too, for that matter."

"My lips are sealed, Bob."

"Okay, look, the rumors are going to fly, but here's the deal. Gene was rumored to have several shady offshore bank accounts and was part owner of a professional woman's soccer team in Moscow, along with a consortium of oligarchs, who were not exactly legit, if you know what I mean. Besides that, she was chairman of the board of the Girl Scouts of America and chief counsel for a global entertainment company, which owned several pornographic websites and a chain of remarkably successful brothels throughout Southeast Asia."

"Busy woman."

"Hell yeah, she was amazing. Look, she wasn't known as "The Castrator" for nothing. Gene was a complicated human being, to say the least, and many details of her life are a mystery, even to me."

I had heard a lot of unverified stories about Gene from other lawyers, but even though I was tempted, I wasn't about to ask Smalley if they were true, certainly not while her suicide was so fresh. Apparently, some of Gene's antics were straight out of the Delta Tau Chi fraternity in *Animal House*, a few in good fun while others were done in retaliation for how people had mistreated her. A couple stories about Gene were mean-spirited and completely over the top, and it was hard to imagine they were true. Jealousy, as in the lawyers who wished they made as much money as Gene, can get people to make shit up.

"Listen, Bob, you don't have to tell me anything. Maybe we should just go home as soon as we can and take a few days to let this cool down."

Smalley grabbed me by the shirt collar and pulled me further away down the hall. He motioned to a policeman that we'd be right back.

"Coleman, shut up and listen to me. Gene has been having financial problems for a long time, so she helped herself to more than $120 million from a Yahoo securities class-action settlement where she was lead counsel, which was settled for more than $595 million. That obviously crossed the line, even for Gene, and put her in great legal jeopardy."

I was dumbfounded.

"Gene had recently been forced to plead guilty to one count of wire fraud and a single count of criminal contempt because she never complied with Court orders. The prosecuting attorney claimed that this was not the first time Gene had stolen money, but it was the first time she had been caught."

"Holy shit! I had no idea."

"Of course, you didn't. Hollis doesn't even know the whole story. Look, the judge was about to sentence Gene to 18 years in prison and full restitution payments. There was no way Gene was going to serve that kind of time or come up with that money. So, with the screws turning extra hard over the past week, I guess she must have felt like she had no other choice."

"You didn't see this coming, huh?"

"No fucking way, Coleman. Gene was a piece of work. Tough as nails."

"Yeah, she was really something."

Smalley didn't look so good. I suggested he go talk to the police, get that over with, and head home to rest up until the funeral. We headed to the ballroom and answered some more questions, but they were minimal because the coroner had already determined that Gene had died by suicide, that there was no foul play and no suspects.

Before he left, Smalley gave me a file.

"Take this with you, Coleman, and consider it a little tutorial on how this class action world really works if you want to use it to its full advantage. But think twice because as you go deeper and deeper you might get in over your head. See you back East."

On my commercial flight back home to Philadelphia, I dove right into the file. I was exhausted and still in shock from the thought of Gene blowing her brains out with a fucking gun, but I had to find out what Smalley had given me.

Normally, when a lawsuit settles the defendant pays the proceeds within 30 days and the funds sit in an attorney escrow account until the Judge enters a final order to distribute the funds. Lawyers grab their fees and reimbursement of expenses almost before the ink dries on the Judge's Order. Since Gene controlled the money, she probably received a majority of the fees.

She held that money in an escrow account at Centennial Bank in Little Rock, Arkansas. She was the lone signature on it, which meant she was the only one who could withdraw funds. Gene was one of the owners of the bank, too, so no one questioned anything. It became clear later that she had been steadily misappropriating those funds to pay her own personal expenses, which included huge alimony payments and God knows what else.

Apparently, Gene was desperate and helped herself to at least $120 million from that class-action settlement. You read that right—$120 million. What the hell was she thinking? When I think back to how she seemed so cavalier about spending money, infatuated with the Gambino crime family, like Smalley, maybe it makes sense that she stole the money just to maintain her lavish lifestyle. Then again, she had plenty of money. The reason she stole all that money is because she was a fucked-up person, probably because she was abused as a kid and then mistreated by men throughout her whole life.

A week before Hollis' Christmas party, Gene found out that she was facing hard times and would be forced to sell off most of her properties to pay the restitution penalties. Plus, if the shit went public in a trial, it could bring down Hollis in a simple case of guilt-by-association. So, Cauley told the judge she would settle up and go to prison as soon as she got back from Vegas. For some reason, the judge let her go. Maybe he was just a pushover and felt sorry for her or maybe he owed Gene a "favor."

Gene had tried to argue that she should be given probation instead of jail time, that if she was not incarcerated, she could earn the money to pay the restitution. That argument was a bit nonsensical as Gene had to give up her law license, so she could not have earned any money—at least not legally. To pay all that money back, it would have taken Gene about 400 years of delivering pizzas, a job she once took during law school. Gene had other sources of income, from the porn sites and the Girl Scouts, but they cut ties with her when she was pled guilty.

All along, Gene was paranoid that *The Wall Street Journal* and other media would blow the story open, which would have ruined her two closest partners, Smalley and Hollis, and embarrassed her family, which she was constantly struggling to make amends with for all her years of neglect. Under that hard shell of a ruthless woman operating in a man's world was a genuine human being who cared about her personal legacy and the people who had helped her become so successful.

"I made false statements to others to explain my failure to pay over those funds," Gene stated in her defense, "which I had used for other unauthorized purposes."

It sounds to me like she did not own up to the fact that she stole the money. I guess in her mind, she didn't. Gene also claimed to have been suffering from depression for a number of years, but as far as I could tell, that was a lame B.S. excuse, which the Court did not believe, and Smalley even hinted was not true.

Gene was a mess. Two failed marriages, estranged children, and no prospects for reviving her legal career once she served her time. I mean, from the file Smalley handed me to read, and considering how Gene Cauley had been sexually abused as a child, it looked like she felt as if suicide was her one and only option. Or maybe if you do something like that, logical thinking and reflection are not even part of the equation. Obviously, Gene was in a shitload of pain and taking her own life was the only way to make it stop.

When I think of her story in human terms, without all the crime and punishment, I am saddened by the tragedy of Eugenia Cauley. I mean, I have to wonder if there was something I missed, something I could have done to save her. I actually liked her, and had to respect her achievements, especially in light of what she had to put up with growing up and throughout her long career.

That said, I definitely do not agree with her overall attitude concerning the reason and purpose of her class-action practice. When Gene told me that she never cared about the Plaintiffs of the Class she was representing, that it was all about making money, I just couldn't bring myself to accept her position, even though I had heard it from Smalley, too, who probably learned it from her. For me, that kind of behavior only helped the little guy get more screwed by the greed of corporate America.

Now, with Cauley in a casket, I had to wonder what I had gotten myself into and if I should continue to pursue these opportunities with Hollis. What would my mother say? Or Beverly? And, how about my best friend, Timmy? What would he think about all this shit?

Even though Gene achieved mythical success at a young age, which I admired, she was human like the rest of us, and definitely had some serious flaws. I have come to conclude that just because someone has a different or contrary moral compass, that does not mean you cannot like and respect the hell out of that person.

That's what I planned to say when I spoke at her upcoming funeral, which Smalley had already asked me to do. By the time we landed in Philadelphia, I had even picked out my suit, a ruby red design by Brunello Cucinelli, with a flamboyant paisley tie and a pair of handmade Italian shoes with golden soles. If I was really going to honor Gene in style, I would need to dress just right for the occasion.

# Forty-Two

## Dog Days in Arkansas:
## Don't Lay Down with Fleas

Less than a week after eulogizing Eugenia Cauley at a small funeral in her hometown of Little Rock, Arkansas, I was dragged back into the EPI class action, the one which had exposed all the shit with the Burn Pits. Dick Dickey was forced to testify and had to answer for a long history of misdeeds and deceit before, during and after his stint as Secretary of Defense and CEO of EPI.

I was still mourning the loss of my friend and mentor, Gene, or should I say her death was making me take a good hard look at my own life. I wanted to make sure that I didn't do anything that might lead me to blowing my own brains out with a gun inside some stupid hotel room in a Las Vegas resort where nobody could give a shit.

I'm running my mouth here because Cauley's suicide freaked me out. First of all, it was just fucking horrible to think about the violence of what she did, I mean, sticking the barrel of a Glock inside her mouth and pulling the trigger. Her whole head must have exploded in a split second. The cops might have seen shit like this before, but the housekeeper had to be having terrible nightmares. I'm sure these people have seen some pretty freaky things left behind in Vegas hotel rooms, but somebody's exploded brains and buckets of blood everywhere? That's way over the top, even for the crazy bastards who go overboard after a night of gambling and who knows what. I almost wish I go could find that housekeeper and give 'em some money to get therapy or something because confronting a scene like that had to mess a person up for a long, long time. I mean, how do you get those pictures out of your head?

It was taking a toll on me, too; that's for sure. The funeral was sad. I mean, brutal, and not just because Cauley was dead. The worst part was that only me and Smalley and one of her kids showed up. Nobody else. Nobody. That's pitiful. I couldn't believe it at first, that we were it. Just us. Okay, maybe it was hard for some people from other parts of the country to fly into Arkansas at the last minute, and maybe some people didn't want to be seen there, you know, associated with a dark death like that from somebody who did what she did. I mean, Cauley was official a criminal with a record of stealing millions and millions of dollars from innocent people. On the other hand, she overcame a lot in her life and rose up to the mega-top of her profession, and she helped a lot of people, women in particular, on her way up the ladder.

She probably hit a lot of people over the head with that same ladder as she climbed her way over whoever she had to step on to succeed. But none of those people came to the funeral. None of her family and friends from back home even showed up. Even the director of the funeral home told me that he didn't want to be there, but it was a payday for him, courtesy of Smalley, so he had to do it. Apparently, they didn't have a wake for two reasons. Nobody in her family wanted one, and they couldn't exactly do a viewing because she didn't have a head. I mean, who wants to stand there and stare at a body without a fucking head? That's too weird, even for Smalley, who wanted no part of that shit. He agreed to pay for whatever everything else cost, and he tipped the funeral home real nice to take her wherever they would take her and bury her and be done with it.

After the brief funeral inside a small chapel, Smalley told me he couldn't go to the cemetery and that I could skip it, too, if I wanted.

"Coleman, this is hard for me, you know. I knew Gene since I was a kid and I looked up to her for such a long time. I wouldn't be where I am today without her, but this whole thing, the way she fucked up and stole all that money and then offed herself; it's just too much. It broke something inside me, and I can't reconcile this with who she was when we were growing up. To tell you the truth, it's completely impossible for me to be associated with her anymore."

"What about Hollis?"

"Oh, no way for him to be connected at all, not in the least bit, especially now that he's an AFL owner. People know he knew her, but that's it. Nothing else. We have to make sure his reputation stays clean as a whistle, like a fucking choir boy."

"We'll do our best, Bob."

I understood the situation, but it wasn't exactly comfortable for me to be associated with Cauley. Fortunately, only a local reporter showed up to the measly service and it ended without incident in about 20 minutes. The funeral director said a few words, the usual stuff about it being a sad day but that we all had to go on with our lives and use the lessons of Eugenia Cauley's life to improve our own. I couldn't argue with that. Smalley opted not to speak, and so did Gene's son, so I was the only one left. I guess Smalley knew this would happen, so that's why he had me get up there, just to make the service feel like an official event, as if somebody had to say something about Gene before we could call it a day and get the fuck out of Little Rock.

Smalley was staying overnight to see some of his family, so I went straight to the airport. I barely spoke with Gene's son, but according to Smalley, it was a clever and cynical move to boost his chances of getting more money from her will.

As I boarded the plane, my phone was ringing off the hook with the EPI case and Dickey's involvement was the primary focus. I spent the entire flight devising a strategy to put him in a corner and make him admit that he received a severance package of $845 million, which he parlayed into billions in profit through illicit deals with the military.

It worked like a charm. Since an explosion had recently rocked an offshore oil rig, resulting in the worst oil spill in U.S. history, EPI was deemed negligent and had to pay a huge fine. Dickey escaped scot free, at least until I got involved and turned the screws on him with a couple of maneuvers I had actually learned from Gene Cauley.

It ended up that Dickey's testimony under oath did not land him in jail, but it smeared his reputation even more than before, enough that he would never be able to purchase a major American sports franchise, not in the AFL or anywhere else, except for maybe a local Little League team or a junior high chess club.

Persona non grata, anyone?

Hollis was thrilled with what I pulled off and sent me a thank you gift of $500,000. Yeah, that's right. Five-hundred-thousand dollars, just for making Dickey's life miserable. This was the kind of appreciation I liked, but I wanted to find a way to keep this money, and all the rest I was earning from Hollis, in a separate account, secret in fact, so in the event of any divorce proceedings, it wouldn't become part of Beverly's haul because I knew she would retain a beast of a divorce lawyer who would stop at nothing to get as much as possible.

As I navigated my way through that maze of financial intrigue, social media exploded with reports of a $40 billion lawsuit as a result of some fossil fuel executives using a complicated web of off-balance sheet partnerships to hide more than $5 billion in debt, which caused the company to file bankruptcy and to fire more than 5,000 people from their workforce of 25,000. Most of those people who lost their jobs overnight had families. The presiding judge awarded the lawyers in that case—Hollis and Smalley—nearly $900 million in fees, more than five times the billable hours they actually submitted.

Smalley put it best.

"Coleman, you're not the only one with an iron set of balls."

How he and Hollis made that happen is anyone's guess. What excuse could the judge have had to award them that much money? What the hell was she thinking? Once again, it had to be razor-sharp lawyers working in secret with company executives to pull off that caper. I didn't ask Smalley or Hollis because I already knew they would only wink and say nothing.

I bet Cauley had her fingerprints all over it because when it came to playing the hardest version of hardball, she was the GOAT, the Greatest of All Time. Unfortunately, to say the least, she killed herself before she could have cashed in on her portion of that windfall.

There was crazy shit going on everywhere. It reminded me of what Smalley had told me when I first met Cauley and he was talking about how rough the legal business can be. He quoted Ben Franklin, who said, "When you lay down with dogs, you get fleas."

I had a hunch that we were now talking about rabid dogs and the kind of fleas that do a lot worse than make you itch.

# Forty-Three

### Get Out Your Condoms:
### Hollis Has a "Date Night"

Randy Hollis left Las Vegas a happy man. He had beaten every charge that Patrick Coyle and Dick Dickey had brought against him, and any damage to his reputation had been quickly repaired, thanks to Bonnie Spencer and yours truly. He was the newest owner of the Flash, an AFL team badly in need of a major reboot, and the football universe was eager to celebrate his aggressive moves to restore a championship level franchise to Los Angeles.

Besides the streak of obvious success, both parties had been a huge hit. The spectacle at the Grand Canyon was unprecedented and elevated Hollis' stature among the world's biggest players. Twitter exploded with photos of his holographic appearance, suspended over the canyon as an A-list of musicians played their biggest hits. The fact that he had managed to rent the Grand Fucking Canyon from the United States Parks Department blew everybody's mind. I mean, no one had ever done anything like it before and it was creating quite a buzz all across social media.

Kanye West was talking about renting the White House for a private launch party for his next music release, an album called *Yeezy Goes to Washington*, a collection of songs about him becoming America's next president. A nutcase can dream, right? I was waiting to see if Smalley was going to arrange for one of his mafia clients to rent out the Supreme Court for a goodbye party before he went off to serve a life sentence in a minimum-security prison.

Crazy shit with Hollis. He created complete chaos when he fired nearly everyone connected with the Flash organization, including the front office, players, coaches and concession workers. No one was immune to his power trip and hardly anyone could object because the truth is most of them sucked. Okay, maybe the popcorn sellers didn't deserve to get canned, but Hollis made sure to smooth that over by making a public show of giving them extremely generous severance packages. He also announced that he would be hiring a ton of new cheerleaders and that many of them would be taking over the concessions, selling popcorn and hot dogs while dressed in outfits that made them look like a bunch of Hooters' employees.

Anyway, Hollis was so busy during the Vegas trip that he apparently did not have time among all his commitments to get laid. Mona tried to arrange this for him, as she usually did, but Hollis was too preoccupied with party logistics and all the AFL stuff to take care of his own primal needs. This was unusual, even for him, as he was consumed with having as much sex as possible before he turned 60, which was fast approaching.

Mona had told me that Hollis had been feeling more and more insecure lately, fearful that he might lose his mojo once he turned the big 6-0. Sounds like he was having a big midlife crisis, but you better believe I was not about to ask him anything about that, not if I wanted to maintain my position and become even more valuable inside his inner circle. One thing you never do with a man approaching a certain age is remind him of the fact and create any doubt about his general desirability and sexual prowess, especially a man of Hollis' stature.

"I got a big dick and I know how to use it."

That was Hollis' mantra, and who was I to challenge him on it? I left that shit to Mona and her team of accommodating women. I only knew that Hollis had no time lately to be with one of the many escorts at his beck and call. Of course, as Mona had explained to me, Hollis was determined to never have a "normal" relationship, certainly not one that would lead to marriage, because he did not trust anyone who might get too close to his money, and he wanted no drama, none at all, that could possibly distract him continuing to expand his multi-faceted empire.

During the party, Gia gave me more intel in that area. Hollis' history with escorts would make Charlie Sheen blush, but he'd been too preoccupied with his purchase of the Flash and all of the class action suits that were bubbling up around him. On top of that, as he had told Mona, he thought he might be losing his mojo and didn't feel confident that even an escort he paid top dollar for would find him sexually attractive. It wasn't enough to pay for what he wanted. That was too easy. He needed his (hired) women to make him feel like he was the only one they desired, as if they really felt that way without turning it into an acting job.

Mona knew exactly what got Hollis excited so she set up what she thought would be a perfect date for her insecure boss when he got back to 220 Central Park, his penthouse condo in New York City, an exclusive property for billionaires with the best views in Manhattan. She secured a night for him with a woman named Lisa O, who Mona claimed was the most exclusive escort in the entire United States. Yeah, that's right. This Lisa O only "worked" when she wanted to and her clients included people like Sheikh Mohammed bin Rashid al-Maktoum, the absolute ruler of Dubai, Xi Jinping, the president of the People's Republic of China, and what's his name, the guy who owns Amazon. Mona said that Lisa O even gave a royal blow job to Prince Andrew, but then again, who hasn't? I was hoping to meet Lisa O so I could ask her if she fucked the Pope.

Here's how Mona described Lisa O.

"Imagine Monica Bellucci, a younger, more beautiful version of Catherine Zeta-Jones, if that's even possible, and a combination of every hot cheerleader you ever wanted to fuck."

Mona was confident that Lisa O would be perfect for Hollis. But just to be sure, to guarantee that Lisa O wouldn't pull an unexpected ego trip and leave Hollis with "blue balls," Mona let me in on her calculated plan. She and Hollis' chef would drug her cocktails, not with anything too heavy, just enough sexual stimulants to make sure she was suitably turned on and ready to do Hollis just right. He had his own custom-made version of Viagra, which supposedly ensured that his junk was ready to rock. According to Mona, Hollis even had a back-up sensor inserted in his penis, which he could stimulate by activating an app on his phone. Jesus, what some guys will do to perform.

*Wait. Was Mona pulling my leg or was this technology possible?*

She swore me to secrecy because even though she had the right intentions, if Hollis found out, he would have fired her and his chef, or maybe something worse, which I didn't even want to contemplate. I mean, I hadn't forgotten what Smalley and Cauley had told me in Atlantic City about that poor guy Paul Budman, who pissed off Hollis and then mysteriously disappeared. That story never left my mind as I became deeper enmeshed in Hollis' inner circle, and it made me wonder what Hollis might be capable of doing now that he was deep in the shit of what appeared to be a serious emotional breakdown, you know, like a mid-life crisis or something. Guys get weird when they get old. Or they just get old. I don't know which is worse.

Anyway, everything was ready when Hollis arrived back in Manhattan. Mona said his place looked perfect. The ambiance was all set up for a classic, romantic date, complete with fresh cut roses everywhere, imported directly from his own flower farm on Long Island. There were handmade aromatherapy candles and world class musicians strategically placed throughout his home. A string ensemble from The Juilliard School of Music was playing in the lobby as Lisa O arrived. Yo-Yo Ma rode with her up the elevator, playing her favorite tunes on his cello.

When she stepped out onto the penthouse level, Lisa O was greeted by Plácido Domingo, singing a medley of Elvis Presley's greatest hits. Inside the living room was a Barry White impersonator, who serenaded Lisa O and Hollis as they sipped on cocktails and a buffet of exotic foods, including braised artichokes, figs marinated in a watermelon puree, and spicy chili peppers, all laced with a healthy dose of some concoction of aphrodisiacs.

Mona had thought of everything. She even hired dancers from the American Ballet Theatre to serve a bouquet of oysters, which are known to increase one's sexual appetite. By the time the Barry White impersonator broke into "You're the One I Need," Hollis was smitten. But he still had to check to make sure that Lisa O met his unusual standards.

You see, according to Mona, each of Hollis' escorts must have an advanced college degree, which makes Mona's job challenging. During dinner, Hollis tried not to be too intrusive about that. As Lisa O described her university experience at Princeton, where she studied linguistics and anatomy, and at Georgetown, where she was supposedly working on a PhD in International Relations, he didn't notice that the drugs were having an effect on her.

As I found out later, that's when the date began to go wrong. As the waiter brought the first course, a pâté of duck liver, asparagus and truffles, Lisa O began to feel woozy and excused herself to go to the bathroom. Hollis thought nothing of it and texted Mona.

"She's amazing! Can't wait to see her naked! Can we stop eating?"

"Relax, Mr. Hollis. I'm sure she'll be right back."

"By the way, Mona, what's the O stand for? Orgasm?"

Mona was concerned, worried that the drug might be affecting Lisa O too quickly and too strong. She checked with the chef, who assured her that this was impossible. He promised her that the combination of maca root, red ginseng, ginkgo biloba and fenugreek would have the desired effect, that Lisa O might just be feeling the first wave, which can often be strong before it levels off into a glowing feeling of perfect lust.

Hollis texted Mona.

"WTF? Anything wrong? Where is she?"

Mona texted Hollis.

"Don't worry. She's probably just excited to be with you for the first time."

"You sure?"

"Yes. You're not like most men she knows. You're special."

Meanwhile, unbeknownst to anyone inside Hollis' penthouse, and something we only found out later, Lisa O was having a severe allergic reaction to the ginseng and the fenugreek. Her throat was closing up, making it impossible for her to breathe. She collapsed to the floor, cell phone in hand, but she was unable to use it to get help.

"Mona, are you sure she's okay?"

"Mr. Hollis, you worry too much. Give an amazing woman like Lisa O her space."

"Okay, you're right. She's unbelievable."

Five minutes later, as Mona was texting me to fill me in, Hollis grew impatient and told Harold Jones, his personal security guard, to find out what was going on. When Jones heard no response from the bathroom, he pried the door open and found Lisa O face down on the floor, unconscious, stuck in a pool of her own vomit. No pulse. Jones knew right away she was dead. Without missing a beat, Jones instructed Hollis to leave and speak to no one. He told Hollis' driver to take their boss to Teterboro Airport a short distance away in New Jersey, and to have his pilot fly him to his estate in Florida, where he was to remain until this could be "fixed."

Hollis didn't hesitate. He knew that he could not be found in his penthouse with a dead escort. Impossible. The truth needed to be erased, as if the evening never happened.

## Forty-Four

### The Fixer:
### Jones Takes Charge, Almost

As soon as Hollis was gone, Jones pondered his options for explaining the situation to the police and the media. That's when he decided to call me. Jones said it was an emergency and I had to come right away. I was working overtime, closing the EPI case, but how could I say no? After all, Jones was huge and scary, and I wasn't about to test his temper.

Once again, I explained to Beverly that this was part of working with a billionaire, and I hightailed it out of Philadelphia. Without traffic, I could make it to midtown Manhattan in less than 90 minutes if I didn't get pulled over for speeding.

I wondered what this was all about. I figured something went south with the Flash and Hollis needed me to fix something. As I cruised up the New Jersey Turnpike, Jones rang again.

"Mr. Jones, I'm on my way."

"Coleman, Hollis is on his way to Miami right now. He can't be connected to what happened tonight."

"Mr. Jones, with all due respect, what the fuck are you talking about?"

"It's terrible, Coleman. The only thing worse would be if Hollis had died."

"What? Somebody died? Who fucking died?"

"I found her in Hollis' bathroom, face down in her own vomit."

"Who? Who the fuck was it? Who vomited in his bathroom?"

Of course, it was Lisa O, the greatest escort in the world.

"Coleman, we're in deep shit here."

We? I thought about that for a second and realized I was definitely part of the we. Why else would I be driving like a maniac all the way to New York City?

Jones filled me in on what he knew, which was not much. This made me wonder if he was covering for his boss. Maybe Lisa O had done something wrong, and Hollis lost his mind and killed her. I had no fucking idea. I was just trying to drive fast and not get pulled over. My head was spinning, trying to process everything. Obviously, it was terrible that Lisa O had died for a reason no one could determine, but this was also the worst thing that could happen to Hollis, especially when the entire football world was waiting for his next moves after he fired most everybody in the Flash organization. The pundits and fans were making a lot of noise about what would happen next. Hollis had to get it right.

"Listen, Mr. Jones, Mona told me about some cocktails she made for Lisa O with some kind of aphrodisiac to get her all relaxed and horny. I mean, she's a fucking escort. Why would you have to make her horny? She's paid to fuck, whether she's horny or not."

"Coleman, what do you know about escorts?"

"I don't know shit, except that the best ones make a ton of money, right, and they know how to make their clients feel like Olympic athletes in the sack, or whatever."

"Sounds like you've had your fair share."

"No way. Never. But I watch TV, so I've seen a few things. Look, I'll be there soon, and we'll figure something out."

I kept my foot heavy on the gas and thought about what Mona had said, that Lisa O slept with international leaders and the biggest corporate bosses you could imagine, that she was the elite of the elite. So, why did Mona think she had to drug her? She better come up with a good answer for that because the police will want to know. I guess she could explain that Hollis had been so insecure lately about his manhood, especially now that he was closing in on collecting social security, that even when he's paying top dollar for the best escort in the world he felt that she might need a boost to find him hot enough to fuck.

That was a crazy notion. He's Randy Fucking Hollis, for Christ's sake, a powerhouse in the business world, and maybe the best lawyer in America, so why would he turn into such a wimp when it comes to women, especially the ones he pays to sleep with him? Where did his fucking confidence go? Go figure. I couldn't believe that Hollis felt the need to drug an escort.

I tried to call Mona, but she didn't pick up. She didn't answer my text, either. I wanted to know if maybe the chef put too much of that aphrodisiac in her cocktail. Maybe she said teaspoon and he heard tablespoon. But Mona would not have fucked that up. She was much too sharp. I felt sure that she and the chef measured out the exact amount of ingredients for a woman Lisa O's size. Mona and the chef probably had no idea that Lisa O would react as she did, like she was super allergic to something in that drink.

My phone rang again. It was Jones.

"Mr. Jones, where's Mona? She's not answering me."

"Mona left with Hollis. We'll decide what to do with her later. And call me Harold."

*Harold? When did we get on a first-name basis?*

I didn't know what to say. His response sounded way too spooky for me. Before I could come up with anything smooth to say, he continued.

"Coleman, we can't let Hollis be connected to this dead woman. It's not because she died in his house. People need to die somewhere. We just can't have him associated with an escort, not even the number one escort in the whole world."

"What is there, a rating system or something?"

"Yeah, according to Mona, there is, and Lisa O has been number one for a few years."

"Listen, Harold, that's fascinating, but I don't think it's important right now."

"Okay. I should call 911."

"Don't."

"Why?"

"We need an alibi for Hollis."

"Shit, Coleman. You're right."

Jones hung up. I was about to exit the Lincoln Tunnel and head cross-town and up to Hollis' place. Alibi. Alibi. What fucking alibi might work to keep Hollis out of trouble?

One thing was sure. Jones had to get someone at Teterboro Airport to erase the flight to Florida from their ledger. Then, we'd need someone in Miami to do the same thing. There could be no trace of Hollis' plane.

This sounded like real gangster shit, but it had to be done or Hollis was toast.

I still had no alibi in mind when I left my car with the doorman and headed up to the penthouse. I'd never been there and now I was supposed to come up with a story to keep its billionaire owner out of hot water.

"So, Mr. Hollis. Where were you when this uh, Lisa O, expired?"

"What was your relationship with her?"

"What were you doing in Florida?"

These questions were basic ones that any cop, no matter how stupid, would ask. Hollis would have a hard time answering them correctly, as in convincingly, with good back-up to corroborate his story. Too much to cover up. This might already be botched beyond repair.

Wait a second. It suddenly occurred to me that Hollis could be setting me up to be his fall guy. Holy shit! That would put me in a real pickle. But then again, I might be Hollis' best alibi.

Before I could test that idea with Jones, I rode with Lisa O's dead body to Mount Sinai Hospital. She had passed away long before the ambulance arrived but since formalities are required in these times I wanted to be sure that the death certificate would be "accurate" under these extenuating circumstances.

I wasn't about to strong arm anybody, but under the right circumstances, people can be convinced to do things they never thought possible, like looking the other way when bad shit happens right in front of them or fudging the truth when it's clearly necessary.

In this case, with a dead escort on our hands, I figured I would need to persuade the coroner or whoever filled out the death certificate that it was in their best interest to "adjust" the time of death and even more important, the cause of Lisa O's untimely passing. I needed to be sure that they would enter certain information that would keep Hollis out of trouble and make my alibi plausible. On top of that, I had to make sure that I was the only one speaking with this official. There was no way we could have Lisa O's next of kin around to muck up the proceedings with a bunch of questions.

"Mr. and Mrs. Orgasm, I'm so sorry about your daughter's death, but please be assured that it was 100 percent accidental, and I will take care of all of the funeral expenses."

As every lawyer knows, when something goes wrong you gotta control the narrative right away and sometimes, the truth be damned, especially if it's not convenient for your client. So, when it came to keeping Hollis in the clear, I knew I had to pull no punches.

I don't know how I even thought of shit like that in such a situation, but I knew this was a time to have some real balls and take a big risk because that's just what I had to do. It didn't escape me in the least that this was probably a real fool's errand, but I couldn't stand by and let Hollis get fucked for something he didn't do. I mean, he didn't fuck her. Jones said that Hollis barely even touched her! Anyway, while I was plotting a crime in one half of my brain, I was trying to legitimize my actions in the other half, as if I had a conscience or something.

I thought about what my mother would tell me to do but running wasn't an option. I was totally on my own. I didn't trust that Jones could figure this out. I could have contacted Smalley, but ever since Cauley blasted her brains out he was a mess. The fate of Randy Hollis rested solely on my shoulders. I figured the police had to investigate the death, which happened in one of the wealthiest buildings in Manhattan. The heat would rise quickly, as investigations often do, and the media would be all over it once they found out that an escort had overdosed inside the penthouse of one of America's richest dudes.

What a disaster for Hollis. Nobody would care that Lisa O was the number one escort in the world because elite men, especially white ones, are known to indulge in all kinds of sex with escorts and even young girls, but that's freaky shit and those guys should be put in prison for that stuff. At least Hollis was picky and only indulged with grown women who were old enough to have serious credentials.

This was my chance to look good to Hollis, I mean, beyond good, like fucking gold, a total lifesaver. If I pulled this off, I would zoom right to the top of his pyramid. But there was a major problem with my idea. I would have to lie to the police and make sure I covered every single bit of my story, which would not be easy at all to do. One false move and I could end up in jail for a long, long time. And, for what?

By the time I got back to Hollis' place, I was a mess. I didn't know what to do or what to tell Jones. I was shocked to find out that he had already decided what was going to happen.

"Okay, Coleman, I spoke with Mr. Hollis, and he decided that he wants you to claim that you are the one who had a date with Lisa O tonight and that you used his home while he was away in Florida. You will tell the police that after Lisa O excused herself and was gone for so long, you found her unconscious and tried to revive her, but nothing doing. She was gone."

"For real? Hollis wants me to cover for him?"

Jones nodded.

"Now that you have the death certificate, we need to coordinate the time of death on that with what you tell the police. I called 911 and they are on their way."

"Holy shit, this is really happening."

"I'm sure Mr. Hollis is grateful for you volunteering to do this and that he will show his appreciation once this all blows over."

"Oh yeah? When?"

"In due time."

That motto again. Fuck. I didn't feel like a volunteer at all. Jones, who was several inches taller than me and much heavier, managed to be intimidating just by being in the same room. I didn't know if he had spoken to Hollis or if he had decided on his own to make me cover for his boss.

For the moment, there was no way for me to know. I had to make a choice. Either leave right away, if I could get out the door without Jones breaking every bone in my body or stay and take my chances with the police and the Manhattan district attorney who was in charge of investigating a questionable death like this one.

# Forty-Five

## The Deceased:
## Could We Please Stop Saying That Word?

Two detectives arrived before I could decide what to do. Since I wasn't a criminal defense lawyer or a prosecutor, I wasn't exactly sure how this would play out or if I should be calling a lawyer before I stepped into any of my own shit. Then again, if the cops saw a lawyer bringing in a lawyer it would make that guy looking pretty guilty before he even opened his mouth.

I would have to navigate my own way through this mess. Above all else, I had to keep my cool and maintain a believable balance of shock and grief over the death of my "date" while crafting and maintaining a plausible story I could remember under repeated questioning.

At least that was the playbook I learned from watching cop shows on TV and maybe even from a class or two in law school. Truth is, I knew all along while I was at Temple that I was not going to become a prosecutor or a public defender. I had my mind set on doing corporate stuff, which yielded the most money and would keep me far away from real criminals. I mean, guys who get nailed for white collar shit are technically guilty of breaking the law, but they are not real criminals, I mean dangerous ones, like killers or rapists or stuff like that. I grew up around enough people like that in my neighborhood and I had no interest at all in being any part of that.

All this was jumping around in my head as I sat down with the two detectives in Hollis' living room.

"Quite a place you've got here, Mr. Hollis."

"Oh no, I'm not Randy Hollis. But you're right. This penthouse is unbelievable."

One of the detectives whispered to the other, apparently to get him up to speed on who was who. Jones had already made a point of telling them that Hollis was not in town, so I didn't know if they were simply stupid or trying to play me.

I had a lot to calculate as I readied myself for their questions. First, Hollis could be charged with conspiring to cover up Lisa O's dead body in his condo. Jones might have taken care of that by getting Hollis out of town, but only if any trace of his flight was totally deleted and they bought my story. I mean, it's not technically a crime to pay a woman to be an escort. If you happen to have sex, it's two consenting adults doing what they do, right? I mean, it would have to be proven that she received money for taking off her clothes. That's prostitution, which is obviously against the law in this country. I'm sure Hollis was paying his escorts in cash, but since Mona was nowhere to be found, I couldn't verify that as a fact. Anyway, escorts advertise their services, and the beat goes on. What else is new? These detectives wouldn't give a shit about another rich guy fucking a hooker. It's just sex between two consenting adults. Or three, if the guy is into that.

"Mr. Coleman, you've confirmed that this is not your home. Is that correct?"

"Yes. This penthouse belongs to Mr. Hollis, and since he is in Miami right now he offered me the use of his place to have a nice date with uh, you know."

"Yes, with a woman identified as Lisa O, now deceased."

"Correct. Unfortunately, and sadly correct."

"How did you know the deceased?"

Man, it was getting to me a little that he kept using the word deceased. It sounded so final and kinda dirty, like you had to do something bad to become deceased.

"Okay, Officer . . ."

He frowned.

"Detective. Sorry. Like I said, I was here tonight on a date. See, I live in Philadelphia, but lately I've been doing a lot of work here for Mr. Hollis, and I'm going through a bad time in my marriage, so he offered to set me up on a date at his place with uh, you know, with an escort."

"Lisa O?"

"Correct. She was very nice. Beautiful. Smart. I mean, she was in graduate school, getting her PhD in uh, I don't remember exactly, but I was enjoying our conversation before she uh, you know, before she became deceased."

"Mr. Coleman, did anything unusual happen before the deceased went into the bathroom, where you eventually found her? Did she mention feeling ill at all?"

"No, nothing at all. Everything was going fine. I was kinda nervous, of course because I never did anything like this before, having a date with somebody while I was married, let alone an escort who I was planning to have relations with, if you know what I mean."

Both detectives smirked and whispered to each other. It's never a good sign when cops huddle up like that. In every crime show I ever saw on TV it goes bad for the person who is being questioned when the interrogators start whispering to each other. Plus, it's fucking rude.

The one doing most of the talking didn't seem to believe me, or maybe it was my imagination because even though I was playing it cool I was falling apart inside. Falsely reporting a crime can be charged as a misdemeanor or a felony and the punishment can be up to a year in jail, or in an extreme case, you could do up to seven years in a state prison. That much I knew. There was no way I was gonna do that, so I had to get my shit just right with those guys.

I mean, I hadn't technically reported a crime. I was just saying that it was me who was there with Lisa O and not Hollis. But that's false representation. You can't make up stories and knowingly lie to a police officer. That's blatantly against the law in any state.

Before I could get this shit clear in my head, and as I was wondering if I should ask to make a phone call, like to my former law partner and BFF at Temple, Timmy, short for Timothy J. Yuskas, the main detective interrupted my thoughts.

"Mr. Coleman, we'd like you to come downtown for questioning."

He actually said the words "come downtown" like we were in the middle of an episode of *Law & Order*, but I had no choice. You simply don't resist when this happens or else you look fucking guilty, and I wasn't guilty of anything except maybe some bad judgment and everything I just described.

I texted Smalley to get him up to speed, but he didn't reply. I knew Hollis would not intervene unless it was under deep cover with one of his contacts inside the police department and he wasn't going to risk that until it was clear that I was in real trouble. I mean, this was no picnic, but I wasn't under arrest or anything like that.

On our way out of the penthouse, I told Jones to let Hollis know what was happening so he could keep me out of jail if it came to that, but I had no idea if that was even a remote possibility. For all I knew, Hollis wanted me to go down for him because it was the most convenient thing possible. Since I had no record and was an officer of the court, so to speak, I might get off with a minimum sentence or probation if I was lucky. But I could lose my law license, which would be even worse than having a record.

I was worried that the police thought I was covering up for Hollis. Finally, after an hour of back-and-forth at the precinct, answering the same questions all over again with another detective, I was released without being charged with any crimes, but they told me I was a person of interest as long as the investigation continued.

It all happened so fast I didn't know what to think. I wasn't sure if I was more afraid of the police or Hollis because I had no idea what he might do if he felt cornered. He had a ton of influence with the New York City Police Department because he donated an enormous amount of money to the Police Benevolent Association, and those guys are faithful to their biggest supporters. Hollis also knew a few judges who would do him a favor, like expediting warrants and shit like that, just in case the cops decided to move fast to arrest me and save Hollis.

By the time I stepped outside the precinct on East 51st Street and headed back to my car, the sun was beginning to rise, even though it felt like my own life was sinking fast. I did a quick search on my phone and confirmed that falsely reporting an incident in New York City is a crime, possibly a felony, but a misdemeanor at the very least, which would be extremely embarrassing for Hollis. Lisa O dying in her own vomit was not an "incident." I didn't even know if it was an accident. But as the detectives kept saying, she was deceased, and no matter what you call it, that fact was not going away.

It was also maybe a fact that Hollis killed Budman, as Cauley and Smalley had suggested that day in Atlantic City, or had someone like Jones do the deed, so I wasn't sure at all if either of them had my back. Hollis was acting fucking whacky with all his midlife crisis bullshit. Jones wasn't exactly forthright about anything, so maybe he killed Lisa O, but why? Why would either of them kill her?

I had no answers as I walked a few blocks uptown. It was too early to call Timmy, to tell him that I had just committed a crime by lying to the authorities. Sure, my intentions were noble, to save Hollis from being linked to a real shit show with a dead body in his house, but what if Hollis actually killed Lisa O? He could have me killed, too, which would solve the whole problem of Lisa O ending up deceased in his penthouse.

As I drove back to Philadelphia, all I knew was that I was in a heap of trouble, and nobody was showing up to bail me out.

# Forty-Six

## Caffeine Paranoia:
## What To Do with My Balls

I was a mess by the time I got home. Luckily, Beverly was gone already on a shopping spree with some girlfriends from work. Apparently, the school where she works as a guidance counselor was closed for the day because a bunch of kids had clogged up all the toilets.

She left me a note to say that they were going to see the directors' cut of *La La Land* and would be home for dinner. That movie was a romantic story set in Los Angeles where the two main characters are trying to fulfill their aspirations for the future. To me, it's kind of stupid when people start singing out of nowhere about everyday shit like that, but this notion of finding your dreams was not so bad.

In that moment, I was dreaming of how I could make all my problems disappear. I mean, all this questionable behavior surrounding me, with Hollis and Cauley's suicide, and God knows what else, was making me take stock of my life, in and out of the legal arena.

I made a pot of coffee and tried to relax. At least for the meantime, like the next few hours, barring any unforeseen bullshit, I would be okay in the relative safety of my own home. It was cold outside, but I needed some fresh air, so I went out onto the patio to collect my thoughts.

That day in court in Dallas when I met Robert Smalley jumped into my mind. So much had happened since then, and so fast, too, but what stuck out to me the most was what he said to me that day.

"You got balls, kid."

That launched me into a world I had never imagined, one that seemed to be changing my life, and not necessarily for the better, despite all the new money I was making. It seemed like with each passing moment it was testing my moral code of ethics. I mean, okay, I had balls, but did I have brains? One without the other spelled trouble. I didn't need a law professor or my mother to tell me that.

At that point, I didn't have the balls to call Hollis and talk to him directly about the situation, maybe ask him what happened, like, did somebody kill Lisa O? Did *he* kill Lisa O? Did Jones kill her? Mona? The fucking chef? I mean, he had to know what happened.

I wasn't ready to make that move. I was still thinking that the police may back off. I was pretty convinced that Hollis would applaud my actions. Then again, I didn't know if I could trust him at all. He had to know what was going on, so why hadn't he called me yet?

Even though I was technically free, I was not in the clear, and I wouldn't be until Lisa O's death was declared an accident, if, in fact, it was a fucking accident. Maybe Mona or the chef messed up and Lisa O overdosed. Maybe Jones told Mona to lay low until things cooled down. Or maybe he was going to set her up as Lisa O's killer because she was jealous of the world's number one escort and wanted Hollis all to herself.

I was all revved up on coffee and thinking some crazy shit. I guess people do that when they're scared and have no idea what's happening. That was me, twisted into a pretzel from working for Hollis. I mean, even if my motives were well-meaning, I lied to the police to cover for Hollis, someone I barely knew, and the pressure was ramping up, at least in my head.

I had to choose. Do I continue lying or disclose everything to the police? Either way, I was in deep shit, and not breaking into a song, like Ryan Gosling did in that movie. My shit was real, and I had to figure it out fast.

My phone rang. Harold Jones.

*Fuck, this better be good.*

I didn't want to talk to anybody unless it was Hollis or the police, telling me everything was fine, that I was no longer "a person of interest." I didn't want to be interesting. I wanted to drink my coffee on the patio and be boring as hell.

Jones wasted no time getting to it.

"What happened with the police?"

"I can't talk now."

I hung up. I had no idea if that was smart, but I was in no condition to rehash all the questioning and lying I had done. I figured Jones knew where I lived and if he wanted to come down or send a goon to rough me up, so be it. I thought about getting a gun, and I knew people from my old neighborhood who would do that for me, but no way. Fuck no.

I tried Smalley again and was surprised when he picked up. I told him what was going on, and that I needed him to level with me.

"Am I safe with Hollis or not? I mean, I remember what you told me about what happened to Budman and I don't want to end up in a ditch or something like that."

Smalley laughed.

"A ditch? What is this, a Mafia movie? Coleman, why would you end up in a ditch? It looks to me like you're taking one for the team and I'm sure Randy agrees."

Is that what I was doing? Taking one for the team? What team? Team Hollis? The Los Angeles Flash? What did "taking one for the team" mean, anyway? That I was going to jail because I lied to the police to save Hollis? What kind of fucking teamwork was that?

"Listen, Bob, I gotta go."

I didn't know which end was up or what I should say next. I wasn't sure anymore if I could trust Smalley, either.

"Coleman, you worry too much."

"Oh, yeah? What makes you so sure? When will I hear from Hollis?"

"In due time."

He hung up. Let's just say his answer, that creepy motto again, sounded chilling and definitely not a confidence booster. I felt clueless. Should I expose Hollis and rat him out or keep quiet and be faithful to the man who introduced me to riches beyond my wildest dreams?

I decided to go see my mother and then drop by Timmy's office to see if my best friend from law school had any good advice. Somebody had to be able to tell me what the fuck to do!

The whole situation was making me reconsider why I was practicing law. I had never taken money from a case that did not belong to me, like Cauley, and I never elbowed other lawyers out of the way, like Smalley and Hollis, but I was feeling dirty from whatever you want to call what I was doing for "the team."

It wasn't the flaws in the class-action system that bothered me, like the fraudulent behavior of business executives or the dicey tricks these high-powered lawyers were pulling. I wasn't looking to become a whistle blower. In fact, I was into cashing in on these exclusive opportunities.

My mother and Timmy both advised me to "do the right thing" and suggested I call Smalley back and put him on the spot to tell me the truth about what Hollis was up to and how it was going to play out for me.

When I got back home, I poured myself another round of coffee and added some whiskey, just to see if that would calm my nerves.

"Listen, Bob, with all due respect, I don't feel comfortable with what's going on and I need you to level with me about Hollis."

"Stop right there, Coleman. I don't take kindly to being threatened. Something I learned from Cauley and Hollis. Look, do you want to know the truth? You are in over your head, especially with the cops, who could arrest you any time for the escort's death, and if that doesn't hold up, if they find out what really happened, they can nail you for lying to them about a fucking murder."

I thought I was gonna throw up, like Lisa O did less than 24 hours ago.

"Am I making myself clear, Coleman? If you don't play this right, if Hollis doesn't feel like he can trust you, he will make you disappear. So, relax, Ryan, and don't do anything stupid."

Smalley hung up, leaving me scared shitless. I did not have clean hands. That's for sure. Maybe I could go back to the police and plead for mercy, claiming I was under terrible duress. I could deliver a dramatic mea culpa and see if they would buy it if I dumped the whole thing on Jones. Maybe he would go to jail instead of me. The only question was, do I claim he murdered Lisa O or that he forced me to take the rap for Hollis?

Forget the coffee. I went straight to a whiskey bottle, desperate to get numb and stop feeling so helpless. Smalley was probably right. I was in over my head.

My phone vibrated. A text from Mona.

Sorry. My battery died. Good luck!

WTF Mona? Good luck with what?

No answer. Easy come, easy go. I didn't hear from her again. I didn't know if she was with Hollis or somewhere in exile, under lock and key, so she couldn't speak to any authorities.

I needed to get my shit together. I went into the bathroom and stared in the mirror, trying to work up some confidence, I reminded myself that I was a fucking lawyer so I should know how to handle this shit. According to Smalley, I had balls, and I needed them now more than ever, but most of all, I needed my fucking brains to max out and save my ass.

I leaned in closer to get a better look and stuck out my chest to prove to myself that I was still the shit, at least in my own house.

"Lawyers rule the fucking world. That's a fact, whether people like it or not. I know it, and they know it, so listen up Ryan Coleman. That's right. You, you stupid bastard. Stand up straight and be the man your father would want you to be right now."

252

I heard myself talking but wasn't sure I wanted to hear it. When I was a young kid, getting pushed around by bullies on our block, my father told me over and over to not be a pussy, to not take any shit from anybody.

"Ryan, my boy, if you want to succeed in life, you gotta stand up for yourself and nobody will mess with you. Got it?"

I always agreed with him, even if I didn't always believe it, but I wasn't sure if my father's words of wisdom applied in this situation because back in the day there were no kids disappearing out of the blue or escorts dying in their own vomit. At least I never heard about it if they did.

But now I was a lawyer, working in a system designed for our benefit. I mean, why do you think litigation takes so long? Attorneys grease the wheels because the system is set up for delays, petitions and motions to keep the cash flowing. It's not rocket science.

Right now, being bullied by Smalley, and for all I knew I was being played by Hollis, too, I felt like the sucker getting bit in the ass by all the fine print people complain about because they never read it until it's too late. That's because lawyers get paid buckets of cash to make up all that nonsense and average people have to pay for it. Only this time, this fancy pants lawyer might be the biggest sucker of all.

I turned off my phone and tried to take a nap.

# Forty-Seven

## Heat Rising:
## "Run!"

During this whole sordid ordeal, Handler was tracking my every move. Apparently, the dick had bugged my phone and jumped into action as soon as Jones called me about Lisa O. By the time I got to the police station, Handler was there, incognito, or at least he thought so, listening to my entire interview and gathering any information he could use to nail me and ultimately Hollis.

How did I know this bastard was doing that? Well, Smalley was tipping me off on some sketchy stuff that was going on and he also had a lawyer friend who knew Coyle. This guy ran into Coyle a night earlier and they got to drinking and shooting the breeze and Coyle spilled the beans on his obsession with Hollis. He also blabbered to Smalley's friend about Handler, which tipped me off that I was being followed.

I had no idea how he might have gotten a device on my phone until I realized we were no longer living in the Stone Age. I mean, it was easy to track someone remotely if you had the right connections and Handler was set up for that with Dick Dickey, who had access to the best surveillance technology in the world.

I was a sitting duck. They knew exactly where I had been and where I was now, which Coyle and Dickey could try to use to leverage me to do their bidding. Who knows what he had already discovered about me, and maybe Hollis, too? Plus, Handler had connections with the police so that made things even worse. I felt like I was getting sandwiched in the middle of two parties that only wanted to use me for their own benefit. Once again, who was my friend and who was my enemy?

I had to turn the tables if I could. By that time, I figured that Handler was convinced that he had me trapped, which meant Hollis was next. Coyle probably thought he had finally struck pay dirt and could bring down his nemesis. For Dick Dickey, that meant one last chance to step in and buy the Flash, securing his foothold inside the AFL.

Then again, Dickey was in serious hot water as a result of what I had done to expose him in the Burn Pits case. His power trip in that arena was about to end, so I guess he was super pissed at me, too, for instigating that debacle. Now, he had two people to ruin: Hollis and me.

Since I wasn't in any imminent danger, as far as I knew, like Jones showing up with a machete in my shower or two detectives banging on my front door, I figured this might be as good a time as any to reflect for a minute on how I had gotten myself into such a mess. Maybe if I could recognize a pattern in my behavior I would be better able to solve my predicament.

I thought back to how I first met Smalley, which triggered this whole sequence of events. Even though I was a relative novice at the time in this huge legal arena of securities class action stuff, and a small player to boot, I became quickly involved, and my position granted me access to inside information and a front row seat to an assortment of dubious practices. I was privy to many types of shenanigans, legal and otherwise, most of which I had not questioned and was only now beginning to see as a fundamental problem.

I used to see class actions as a way to help little guys fight back when big corporations harmed them. I was raised with values like that and then in law school I learned that I could do something about it. But I was fooling myself. People were being fucked, especially by lawyers like Smalley. I thought back to when we first partied in Manhattan, and he told me he didn't give a shit about any of the Plaintiffs. That didn't sit right with me at the time, but I let it go because I was so eager to get in good with him. Instead, lawyers like me were making lots of money off defenseless victims. That means some could say I had dirty hands, that I was guilty by association, and it might be time to come clean.

How does that apply to you? Maybe you, or someone you know and care about, have invested your life savings in the stock market, thinking you stand a chance of winning the jackpot. Are you sure? Any of us who throw our money at Wall Street are taking a huge risk of being taken for a ride by greedy, self-interested corporate executives.

As a securities class action lawyer, supposedly helping investors fight back against these modern-day outlaws, I used to think I was helping, and maybe I did once in a while, but I was also taking people for a ride while us lawyers got filthy rich, hand over fist. It's just that the levels of filthy vary a lot and who am I to say whether that makes me a scumbag, too?

For the moment, I didn't care about the bigger picture. I would have to leave the philosophizing for another day. As a willing (and maybe unwilling) player in the Hollis Freak Show, I had to find out where I stood and decide what to do.

My mother had jokingly said "run!" when I told her what was happening, as if I could just disappear and pretend none of this ever happened. I sure would've been happy if I could've done that. It would've saved me a ton of anxiety and I may have even skirted more aggravation with my marriage. But above all else, no matter how stupid I might have been, I was a realist.

I couldn't run. I could only suck it up and figure out what to do next, and I had to do that completely on my own. I felt like Smalley and Hollis were not going to lift a finger to help me, not unless it benefited them. Hollis was MIA and Smalley was playing games.

Meanwhile, I was stuck in the same loop. Do I confess to the cover-up and expose Hollis? Or do I play out the ruse and ensure my position as Hollis' new and faithful right-hand man? Lying to the police could jeopardize my license to practice law and put me in jail. Yeah, I know, I've said that a million times, but I was obsessing, for Christ sake. Wouldn't you, too, if your ass was on the line like mine?

As I heard a car pull into the driveway, I hoped for once it was only Beverly.

# Forty-Eight

## Heed the Signs:
## No One Gets Out of Here Alive

Everything went radio silent overnight. No communication from anybody, not a peep, except my mother, who called that night to make sure I hadn't committed suicide and left any perishables in the refrigerator. I reminded her that Beverly was around to clean up but since Cauley had just taken her own life, I would try to do something more original.

I was laughing a little as I got into bed. Beverly was feeling all romantic after buying some new clothes and watching Ryan Gosling go topless and play the piano. Maybe she mistook me for him because she was unusually energetic in bed that night, which took my mind off my troubles for at least a few minutes.

The next morning, after a fitful night of sleep, I said goodbye to Beverly and headed into Center City to file a Motion in room 691 of the courthouse at City Hall. I was doing my due diligence, taking care of Smalley's class action suit. In all honesty, I was relieved to be back in a place where I could do normal things, but I didn't feel normal at all. I kept looking over my shoulder, wondering if anyone was following me. Handler could have had eyes on me, or Jones, too. For all I knew, a New York City police detective was undercover inside the courthouse, waiting to corner me in the bathroom and make me confess. I could be walking into a trap and become the first lawyer ever arrested for murder during a class action hearing.

While I waited for my turn, a colleague approached and stared at me until I looked up.

"You seem kind of ruffled, Ryan. You don't look like yourself. Are you okay?"

"I have no idea what you're talking about."

"Ryan, I've been watching you for a few minutes already and you're rocking back and forth there, mumbling to yourself about I don't know what, but you seem pretty disturbed."

"Oh no, not at all. I'm just wiped out, you know, from too much sex with the wife."

"Really? I've known you for a long time, Ryan, and I've never heard you complain about too much sex."

I laughed.

"Oh, you know, just getting older, and uh . . . you know."

I couldn't have fooled anybody at that point. I was wearing a heavy heart on my sleeve, wondering why I was feeling so bad for doing something noble for Hollis. I still couldn't believe he hadn't contacted me. Maybe he was mad for some reason. Maybe he was going to have me rubbed out, like Budman. Maybe there would be two guys in ski masks inside the parking garage waiting for me by my car, and they would hit me with a stun gun and throw me into the back of a van and take me to see Hollis out in the middle of the woods somewhere to meet my fate.

That's when I nearly smacked myself in the face. I had seen way too many kidnappings on TV. I had to stop making up shit like that or I would go crazy and end up in the psycho ward next to my mother's nursing home. I nodded to my colleague, who was still waiting for me to convince him that I was okay.

"Don't worry man, it's all good."

"Okay, Ryan, so when do you want to get together for a drink?"

"In due time."

"What? What does that even mean?"

You heard what I said. In due time."

I shook his hand, filed the Motion with a clerk, and left the court-house. I had parked my car about four blocks away in a six-story garage. It felt so good to be walking and breathing in some fresh air. From what I had heard, the air inside a jail is not fresh at all. In fact, it stinks from grown men sweating and farting and not taking enough showers. I figured I better enjoy it while I could, just in case. I walked slowly inside the lobby, paid for my ticket and headed up to the top floor. I thought I recognized a woman inside the elevator. She looked like one of the women I had met on Cauley's yacht, but I must have been wrong.

As the doors opened, she went one way and I headed to my car, just a few steps away. That's when everything went dark.

# About the Author's

**Brian Felgoise, Esq.,** has enjoyed an extremely varied professional career. He is a graduate of Temple University Law School and has been practicing class-action law for more than 25 years. He has been appointed lead counsel, co-lead counsel, and class counsel in numerous cases throughout the country. Felgoise has been involved in cases where billions of dollars have been recovered for class members who lost a significant amount of money.

Felgoise has represented numerous individuals in many "garden-variety" personal injury matters, where he recovered millions for his injured clients.

In addition to practicing law, Felgoise was the driving force behind the creation of TeachPrivacy, a consulting company he co-founded, which provides e-Learning to businesses, and training for companies such as Intel, Caterpillar, American Express, and McKesson.

**David Tabatsky** has authored, co-authored and edited several novels, including *The Boy Behind the Door* (Amsterdam Publishers), *Friends Like These* (Speaking Volumes), *The Marijuana Project* (SDS Publishing), *The Battle of Zig Zag Pass* (Speaking Volumes), *Slipping Reality* (Author House), *Drunk Log* (Speaking Volumes) and *So Much for Happy* (WE Edutainment).

He has also written, co-written and edited many inspirational memoirs of people surviving mental and physical health challenges as well as self-help guides, including *Chicken Soup for the Soul's, The Cancer Book: 101 Stories of Courage, Strength & Love, The Intelligent Divorce: Because Your Kids Come First* (Intelligent Books), *The Overparenting Solution* (Rowman & Littlefield) and *Write for Life: Communicating Your Way Through Cancer and Chronic Disease.*

His memoir, *American Misfit*, was published in 2017. Visit David at www.tabatsky.com

*Upcoming New Release*

# BRIAN FELGOISE
# DAVID TABATSKY

# FILTHY RICH LAWYERS

## BOOK TWO
## IN DUE TIME

*It's not a novel. It's a lifestyle.*

Attorney Ryan Coleman is kidnapped in downtown Philadelphia, drugged and "delivered" to Randy Hollis, who greets his prodigal son on a yacht off the Miami coast. Coleman discovers that Hollis, who he thought might be framing him for the death of an escort in his Manhattan penthouse, has chosen him to carry on his legacy as the one-and-only heir to his enormous fortune. When Hollis mysteriously disappears, Coleman must assume control of Hollis' empire while saving himself from losing his license to practice law and going to prison…

**For more information
visit:** www.SpeakingVolumes.us